SLINGSHOT

SLINGSHOT

Stuart Jackman

FABER AND FABER
3 Queen Square, London

01397216

First published in 1974
by Faber and Faber Limited
3 Queen Square London WC1
Printed in Great Britain by
Latimer Trend & Company Ltd Plymouth

ISBN 0 571 10620 X

87412274

© Stuart Jackman 1974

For ANDREW, to await his pleasure

Then David chose five smooth stones from the brook and put them in his shepherd's bag; his sling was in his hand and he drew near to the Philistine.

1 Samuel 17:40

And among the rebels in prison, who had committed murder in the insurrection, there was a man called Barabbas.

Mark 15:7

The third week in March they found what they were looking for: a top-floor room in an empty house at the end of Chain Street.

It wasn't much of a place from which to direct the liberation of two and a half million people; just a little square box, dirty, unfurnished, the white walls grey with dust, the laths showing through the broken ceiling where the plaster had come away. But it was central, in the heart of Jerusalem, with a window overlooking the great courtyard of the Temple. That was what they needed.

They took the room from the beginning of April, paid a month's rent in advance and left it unoccupied, waiting for Davidson to show his hand.

Jesus Davidson was the key to SLINGSHOT; the x factor in a complicated equation of weapons and manpower and timing. Until he gave the word they dared not move.

On Sunday 1st April they went to twelve hours' readiness and waited.

The word came nine days later when Simson walked down to the phone box outside the Bethany Post Office, dialled Rocci's private, ex-directory number, identified himself and said, "Tomorrow afternoon. One-thirty."

They moved into the room the next morning. Tuesday 10th April, three days before the Passover.

PART ONE: Tuesday

1

Jacobson brought them up from Masada in the Land-Rover, coming in by the southern route through Arad and Hebron to the Jaffa Gate. The city was crowded with pilgrims and tourists, unbelievably noisy after the empty silence of the desert.

He drove into the little cobbled yard behind the house, shut the wooden gate and helped them to off-load the equipment and carry it upstairs. Two camp stools and a trestle table, the bulky, multi-channel radio receiver/transmitter, a Mark I rocket launcher, two automatic rifles, a wooden box of ammunition, a four-by-two sheet of plaster-board, a canvas grip and a cardboard carton of rations. No bedding. If things worked out they would sleep that night in the Residency. If not, they would be in prison. Or dead.

When Jacobson had driven away to park the Land-Rover and join his commandos Barabbas closed and locked the yard gate, secured the door at the foot of the stairs and went up to help Hodor.

It took them an hour to set up the Command Post.

They began with the radio, mounting it on the trestle table against the outer wall, running the aerial up through the laths and out of the skylight in the roof. Hodor hooked in the loudspeaker, tested the circuits and left the set switched to RECEIVE.

From the canvas grip they took a hammer and a box of one-inch masonry nails, a packet of drawing-pins, another of coloured marker pins and a large-scale street map of the city and suburbs. They nailed the plaster-board to the wall above the table and pinned the map on it.

Then they removed the window from its frame and carried it out on to the landing at the top of the stairs. They lifted the six-and-a-quarter-pound projectiles out of the ammunition box, stacking them on the floor under the window opening, inverted the empty

15

box and used it as a base for the rocket launcher. Barabbas screwed in the telescopic sight and centred the cross-wires on the massive wrought-iron gates of the Temple.

They worked well together, anticipating each other's needs with an instinctive understanding which bypassed the need for words. Their movements were calm, economic; the two pairs of hands working like parts of a single machine. Only the shine of sweat on their faces and an occasional impatient grunt when a wire frayed or a nut cross-threaded betrayed the tension building up between them in the quiet room.

And yet they were an oddly dissimilar pair, the giant and the little cripple; as different in temperament as they were in physique, alike only in their common devotion to the dream.

The dream was their shared inheritance, their reason for living. It was a dream of freedom; the ancient Jewish dream handed down in blood from generation to generation through the bitter centuries of oppression since the Exodus. The dream Isaiah had sung about. The dream the Maccabee brothers had died for. The dream at the heart of SLINGSHOT.

Slight in build, twenty-seven and already balding, Ben Hodor was the brains behind SLINGSHOT. Crippled by a Roman anti-personnel mine which had smashed his left ankle and taken three toes off his foot, he moved awkwardly, dragging a built-up boot, relying on a heavy intake of codeine to keep the pain under control. His eyes were deep-set in his narrow face; dark, intelligent eyes, seldom smiling. Behind them a brain like a computer, pro-grammed with the detailed operational plan, produced a print-out of times and objectives designed to turn the dream into a reality.

It was Hodor who had thought up the name SLINGSHOT. The five Pebble commando groups, waiting now at their jumping-off points around the city, represented the five smooth stones David had taken from the brook that day in the Valley of Elah when he had run with his sling in his hand to meet the Philistine giant. But for those waiting guerillas the enemy was not Goliath of Gath. The enemy was His Excellency Lord Pilate, Governor-General of Judea, with all the might of Imperial Rome behind him.

Hodor made the plan and gave it a name. But Barabbas breathed life into it.

Six foot two and built like a tank, with brown, almost black, eyes and bright red hair cut close to his head, Jesus Barabbas was in command of SLINGSHOT. He had all the attributes of leadership: presence, authority, great physical strength. And something else: some magic, elusive quality compounded of courage and compassion which compelled the loyalty, even the affection, of the desperate men he commanded. At thirty-five he was already a legend, the scourge of the Romans from Safad to Beer Sheba.

For him the dream was a violent one, seething inside the prison of his cropped head, waiting for the right man at the right time to come and set it free. In Jesus Davidson, the Galilean joiner turned revolutionary, Barabbas believed he had found that man.

They finished their preparations just after eleven. Hodor opened the carton of rations, took out the big thermos of coffee and poured two cups. They lit cigarettes and sat on the camp stools, smoking and drinking the hot, sweet liquid. The babble of voices from the people crowding into the courtyard below came to them clearly through the empty window opening. The room was hot and smelled of dust. The little red eye of the warning light on the RT set stared at them, mocking the semi-obsolete rocket launcher on its makeshift base, the cheap map from the Tourist Office, the cobwebs dust-furred in the corners of the room. Outside, above the Antonia Fortress beyond the Temple, four kite-hawks floated lazily in the warm morning air. Hodor watched them morosely, stubbed out his cigarette and lit another. This was the bad time, the waiting time.

At eleven-thirty the loudspeaker suddenly crackled into life.

"Hullo, Slingshot. This is Seeker. Do you read me? Over."

Barabbas grinned with relief as Hodor switched to TRANSMIT. "Slingshot here. Reading you fives. Over." He tore open the packet of marker pins and tipped them out on to the table.

"Seeker to Slingshot. I have details of the opposition's armed patrols in the city area scheduled for today. Over."

"Roger, Seeker. Go ahead. Over."

Hodor picked up a black felt pen and began to mark in the sector squares on the map as Seeker gave him the co-ordinates. Barabbas got up and went to stand behind him, watching the squares grow into a grid spreading across the city from the northern suburbs to the Gaza road. This was vital information which could be worth a couple of commando groups to them later in the day.

Seeker's voice was cool, almost casual. Barabbas smiled, visualising him sitting in his Post Office Telephone Service pick-up in some quiet cul-de-sac out near the University, the walkie-talkie set cradled on his shoulder, calmly spelling out the results of an hour's dangerous work in Imperial Army HQ that morning.

Hodor completed the final square and began to stick the coloured pins into position.

Seeker said, "I also have the strength of the opposition forces in HQ. There are figures 5 Romulus armoured personnel carriers on stand-by. That's figures 60 men. Apart from them—taking out patrol crews and men assigned to special duties at the Residency and the airport—I estimate the total complement to be not more than figures 100. Over."

"Roger. I'll get that through to Pebble 4. Thanks, Dave. Great job. Over and out."

"He's a bloody wonder, that boy," Barabbas said happily.

Hodor nodded, "What about these five carriers? That's a big bite to chew on. Those Roman APC crews are mustard."

"Tigal can handle 'em, don't you worry," Barabbas said, confident at the prospect of action.

"I hope so." Hodor looked at his watch. "So all we need now is our young friend from Nazareth."

Barabbas heard the wryness in his voice and grinned. "OK, Ben. We all know you don't like Davidson."

"It's not a question of liking," Hodor said. "I just can't get to him." He looked at Barabbas. "He's unpredictable. A loner."

"What's the matter?" Barabbas said. "Don't you think he'll come?"

"Oh, he'll come. For what it's worth."

Barabbas's face reddened, the quick temper rising. "Look, let's get this on the line, Ben. I don't . . ."

"Yes, let's do that," Hodor said evenly. "He came last Sunday, right? Messiah on a donkey. Palm leaves, cheering crowds, the lot."

"So?"

Hodor shrugged. "So nothing. That's what I'm saying. It was there waiting for him. And he turned his back on it."

Barabbas scowled. "We weren't ready last Sunday."

"For God's sake," Hodor said. "We've been ready for weeks. What you mean is, he didn't bother to let us know."

"Davidson fixes the time," Barabbas said doggedly. "Whatever it looks like to us, he makes the decision. We agreed on that."

"God knows why." Hodor shifted on the camp stool, his injured foot in the clumsy boot thrust out awkwardly under the table. "It's not as though last Sunday was the first time. In the past two months he's had a dozen chances to take over. All he had to do was say the word and we'd've been in there. But every time, every single time, when it comes to the crunch he chickens out."

Barabbas shook his head uneasily. Sunday's curious non-event has shaken him more than he wanted to admit even to himself. But Davidson was like that; difficult, moody, full of disquieting surprises. It was no use trying to understand him. He was too deep for that. In the end all you could do was trust him.

He said, "This time it'll be different."

"Will it?" Hodor said, half sceptical, half hopeful.

The question hung unanswered between them. They had been over this ground too often before to commit their hopes to words.

After a moment Hodor said, "You still think he's who he says he is?"

"Messiah?"

"Yes."

Barabbas shrugged and looked away. "The people think so."

"That's not what I asked you," Hodor said quietly.

Barabbas hesitated. Everything depended on this. SLING-SHOT; the lives of his men; the hope of Israel—all balanced precariously on the identity of Jesus Davidson. The Messiah would be a conqueror. Everybody knew that. The Soldier King who would come to lead his people to victory. It was not easy to recognise such a leader in the lonely young man whose classic Messianic donkey ride into the city last Sunday afternoon had led not to the triumphant proclamation of the Kingdom but to a shy, almost furtive retreat.

And yet—and yet there was something about Davidson that fascinated him. A sense of destiny; a feeling of immense power waiting in the wings for the cue that would unleash it.

But the nature of that power and what it would accomplish for Israel—these were mysteries.

Looking at the face of Davidson—seeing it clearly in his mind's eye—Barabbas had the curious feeling that he was looking at himself. But himself strangely altered, transformed, set in a new perspective.

Elbows on knees, chin cupped in his hands, he said then, "It doesn't matter a damn what I think. Whoever he is, we need him. Maybe he doesn't measure up to what we expected. But he's still got something we can never have." He felt the old wound open in his mind. That was what she had said, the girl with the red hair whose astonishing love for him had cooled, since she had met Davidson, to kindliness. The wound was angry, inflamed. Passion he understood. And hatred. But not kindliness. Kindliness was a little emotion, for little people. He pinched the wound shut with the fingers of his will and jerked his head towards the window. "That lot down there wouldn't follow us across the street. We scare them a damn' sight more than the Romans do. But they'll follow Jesus Davidson to hell and back."

Hodor nodded. "To hell, anyway."

Barabbas looked at him sharply for a moment and then grinned, his mood changing. "You know your trouble, Ben? You worry too much."

Hodor smiled, a small, unconvinced smile. He looked up at the map, pinpointing the five Pebble commando groups. One hundred and sixty men ready and waiting. It seemed to him far too many lives to gamble on the record to date of Jesus Davidson.

"This time tomorrow," Barabbas said, "we'll be living in Free Israel."

"That is my hope," Hodor said. He switched the RT set to TRANSMIT and began to call up Pebble 4.

20

2

At twenty past one Andrew Jacobson, eighty feet up on the city wall, looked out across the Kidron valley and saw the bus come round the corner on the Bethany road and begin the long descent to Gethsemane. Thin and muscular, wearing the black, ankle-length cloak of a desert nomad over khaki shirt and slacks, Jacobson stood stiff-legged, the walki-talkie set under his arm, a short-barrelled sub-machine gun strapped to his thigh under the cloak. He was thirty-one, quiet-spoken, intelligent; a man Hodor trusted. Which was why he was there, above the Temple courtyard, at the flashpoint of SLINGSHOT.

Jacobson was an accountant whose career had come to an abrupt end a year earlier when the firm in which he was a junior partner had been implicated in a major tax evasion scandal involving a number of important clients holding government contracts. He had been personally cleared of any responsibility but some of the mud had inevitably stuck and his reputation was gone. Embittered, his sense of justice outraged, his honesty affronted, he had turned his back on society and joined the guerillas, contributing to their planning sessions the kind of single-minded dedication Hodor admired.

The bus pulled in to the stop below the Golden Gate. About twenty people got off. Jacobson stared down at them, narrowing his eyes against the glare of the afternoon sun, his face tautly expectant in the white frame of his black-circled burnous.

He recognised Johnson first, the big, shaggy fisherman so sure-footed in a boat, so ungainly on land. John Zebedee was on his right, talking as usual, and between them Jesus Davidson in checked shirt and denim jeans, coming up the steep path with an easy, effortless lope. Lagging a little behind the group was a slight, narrow-shouldered man Jacobson recognised as Simson. He swallowed with excitement as he saw him step on to the worn grass beside the track, take off his glasses and begin to polish them with a handkerchief, holding them up at arm's length, turning them in the sunlight as if to make sure they were clean.

Jacobson blinked and grinned as the reflected light from the glasses flashed the agreed signal in his eyes. He turned, moved in beside a buttress and pulled up the aerial of his walkie-talkie.

"Pebble 2 to Slingshot." Jacobson's voice came in through the RT speaker, metallic, urgent. "The King is here. I say again, the King is here. Over."

Hodor depressed the TRANSMIT switch. "This is Slingshot. Roger, Pebble 2. Your message received and understood. Out." He checked his watch. Thirteen-thirty hours.

"Right on the button," Barabbas said.

Hodor nodded and spoke into the microphone. "Hullo all Pebbles. All Pebbles, This is Slingshot. Condition Red. Condition Red. Out."

Silhouetted in the window opening Barabbas said, "This is it, Ben."

Hodor heard the controlled excitement in his voice, saw the big hands clench into fists itching for action, and was suddenly afraid. Not for himself. For Barabbas.

Jacobson took up his command position at the top of the stone steps leading down into the courtyard. Below him, penned within the high walls under the blazing sun, two thousand people jostled and shoved, noisy, irritable, ripe for trouble. Seeded among them like neutrons in an atomic pile his commandos waited in their black desert cloaks, poised now to trigger off a chain reaction of violence with Jesus Davidson, code-named the King, at its centre.

And like a king Davidson strode in through the gate, his twelve men packed tightly round him. Jacobson felt his heart jump. This was no meek Messiah on a donkey. Not this time. This time there was purpose, drive, an iron touch of anger. This time he meant it.

The group crossed the corner of the courtyard, marching like a phalanx, Davidson in the centre, his head up, his face set, the sunlight gleaming on the copper in his thick brown hair. It was a good head, well set on broad shoulders; and a good face, the chin firm, the nose finely chiselled, the eyes dark and lustrous. The head and face of a man born to be king.

Jacobson watched them drive through the crowd towards the steps of the portico where the money-changers had set up their tables, and nodded approvingly. The money-changers were a natural target; a built-in, ready-to-light fuse. Charging exorbitantly high commission rates to convert the common coinage into the special Temple currency used in the outer court market, they had been hated for years by the ordinary citizens. An attack on them would win immense popular support. Looking down he saw the people swirl in a pattern round Davidson, opening a way in front of him, moving back and curving in behind like iron filings forming a field round a bar magnet. This was part of the Davidson mystique, this ability to dominate and control, to rearrange the world in a circle of power with himself at the centre; and to do it effortlessly, casually, simply by being there. It was what Barabbas had seen and understood, the quality Davidson had that they could never have.

Jacobson whipped up the aerial of his walkie-talkie as the group reached the first table and Davidson stepped forward to confront the money-changer. The crowd went quiet and he saw the money-changer shrug and spread his hands, saw Davidson shake his head angrily, turn quickly and run up the portico steps. On the fifth step he swung round, head thrown back, arms spread wide in the sunlight. Snatches of what he was saying floated over the heads of the people to Jacobson.

". . . the house of my Father . . . prayer and praise . . ."

Jacobson clenched his fists, his mouth dry, his heart thumping in his chest. "Come *on*, man. Don't lose it now. Never mind the sermon. Let's get to the action."

He saw Davidson's right arm shoot out, the index finger stabbing down at the money-changers below him. His next words came with splendid clarity, ringing iron-hard off the enclosing walls. "You have turned this holy place"—the voice rose to a great shout of anger—"*into a den of thieves and robbers!*"

23

And he went down the steps in three long strides and stooped and slid his arm under the edge of the table, and gripped and straightened his back, all in one quick, smooth, fluid movement.

Jacobson flipped the switch of the walkie-talkie and held it to his mouth.

Barabbas saw it all with an intense, dream-like clarity, like a film run in slow motion. The money-changer's table reared up on end, the silver spray of coins hung in the air above the upturned faces, the arms reaching up to catch them waved slowly, gracefully, like fronds of seaweed in quiet water.

"Pebble 2 to Slingshot." Jacobson's voice broke the spell. "The fuse is lit. Repeat, the fuse is lit. Over."

Barabbas swung round to face Hodor, his eyes burning. "He's done it, Ben. By God, he's really done it."

Hodor nodded and switched to TRANSMIT. "Roger, Pebble 2. Out."

Down in the courtyard there was a sudden quiet, a second or two of shocked silence in which the tinkle of coins on stone sounded unnaturally loud. Then one of Jacobson's commandos shouted, "Pull the thieving bastards down."

Instantly two thousand people erupted in fury, rampaging across the cobbles, overturning table after table, ripping apart the stalls selling religious souvenirs. Released from their pens by the Pebble 2 commandos, the sheep and cattle plunged into the mêlée, bellowing and bleating in terror.

The commandos were everywhere, their black cloaks discarded, their rifle butts swinging, creating whirlpools of panic as the chain reaction began to run free.

The noise now was unbelievable; a sustained, bellowing shriek, high-pitched, savage, beating bedlam fists against the high enclosing walls, reaching up to crack the sky. A mindless, apocalyptic howl of rage. But to Barabbas it was music; the splendid opening statement in a symphony of freedom.

He stood by the window, his hand resting lightly on the barrel of the rocket launcher, his mouth curved in a hard smile. This was how they had planned it, down there in the caves below Masada.

A major riot in the heart of the city to draw some of the opposition and shorten the odds against Tigal and Rosh and Sorek. He turned, shouting to Hodor, "OK, Ben. Get 'em started!"

Hodor nodded and crouched over the microphone. "Hullo all Pebbles. All Pebbles. This is Slingshot. *Go! Go! Go!*"

3

Jack Tigal swung the bulky furniture van into the traffic stream moving down the Rehov Hanevi'im towards the Damascus Gate.

Tigal was from Beer Sheba; a big-boned, leather-skinned desert man, five foot eleven, hook-nosed, with dark, dangerous eyes. He was twenty-nine and a widower. Five years earlier his young wife had died unpleasantly and without dignity, spread-eagled naked over the tailboard of a Tenth Legion liberty truck, a first field dressing wadded into her mouth.

Tigal was not interested in freedom, only in vengeance. Barabbas and the other Pebble commanders saw SLINGSHOT as being a means to an end. But to Tigal it was an end in itself. What happened afterwards was unimportant.

Behind him in the stuffy gloom of the van fifty men of Pebble 4 Commando, sweating in denims and jump boots, eased the chinstraps of their para helmets and took fresh grip on their automatic rifles. Tigal's Tigers, they called themselves; the toughest troops in Barabbas's tough little guerilla army. Big men in the peak of condition after ten weeks' intensive battle training in the wadis south of Arad, on their way now in a latter-day Trojan horse to seize control of Imperial Army HQ, Jerusalem.

A truck-load of dynamite, running out of control into the crowded city, could not have been more dangerous.

Outside Radio House opposite the Jaffa Gate the chartered EGGED bus pulled into the kerb. Carrying small airline bags the men of Pebble 1 Commando, looking like tourists in crimplene suits and flowered shirts, stepped out on to the pavement and clustered casually round Sorek.

The youngest of the Pebble commanders, Peter Sorek was twenty-two, long-legged, foot-loose; as good with words as Tigal was with a gun. Behind his quiet poet's eyes they shimmered in brilliant kaleidoscopic patterns of beauty and meaning. When he talked about freedom even Shad Rocci listened.

Nobody knew what his background was. He had drifted into the camp below Masada one afternoon, bearded, in faded, sweat-stiffened jeans, with a sleeping-bag and a guitar, sensed the dedication burning in the tough, silent men who had come out of the caves to stare at him, and joined them, asking no questions, offering no explanations. Just being there, as if he had always been there, and fitting in.

The common denominator was freedom. To Sorek, drop-out, visionary, freedom was what it was all about. The only reality. A gate in the wall of time through which he could glimpse another world where men might live in dignity, at peace with their neighbours, unafraid, without envy. He recognised in SLINGSHOT the key to that gate. The key was an iron one, ugly as the grenades packed now into those airline bags his commandos carried. But the gate itself, like the world beyond it, was pure gold.

Astonishingly neat now in the dark-blue uniform of a Trans-Med Tours courier, freshly shaved, shoes polished, his fair hair cut short, Sorek slung the strap of his walkie-talkie over his shoulder, grinned at his men and began to lead them up the steps to the main doors of Radio House. Once inside, the doors sealed, the microphones open, he would come into his own as the voice of Free Israel.

Four miles away up the Nablus road the black Fiat hearse turned into the approach to the Kalandia Airport terminal building. In the five funeral cars behind it thirty men of Pebble 3 Commando sat upright in black coats and black trilby hats. Thirty men and one woman in full mourning, her face heavily veiled. Beside the driver in the hearse, with the flower-covered coffin crammed with high explosive at his back, their commander, Tzev Bruchman, slid a new battery into his hearing-aid, clipped it back into place and hooked the small plastic box on to the outside of his breast-pocket. He lodged the tiny speaker more comfortably in his left ear and adjusted the volume.

"Easy, now," he said in his flat, deaf man's voice. "We're not pushed for time."

Five foot five, thin as a winter fox and as cunning, with a pale oval face and eyes like black olives, Bruchman was SLING-SHOT's explosives expert. A withdrawn, self-contained man, he moved deftly through a microcosmos of wiring-circuits and time-clocks, setting trembler fuses with the delicate precision of a master watchmaker. Which he had been, until a Roman bull-dozer had demolished his shop to bring through a new motor-way.

A dispassionate man, he had turned without bitterness from re-pairing watches to blowing bridges and booby-trapping ball-point pens. For those he destroyed he felt neither hatred nor pity, nothing. His intensely orderly mind, insulated by his deafness, rejected emotion, finding it crude and untidy. Nor was he moved by dreams of freedom. His world rotated smoothly on the axis of fuse and detonator; a fascinating, predictable world in which, being the master, he was completely free. The fact that it was a maverick planet careering through the universe leaving a trail of destruction behind it troubled him not at all. Everything was focused on the explosion; the correct charge at the precise second in the exact place. What happened after was unimportant.

"Give me the airport, Barabbas," he had said at the briefing for SLINGSHOT. "I'll dig a grave in the main runway big enough to bury a regiment."

In the full-dress uniform of a colonel of the 3rd Hussars, the transistorised walkie-talkie concealed under the short cavalry cloak slung by its chain from his left shoulder, Paul Rosh climbed out of the staff car and walked coolly up the steps of the Residency. The sentry presented arms. The duty sergeant opened the door to him and saluted.

"Afternoon, sar'nt." Rosh's lazy drawl matched his aristocratic face, the row of good medal ribbons on his tunic. Odd man out in the SLINGSHOT team, he had been given the critical assignment: to kidnap the Governor-General and deliver him safely to Sorek at Radio House.

He handed the forged special pass to the sergeant. "Colonel Rosh, representing the C-in-C Egypt."

"Sir." The sergeant looked at the pass. "I'll have to check with Security, sir."

"So I should hope," Rosh said frostily.

The sergeant withdrew into a small side office. Rosh took off his gloves and stood waiting, relaxed, assured. Tall, educated, polished, with grey eyes and a short, straight nose, he looked the part exactly: from silver spurs to gleaming cap badge the epitome of military sophistication.

He had joined SLINGSHOT nine months earlier, driving down the wadi into the camp one blazing July day in a brand new long-wheel-base Land-Rover, calmly ignoring the dozen rifles trained on him from the rocks on either side. With him in the Land-Rover were a suitcase full of expensive clothes and a tin trunk containing twenty thousand pounds in Roman Occupation currency.

In spite of the money, without which SLINGSHOT could not have got off the ground, he was not popular with the other Pebble commanders. They were suspicious of his upper-class background and resented the contemptuous line of his mouth, the inborn arrogance of his manner.

"OK, so we need the bread." Sorek had said that night. "Him we can do without."

There had been a growl of assent from the others crouched round the fire in the entrance of the cave.

"We need him," Barabbas had said simply. Only he knew of Rosh's encounter with Jesus Davidson and the subsequent selling-up of his estates north of Haifa. Only he recognised the value to SLINGSHOT of a young aristocrat for whom the good life had suddenly gone sour and whose disenchantment had crystallised into a calculated, diamond-hard devotion to the dream.

"He's useless," Tigal had said then. "Fancy clothes, hands as soft as a bint's. And he stinks like a Greek whore."

Barabbas had grinned. "A little after-shave never hurt anyone."

Tigal had scowled. "He's not one of us. Any fool can see that."

"For God's sake, Jack, use your head," Barabbas had said. "That's why we've got to have him. If anyone can talk Pilate out of the Residency and over to Radio House, he can."

Rosh looked through the glazed doors, over the sentry's shoulder, to the flower beds in the lawn fronting the Residency. Half a dozen gardeners with hoes and a wheelbarrow were weeding the beds; six members of his Pebble 5 Commando. He knew they had automatic rifles hidden in the barrow under a layer of weeds and dead flowers; knew also that on both sides of the house and round at the back more of his men were posted, ready to close in if he gave the signal.

The sergeant came back with his pass. "Thank you, sir. You're cleared to go in now." He pressed a bell-push in the wall. "Sorry for the delay, sir. Security's a bit tight just now. It's the Passover, sir."

Rosh nodded. Not tight enough, laddie, he thought. Not nearly tight enough.

A footman came through the far door at the end of the hall. The sergeant said, "Take this officer to the ante-room." He saluted Rosh.

Rosh returned the salute, casually flicking his gloves at the peak of his cap. "Thank you," he said. "Oh, and sar'nt."

"Sir?"

"That man outside."

"Sir?"

"I suggest a little extra arms drill. I've seldom seen a sloppier Present."

The sergeant flushed. "Sir."

Rosh followed the footman down the hall. The sound of his black cavalry boots echoed off the parquet floor like the sound of drumsticks on the rim of a drum. Or the ticking of a bomb.

4

Tigal took the furniture van in through the Damascus Gate, turned sharp right into the little square outside Army HQ, drove in under the raised barrier and stopped outside the main guardroom.

A Roman soldier with a sub-machine gun slung over his shoulder and the green and white flash of the Tenth Legion on his sleeve pulled himself up on to the running-board. "What's all this then?"

Tigal gave him the docket. "Load of junk for the Officers' Mess."

The soldier looked at the docket. "Oh, ah? First I've heard of it."

Tigal shook his head. "Always the same, innit? Sweat your guts out to deliver the bloody stuff and when you get there nobody wants to know."

"Hang about, then," the soldier said. "I'll get through to the Mess Sergeant and check."

"You do that, mate," Tigal said, putting his right hand into the pocket of his dust-coat and slipping his middle finger through the ring on the grenade.

The soldier dropped off the running-board and went up the steps on to the veranda that ran along the front of the guardroom. Tigal eased the grenade out of his pocket and cradled it in his lap under the rim of the steering-wheel. With his other hand he banged twice on the back of the cab to alert his men.

The soldier opened the guardroom door and put his head inside. Watching him, Tigal was aware of the noise coming faintly across the city from the Temple, growing in volume, like the roar of some gigantic waterfall.

The knuckles of his right hand whitened as the klaxon mounted on the veranda roof blared its warning.

The soldier came running back, waving his arms, shouting. "Get that bloody great thing out of the way." His voice was thin against the full-throated klaxon.

Tigal grinned, dropped the grenade back into his pocket and slammed the gear lever into first.

"Come on, man," the soldier yelled. "Move, for God's sake."

Tigal revved the engine and drove up the concrete road, past the Stores and round into the yard. He was just in time. As he turned the corner the first Romulus APC lurched round the end of the Armoury, tilting on its massive springs, thundering down towards the main gate, its siren screeching as the driver kept the heel of his hand on the button. Watching in the wing mirror Tigal saw two more come down behind it, their commanders standing upright in the turrets; heard the harsh whine of gears as they slowed for the gate, the deep snarl of the big, eight-cylinder engines accelerating away into the city.

He grinned and took the van up beside the Stores, turned left round the back of the NAAFI and left again into the road that bordered the parade ground. Behind him now two more Romulus carriers were drawn up outside the Armoury. In the mirror he could see the crews standing in a disciplined rank beside each one.

In a hundred yards he swung right, crossing the width of the parade ground, travelling at a steady fifteen miles an hour. He turned into the road leading to the HQ Admin Block, rounded a bend and drew up neatly outside the Orderly Room. He cut the engine, got down from the cab and slipped out of his dust-coat, transferring the grenade to the thigh pocket of his combat denims. Like his men waiting in the back of the van he had the Tenth Legion flash sewn to his sleeve. He reached in the cab for his automatic rifle and the para helmet with a captain's stars painted back and front, walked unhurriedly to the rear doors and slid back the bolts.

"OK, Tigers," he said. "Let's go."

The ground hostess at the EL AL check-in counter put the phone down and smiled. "That's all in order then, sir. You're cleared with Traffic to use the perimeter road to Bay 8. This is your pass." She clipped a green card to the sheaf of documents and handed it to the solemn little man in the black suit and crêpe-banded top-hat. "Second bay past the tower. The aeroplane is waiting. A Caravelle. There'll be an air hostess to meet you there, as you requested."

Bruchman nodded, hearing her voice thin and clear, the warmth filtered out of it by his hearing-aid. "Thank you. Madam is bearing up very bravely, but seeing the coffin go on board might be a difficult moment for her. A woman's touch at that point . . ." He tucked the papers into his pocket.

The girl said sympathetically, "A close relative?"

"Her husband," Bruchman said. "Only forty-one." He looked at his watch. "Take-off is at half past two, I believe?"

"Fourteen-forty now, actually. We've had to put it back a little. There's a special flight from Rome coming in at fourteen-twenty."

"VIP?"

"Very important." The girl indicated the soldiers positioned about the terminal; by the Customs barrier, inside the main doors, on the stairs leading up to the spectators' lounge; big, un-smiling young men in battle fatigues, their blunt-barrelled rifles held ready across their chests. "Hence the security guards." She smiled. A pretty girl with a warm, reassuring smile. But it was wasted on Bruchman. "Gives you that little bit more time to get loaded on before they taxi down to pick up the other passengers at Gate Six," she said. "Goodbye, Mr. Bruchman. Have a good trip." She stopped short, staring embarrassedly at his funeral clothes, and blushed. "I mean—er—I'm sorry. I . . ."

Bruchman raised his hat gravely, turned and walked out between the banquettes crowded with waiting passengers to the hearse standing under the canopy outside the big glass doors.

"On to the peri-track. Turn left," he said to the driver. "Bay 8. Slowly now." He settled into his seat as the cortège began to roll. "Largo's on schedule. Due in at twenty past."

The driver pursed his lips. "Doesn't give us too much time."

"Enough. Once we move we've got to be quick anyway." Bruchman lowered the window as they came to the junction with the perimeter road.

The soldier on duty there took the green card, examined it and handed it back. "Thank you, sir." He saluted as the coffin passed him.

The girl on the reception desk in Radio House was a young blonde, chosen for her looks. She looked up at Sorek and smiled, turning the visitors' book round on the desk and giving him a biro. "If you'll sign just here, please."

Sorek signed, gave her the pen back and shepherded his men across the entrance hall to the lift. They bunched together round the doors, covering for the two who slipped quickly into the men's lavatory, giving Farat the chance to get down the stairs to the basement.

When the lift arrived they crowded in and rode straight up to the World Television Authority suite on the fifth floor. Two men got out there and the lift started down again, stopping briefly at each floor to let men out.

The two men in the ground-floor lavatory opened their airline bags, strapped on ammunition belts and stood behind the door with their machine pistols loaded and cocked.

Down in the basement Jim Farat put down his bag and pressed the button to call the lift. He watched the lights flashing on the indicator, aware of the deep humming of the generators behind him; a compact, well-muscled man in his late twenties, with side-boards and a heavy, Greek-style moustache.

One of the maintenance engineers came down the corridor and looked at Farat's cream shirt overprinted with large purple flowers. "Lost your way, mate?"

Farat smile apologetically. "Damned stupid, really. Going round with one of these conducted tours. Nipped into the gents for a minute. When I came out they'd disappeared."

The engineer nodded. "Won't find 'em down here. Out of bounds to the public, this is. Try the third floor. That's the telly studios. They usually make for them first."

"What's down here, then?"

"Generators. Air-conditioning plant. One or two bits of electronic gubbins." The man grinned. "What you might call the throbbing heart of Radio Jerusalem."

Farat heard the lift come down and stop. "Well, thanks. Third floor, you said?"

"That's where they'll be, mate."

Farat watched him go round the corner and stepped into the lift. He closed the doors, unscrewed the plate on the control panel and disconnected the main fuse. Working quickly in the dark, he prised open the escape hatch above his head, pushed his bag through and climbed out on top of the lift. It took him less than a minute to wedge the smoke canister securely in place and rip off the plastic cap. As the smoke gushed out into the shaft he dropped back, closed the hatch, reconnected the fuse and screwed the plate back into place. He pressed the DOOR OPEN button, stepped out into the corridor and made for the stairs.

The salon was at the back of the Residency; a long, high-ceilinged room with tall windows opening on to a terrace above the water gardens. The silk-lined walls were hung with full-length portraits of former Governors-General, a massive head-and-shoulders in oils of the Emperor Tiberius in the dominant place over the marble fireplace in which stood an enormous vase of flowers.

Completely at ease in a well-remembered world, Rosh stood near the windows at the end of a long buffet table, a glass of wine in his hand. There were about sixty officers in the room, chatting in small groups under the great crystal chandeliers which fractured the sunlight into patterns of brilliant colour. The Governor-General moved slowly from group to group with his aide, working his way down towards Rosh.

In his middle fifties, bulky and upright in the gold-piped dress blues of an Imperial Field Marshal, His Excellency Lord Pilate, Governor-General of Judea, Honorary Colonel of the Praetorian Guard, Knight of the Illustrious Order of the Eagle, looked as impressive as his titles. Seen like this across a room blazing with magnificent uniforms, he radiated confident authority, his silver-grey hair brushed back in wings, the straight Roman nose supporting a broad forehead. Only his petulant mouth with its over-full lower lip betrayed the anxiety that gnawed him like a cancer.

And, as he drew nearer, his eyes. They were muddy brown, a little too small for his face and very slightly unfocused, like the eyes of a myope too vain to wear glasses. But in Pontius Pilate, vacillator, political blunderer, the myopia was the result not of weak muscles but of a weak will. Inside the heavy body under the impeccably cut tunic crouched a small, unhappy man who lived in a haze of fear and suspicion, stumbling uncertainly down the corridors of power haunted by his past mistakes, envious of his superiors, uneasily conscious of the contempt of those who served him.

As he approached, Rosh set down his glass on the white-clothed table and stiffened to attention.

The aide, a bored-looking major, round shouldered and running to fat, inquired his name and made the introductions.

Pilate offered his hand, smiling. "Good to see you, Rosh."

Rosh shook hands, feeling the bones small in the soft padding of flesh. "Thank you, sir." Perhaps an inch taller than Pilate, he looked down into those muddy eyes, detecting the uncertainty that underlay the smile.

"Weak as water and suspicious as hell," Barabbas had said. "How're you going to handle him, Paul?"

"Flattery spiced with menace," Rosh had said. "The right words in the wrong tone of voice."

"And how's my old friend Brigadier Mors?" Pilate said.

Rosh looked at him coolly. "The C-in-C asks me to convey his sincere apologies, sir." He kept his voice level, with just a hint of something unspoken behind the formal words. "He deeply regrets that he cannot be here in person today."

Pilate's smile slipped a little. "Trouble?"

"Trouble, sir?" Rosh raised his eyebrows as though hearing an indelicate suggestion. "Not really, no." He paused, timing it carefully, then flung in half-a-dozen words, like a fisherman scattering ground bait. "No more than usual, that is."

"So why isn't he here?" Pilate said. It was obviously meant to sound peremptory; the question of a man used to being obeyed. Instead, it sounded peevish.

Rosh smiled reassuringly. "The Brigadier's war wound is playing him up a little."

36

"War wound? Jumbo Mors?" The little brown eyes peered at him suspiciously. "Is this some sort of a joke, Rosh?"

"A diplomatic one, sir. Actually, it's his gout."

"Oh, that." Pilate's grin was relieved, finding the ground bait innocent of hooks. "Giving him the jumps, is it?"

Rosh nodded. "Nothing seems to help much."

"He could try signing the pledge, eh Max?" Pilate said.

The aide smiled politely.

"It's a great disappointment to him not to be here, sir," Rosh said. He paused and baited the hook this time. "Especially in view of the situation."

The hunted look came back into Pilate's eyes. "Situation? What situation?"

Rosh heard the anxiety nibbling at his voice and dropped the hook neatly. "In the Negev," he said. "It's really of no consequence, sir. Straws in the wind. No more than that."

Pilate cleared his throat. "Colonel Rosh, would you mind telling me just what the hell you're talking about?"

Rosh looked at him speculatively. Timing was everything now. The bait had been taken, but had it been swallowed?

"Well?" Pilate said irritably. "I'm waiting, Colonel."

Rosh decided to strike. "Jesus Barabbas," he said quietly. He saw the flicker of pure terror as the brown eyes narrowed momentarily into focus, and knew the hook was in.

"Barabbas?" Pilate's voice was suddenly hoarse. "What about him?"

Rosh looked pointedly at the room full of officers and half turned towards the door that led on to the terrace. "With your permission, sir. We'd be more private outside, I think."

Tigal's Tigers took the HQ Admin Block in three minutes flat, exploding out of the back of the furniture van and into the long, low building on a shock wave of violence, kicking open the doors, hosing the offices with their automatic rifles.

In those three terrible minutes fourteen men died; seven in the Signals Section, six in the Orderly Room, and the Adjutant who was in the CO's office at the end of the block.

Tigal killed the Adjutant. He was arranging some papers on the Colonel's desk when the big, hook-nosed man from Beer Sheba burst in.

"You Macer?" Tigal rapped.

"The Colonel's down at the Armoury." The Adjutant swung round and stared at Tigal. "Who the devil are you?"

Tigal grinned. "The new CO," he said, and shot him.

They bundled the bodies into the van and drove it round behind the block, locked the doors of the Adjutant's and CO's offices and occupied the Orderly Room and the Signals Section which were connected by a wall-hatch.

Tigal picked up the phone, checked the numbers on the list pasted to the wall above the Orderly Room Sergeant's table, and dialled.

"Armoury. Sergeant Gramer."

"Adjutant here," Tigal said crisply.

"Sir."

"Let me talk to the Colonel."

"Sorry, sir. The Colonel's not here. He went out in the first Romulus."

"The devil he did," Tigal said. "Have you had a sit-rep from him?"

"Not yet, sir. They're in action, though. We heard a fair bit of firing just now."

"From the Temple area?"

"Over that way, sir, yes. Sounded a bit close, actually. But you know how sound carries this sort of weather, sir."

Tigal grinned. "Right. Now listen to me, sar'nt. I'm taking one of the stand-by Romuluses out after him."

"Sir."

"Have it sent round to my office, will you?"

"Sir."

"And sar'nt, I want a loud-hailer hooked up in the turret."

"Sir."

Tigal grimaced. It was like talking to a dummy. "Well, get on with it, man," he said. "Should be here now."

He put down the phone and grinned at his men. "OK, lads. Sort yourselves out. I want ten volunteers to go on parade outside."

The commandos pressed forward eagerly.

"Knives, not rifles, this time," Tigal said. "We do it quietly. You know the drill." He turned to his second-in-command, a thick-set man with sergeant's stripes sewn on his sleeves. "Right, Matt. Fall 'em in on the road. The rest of you stay put and keep your heads down."

When the Romulus rounded the corner two minutes later the young lieutenant standing in the turret saw the ten men, anonymous in para helmets and combat denims, lined up outside the Orderly Room with their sergeant, and Tigal standing a little apart from them by the door of the Adjutant's office, his thumbs hooked into his webbing belt. The driver had his hatch open and he pulled the Romulus in past the waiting men and stopped beside Tigal. The lieutenant saluted.

Tigal returned the salute, standing well back, his face in shadow. "I'll have the men out please."

"Sir." The lieutenant ducked his head inside the turret and shouted an order.

The armoured steel doors at the back of the Romulus swung open. Ten Roman troopers with automatic rifles jumped out and formed up in line in front of Tigal's men.

"Come on, come on," Matt shouted. "Pick up your dressing. That man there. Move yourself. Right. Still now. *Still*, I said."

The lieutenant climbed out of the turret and dropped down beside Tigal. While he was still off balance Tigal stepped up to him, pushing him back against the middle nearside wheel of the Romulus so that the open rear door hid him from his men, and thrust in his heavy, double-edged knife under the rib cage, dropping his wrist sharply to drive the blade up into the heart. The lieutenant's eyes bulged in shocked surprise and set in a glazed stare. His throat contracted. Blood came out of his mouth.

Tigal withdrew his knife and let the body slump down. He tucked the knife down the side of his boot, pulled himself up on to the Romulus and stood by the turret looking down on the two ranks of men. "Thank you, sar'nt," he said.

Matt recognised the signal, saluted, called the men to attention. As the Romans in the front rank obeyed the order—eyes front, feet together, backs straight—the commandos took one pace forward, clamped their left hands over the Romans' mouths and knifed them in the back. It was done quickly, smoothly, with the precision of a drill movement. Watching, Tigal remembered the count: "One. One-two. Pause. And out," which the commandos had shouted in the wadi during rehearsals.

"Right, Matt," he said then. "Get 'em aboard." He dropped down through the turret, knife in hand, and killed the driver sitting at the controls. Coming in through the rear doors, Matt pushed past him, heaved the driver's body out through the forward hatch and climbed into his seat. The last of the commandos jumped in and pulled the rear doors shut.

Standing in the turret, the loud-hailer hooked into the circuit, the intercom lead plugged into his helmet, Tigal pressed the microphone button. "When you're ready, Matt."

The girl on the reception desk in Radio House smelled something burning, looked up from her book and saw the smoke drifting out round the lift doors. She let the book fall, reached across and pulled the alarm switch. Right through the building the bells began to ring.

The girl started round the end of the desk towards the lift and stopped short, her face suddenly white, as the two commandos burst out of the lavatory, their machine pistols levelled at her stomach.

Farat came racing up the last flight of stairs from the basement. His shirt was smeared with black grease from the lift cable gear, his hands and face streaked with oil and smoke stains. The girl screamed and ran for the phone at the far end of the desk. Before she had taken two paces a spatter of bullets from the machine pistol shattered the instrument. The girl screamed again and swerved towards the main staircase. Farat ran across, scooped her up in his arms and bundled her out through the main doors.

One of the commandos went quickly down the basement stairs and crouched in the angle of the wall on the first corner, positioned to prevent any of the maintenance staff from coming up. The other stood with his back against the lavatory door; a big, bearded man in a fawn suit and suede, slip-on shoes, the pistol like a toy in his hand.

By now a great column of smoke filled the lift shaft. Up on the top floor one of the commandos thumbed the button. As the lift went up the shaft the smoke was forced out under pressure round the doors on each floor, swirling down the corridors and into the studios and offices in a dense, oily cloud.

The internal phone on the reception desk began to ring, its bell cutting thinly through the clamour of the alarms. Farat grabbed it, shouted, "Fire. Fire. Everybody out!" and slammed it down.

The plan was gathering momentum now. From the fifth floor down the commandos swung into well-rehearsed action, racing along the corridors, kicking open the fire exits, bursting into rooms, whooping and yelling incoherently, creating an infection of blind panic which spread rapidly through the building.

Farat stood at the foot of the main staircase listening to the shouts and screams, the thud of running feet, the strident hammering of the alarm bells. He ran across to the main doors and whipped them open as the first typists and clerks from the administration offices came stumbling down the stairs, gasping for breath, eyes streaming from the smoke.

"Outside. Outside." Farat made his voice a yelp, feeding the hysteria. "Come on. Come on. Everybody out. Quick, quick, quick!"

The cast of the Tuesday play, wearing period costume, ran out from a recording session in Studio 2 on the fifth floor and were herded down the corridor to the stairs by the commandos. Two floors down, Radio Jerusalem's Chief Announcer broadcast a calm statement which regretted the unavoidable break in programmes and promised that normal service would be resumed as soon as possible, pulled off his headphones and ran for the door as the engineer on the control panel shut down the transmitter.

A commando on the top floor ran to the lift, yanked the pin out of a grenade and lobbed it inside. He reached in to press the GROUND FLOOR button and stood clear as the doors slid shut. Three seconds later the grenade exploded, blowing the roof off the lift, severing the cable. The lift dropped down the shaft, knocked off the vertical by the explosion, and jammed itself at an angle just below the ground floor.

Through the buckled doors a huge cloud of dust and smoke

eddied out across the entrance-hall. By now the staircase was bulging with screaming, shouting people fighting to get out of the building. They fell back as the blast of the explosion hit them, going down in a tangle of arms and legs to be trampled on by those being chivvied by the yelling commandos behind them. For a few seconds the staircase was completely blocked by a mass of struggling bodies.

Farat shouted, "Get 'em moving. Quick, for God's sake."

The bearded commando raised his machine pistol and fired into the ceiling, bringing down a shower of plaster through the drifting smoke. Goaded by the harsh rattle of the pistol, demoralised by the insistent clanging of the alarm bells, the choking smoke, the high-pitched yelping of the commandos, the terrified people on the stairs broke free, clawing their way out of the heap to go plunging across the entrance-hall to the open doors. As they streamed past him Farat looked up at the clock on the wall above the reception desk. It was just six minutes since the girl had pulled the alarm switch.

The three Romulus carriers came down Chain Street in convoy, drivers' hatches open, the commanders standing with head and shoulders out of the turrets. In the leading vehicle Colonel Titus Macer MC, Officer Commanding the Tenth Legion, looked with cold grey eyes at the seething mob behind the iron gates of the Temple courtyard, ordered his driver to halt and picked up the loud-hailer.

Up in the Command Post Barabbas went down on one knee beside the rocket launcher, pressed his eye to the rubber-mounted sight, curled his finger round the trigger.

"Go for number two," Hodor said.

Barabbas grunted, swinging the barrel left. The head of Colonel Macer slid across the sight and disappeared as the large-bore barrel traversed, leaving the first Romulus and picking up the second in line. The cross-wires of the sight settled on the driver's hatch, dipped a little, focused on the triple-barrel smoke gun mounted on the superstructure above the nearside front wheel, and steadied.

". . . *Unless these gates are opened in ten seconds, I'm coming through them.*" Macer's voice boomed out through the loud-hailer, bouncing over the heads of the suddenly silent crowd. "*One. Two. Three . . .*"

Listening to the clipped Roman voice Barabbas said softly, "Oh, you bad bastard," and squeezed the trigger.

A gout of flame and exhaust gas licked across the room behind him as the big hollow-charge projectile began its brief flight to the target. The cone-shaped warhead, charged with high explosive, sliced through the smoke gun on the Romulus, penetrated the plating below and entered the driving compartment between the driver's feet, killing him instantly. The flash of the explosion was smothered in a thick surge of black smoke as the bombs ready-loaded in the smoke gun erupted.

On his knees at the window opening Barabbas saw Macer's head whip round, mouth wide open in a useless shout of warning; saw the steel doors at the back of the leading Romulus fly open and the troopers stumbling out, coughing and retching in the acrid smoke. He reached up and dropped another round into the muzzle of the rocket launcher, training the barrel back now to the leading Romulus.

Standing on the steps of the Temple portico Jacobson fired a short burst into the air to rally his commandos. Above him in the shadow of the marble columns, Jesus Davidson and his men stood in a close-packed bunch, dominated by the huge figure of Peter Johnson, looking even bigger in a blue-and-white checked shirt. Over to their right several members of the Sanhedrin, wearing their ceremonial robes, watched the crowd with anxious faces.

Battered and grinning, their faces streaked with sweat, the commandos shoved their way out of the crowd towards Jacobson and began to form up in line across the foot of the steps. Jacobson looked over their heads and saw the black smoke filling the street beyond the gates and the flash from the upstairs window as Barabbas fired the second rocket.

It hit the front offside of the leading Romulus, smashing the giant wheel and exploding in the engine compartment. Caught half-way out of his hatch, the driver was cut to pieces by shards of flying metal.

A wave of cheering swept across the courtyard. Jacobson turned on the steps, looked up at Davidson and flung out his arm towards his commandos. "Your Guard of Honour, sir," he shouted. "Ready to move when you say the word."

The people in the crowd immediately below him swung round. Three hundred arms went up like spears as they stood in the dusty sunlight, saluting the young man who would, before the day was out, be crowned King of the Jews.

5

"A detachment of the Tenth?" Surprise and anger struggled in Pilate's voice. "Mors expects me to send half my garrison out on some wild-goose chase down there in the Negev?"

"Hardly a wild-goose chase, sir," Rosh said. "They're gathering in the hills east of Kadesh. We know that."

"How many?"

Rosh shrugged. "Not easy to answer that, sir. At least a thousand. Could be twice that." He looked at Pilate. "It's a force to be reckoned with, sir."

"It's a rabble, Colonel."

"With Barabbas in command?" Rosh shook his head. "I think not, sir."

They reached the end of the terrace and turned back towards the aide standing outside the glass door of the salon. Pilate took out his handkerchief and dabbed at his face. He was sweating heavily. In the few minutes they had been pacing the terrace he seemed to have aged ten years.

Which was part of Rosh's plan; an anxiety neurosis, created by a mythical crisis in the desert, to soften him up for the snatch.

But you're not part of the plan, my friend, Rosh thought, watching the aide out of the corner of his eye. I didn't reckon on you being here on the wrong side of that door.

"It's not on, Rosh," Pilate said then. "You go back and tell Mors it's just not on."

Rosh nodded. "I understand, sir. It was only a suggestion on the Brigadier's part."

Pilate grunted. "Not one of his brighter ones. Doesn't he realise we're in the middle of the Passover here?"

45

"I doubt it, sir. The Brigadier takes very little interest in religion. Especially other people's religion."

"Then it's time he woke up."

"Sir?"

"The Passover's not just a religious event, Rosh. I learned that very early in the piece. It's political with a capital P. Oh, they dress it up with a lot of high-flown nonsense about unleavened bread and half-cooked mutton. But basically what they're talking about is revolution. Freedom, Rosh. Jewish Independence. That's what the Passover's about."

They turned again at the head of the steps leading down into the garden. Rosh was poised, ready on the balls of his feet. But the aide was still there by the door.

"This Barabbas," Pilate said. "I'll concede he could be dangerous. But he's not the only one, you know. Good God, no. His kind come by the dozen. And you don't have to go ferreting round in the Negev to find 'em. They're here in Jerusalem. The city's full of them this week. Anarchists. Rabble-rousers. Agitators. Prospective kings of Israel, every damned one of 'em." He looked up at Rosh. "We've been at Red Alert here since last Friday, Colonel. Did you know that? All leave stopped. Special security measures. Round-the-clock armed patrols." His lip curled. "And Mors calmly sends you to ask for reinforcements to help him cope with a rabble of desert cut-throats who may or may not be planning some kind of mischief in the Negev. Doesn't make sense, does it?"

"Put like that, sir, no."

"Unless, of course," Pilate said uneasily, "somebody's put him up to it." They stopped at the end of the terrace and he looked over his shoulder quickly and then said, "You know who's coming here today? Who this reception's for?"

"Senator Largo," Rosh said. He looked down the terrace, willing the aide to go inside. Time was running out.

Pilate said, "Julius Largo. Hallum's private jackal. The trickiest, craftiest political lackey in . . ."

"I'm sorry, sir," Rosh said stiffly. "I don't see what the Senator's reputation has to do with Brigadier Mors's request for troops." He took a pace forward.

Pilate fell into step beside him. "On the surface, nothing at all,

Colonel. But is it really just a coincidence?" He shook his head. "Why does Largo suddenly decide to visit Jerusalem in Passover week? I don't like it, Rosh. There's something going on. Something ugly brewing-up here in the city with my name on it, designed to pull me down. A neat little coup hatched out by those bureaucrats in Rome with their secret files and their private little empires. Something that needs the Tenth out of the way for a few days. Something Largo has come to master-mind." He looked up at Rosh and away again. "They want me out of the way, Colonel. I've known that for long enough."

Rosh saw the sweat beading on his forehead, the pallor spreading under his tan. This time, he thought. Aide or no aide, this time we go.

"Odd you should say that, sir," he said.

Pilate stopped. "What?" His muddy eyes peered at Rosh. "You know something, don't you?"

Rosh took him by the elbow and began to walk again. "It's just something I happened to overhear, sir. I didn't attach any importance to it at the time. But in view of what you've just said I . . ."

"Yes? Out with it, man. What have you heard?"

They drew level with the aide. Rosh looked at him pointedly and then at Pilate. "Perhaps a glass of wine, sir, while we're talking?"

"What?" Pilate looked at the aide. "Oh yes. Of course. Excellent idea. Some wine, Max."

The aide said, "Out here, sir?"

"Of course, out here."

The aide nodded and went inside. Rosh held the door for him, slipped out the key, closed the door quietly and locked it from the outside. He took Pilate's elbow and began to walk him towards the steps. "This is extremely confidential, sir."

"Of course. Of course." Pilate hesitated as they reached the top of the steps.

"Just keep walking," Rosh said pleasantly. "There are, at this moment, at least five sub-machine guns trained on you." He felt Pilate sag and gripped his arm more firmly. "No need to panic."

They began to descend the steps, Pilate feeling his way with his feet like a blind man. "Look here, Rosh, I . . ."

47

"You really ought to choose your gardeners with more care," Rosh said. "Rough-looking chaps, some of them. And so numerous. Front garden. Back. Both sides too, I shouldn't wonder."

They walked along the path between the bushes that led to the cobbled yard and the garages behind the west wing of the house. Two of the commandos stepped out of cover and fell in behind them. Six more were moving quickly from bush to bush, working their way towards the terrace; purposeful, quiet-footed men armed with sub-machine guns.

"I demand an explanation of this extraordinary behaviour." Pilate's voice was thin, eaten away by fear.

"Ever read the book of Job?" Rosh said. His hand tightened, his fingers digging into Pilate's arm. "No? You should. There's a sentence in it sums up the situation rather well, I think. 'The thing I greatly feared has come upon me.' "

Rosh's driver had parked the staff car in the yard and run out Pilate's black four-litre Lancia. He had the back door open and the engine ticking over as Rosh and Pilate came into the yard.

Rosh said, "In you get. Quickly now."

Pilate hesitated, saw the four commandos strategically placed around the yard with levelled rifles, and climbed in.

"Any trouble?" Rosh said.

The driver grinned and shook his head. "Chummy's chauffeur was a bit stroppy. Seemed to think we might scratch the coachwork."

"And?"

The driver shrugged. "Situation vacant." He struck a pose. "How does the uniform grab you? Not a bad fit, eh?"

Rosh nodded and got into the back of the Lancia where Pilate was huddled miserably in the corner, white-faced above the tunic which now looked a couple of sizes too big for him. The driver slid in behind the wheel with one of the commandos beside him; a neat, unremarkable man, looking every inch the Special Branch inspector in grey flannels and a dark-blue blazer which bulged slightly over the 9 mm. pistol in its armpit holster.

"Right," Rosh said.

The gold-on-black Governor-General's pennant lifted and stiffened above the long bonnet as the Lancia accelerated out of the yard. Rosh pulled up the aerial of his walkie-talkie. "Pebble 5 to Slingshot." His voice was coolly matter-of-fact. "The goods are undamaged and in transit. Over."

Hodor rubbed his knuckles over his stinging eyes and grinned at Barabbas through the smoke drifting in over the window sill of the Command Post. "He's done it. He's got Pilate out."

The low-ceilinged room, stinking of smoke and exhaust gases from the rocket launcher, reminded him of the gun deck in a painting of an old naval battle. The roar of the crowd, like an angry sea beyond the window opening, and the sweating figure of Barabbas, crouched stripped to the waist over the rocket launcher, added to the illusion.

Barabbas nodded and grinned. He slid another projectile into the barrel, spat plaster dust out of his mouth and raised his head cautiously above the sill. "Time we heard from Sorek."

Hodor looked at his watch. "Time yet. It's not Sorek I'm worried about. It's Davidson. What the hell's he doing down there?"

Barabbas got his right shoulder under the rocket launcher and swung it left, searching for his target. "Ah, come on, Ben. Stop knocking him, for God's sake." He grunted, identifying a gleam of metal in the sight as the command turret poking up through the smoke that filled the street. "He can't do a damn' thing yet, can he?" he said and took first pressure on the trigger. "Not till we've clobbered this last APC."

In Radio House the Pebble 1 commandos were mopping up. The smoke was clearing a little now, drifting out through the open windows.

Sorek stood by the stairs on the first floor and shook his head with relief as Farat cut the alarm bells. In the sudden silence he heard the clatter of feet on the stairs. The commandos came running down, driving before them at gun-point a middle-aged executive in an expensive suit.

"He the last?" Sorek said.

The commandos nodded, their faces glistening black masks of sweat and smoke, as incongruous above their flowered shirts as the short-barrelled guns in their hands.

49

"OK," Sorek said. "Let's go down and wrap this up."

A small crowd had gathered on the pavement outside, talking to the staff members, staring at the ragged black curtains of smoke floating out of the upper windows. An armed Land-Rover of the sector patrol swung across the traffic and into the kerb. Two soldiers, wearing side-arms and white-painted helmets, jumped out, pushed through the crowd and came racing up the steps.

The middle-aged executive was floundering down the last few stairs into the entrance-hall when the soldiers charged in. His warning shout changed to a hoarse shriek as the bearded commando swung his machine-pistol in a tight arc and chopped them down. The commandos on the stairs grabbed his arms and ran him out of the building. He lost his footing on the steps outside and fell awkwardly, rolling down into the crowd below.

"That's it," Farat shouted. "Get those doors shut."

The commandos dragged the bodies of the soldiers to one side, slammed and bolted the doors and took up their positions by the windows, breaking the glass with their gun barrels. In the crowd outside somebody screamed.

Farat turned to the bearded commando. "Cover the back entrance, Dave. They'll be bringing Pilate in that way." He pointed to the dead soldiers. "Two of you get those uniforms on. He'll need a guard when we take him out to say his piece." He glanced up at the clock on the wall and looked at Sorek. "Now it's a toss-up who gets here first, Pilate or the Riot Squad."

Sorek looked at his smoke-streaked face, the sweat shining in his moustache, and grinned. "Let 'em all come. We've got this far. They won't stop us now." He took off his uniform jacket and dropped it on the reception desk, loosened his tie, rubbed a hand over his strangely short hair. He was smiling and excited, his eyes bright, patterns of words like chord groups clustering round the visions in his head. He picked up his walkie-talkie and extended the aerial. "Pebble 1 to Slingshot. Over."

Calm and clear Ben Hodor's voice came back. "Hullo Pebble 1. This is Slingshot. Over."

"OK, Ben," Sorek said. "You are listening to the voice of Free Israel."

They had taken out the last three rows of double seats on the port side of the Caravelle to make room for the coffin. The bearers eased it down into position and stood back, shielding Bruchman from the air hostess while he draped a white dust sheet over it and checked that the firing mechanism built into one of the chromium-plated handles was properly connected to the aerial soldered to the lower inside surface of the chromed rail running round the coffin just below the lid. Satisfied, he stood up and smiled gravely at the air hostess. "Thank you."

She nodded uncertainly, watching the men troop back up the aisle. Trained to cope with drunks, babies, hysterical women and men who tried to pinch her bottom as she moved past them, she was a little out of her depth with a coffin.

Below on the tarmac the mourners began to get back into the cars. At the forward end of the aisle Bruchman was talking to the woman who stood, a lonely, veiled figure, just inside the door of the aircraft. After a moment or two he came back down between the seats and said to the hostess, "Madam would prefer to go back to the Departure Lounge and board with the other passengers. Is that all right?"

The hostess looked doubtful. "I was told you'd both be boarding here, sir."

"Yes, I know. The fact is—" Bruchman lowered his voice "—she wants to, you know, use the toilet."

The hostess nodded. "Of course, sir. I quite understand. You've got your boarding-cards?"

"Yes."

"No problem then." She looked at her watch. "Time for a cup of tea, too, if she feels like it. Boarding will be at Gate Six. You'll hear the announcement."

She walked back with him and stood at the open door as he took the woman's arm and helped her down the steps and into the back of the first car. The car turned in a wide circle, passing the tug attached to the nose of the Caravelle, and headed down the perimeter road towards the Control Tower. The hearse and the four other cars turned after it and moved away in a long stately line.

The hostess waited until two EL AL technicians had moved

51

the steps away and then closed the door and went through on to the flight deck.

The flight engineer looked up and said, "All right, love?"

She nodded.

He grinned. "Cheer up then. It's not your funeral."

Five hundred yards away the first car slowed, pulling over to let the hearse and its convoy go through and turning in towards the Control Tower. The driver edged in close to the wall so that the car was hidden from the slanted, anti-dazzle windows above, and stopped a few feet from the door. A radio-equipped Land-Rover, painted bright yellow, with a big, rotating loop aerial mounted on the roof of the cab, was parked just beyond the door. Bruchman got out of the car and stood with his jacket unbuttoned and his hand on the butt of the pistol tucked into the waistband of his trousers, waiting for someone to come out of the tower. He waited a full minute but nobody came. "All clear," he said and walked across to the Land-Rover.

The woman and a commando got out of the car carrying two suitcases, went over to the door of the tower, opened it and stepped inside. The lift-shaft was set off centre with the stone staircase going up round it to the radar room on the first floor and the hexagonal, glass-sided control room at the top. The commando put the suitcase containing the UHF transmitter on the floor by the lift, opened the other case and took out a length of rope, a machine-pistol, three spare magazines and a black leather satchel with a shoulder strap. He gave the satchel to the woman, picked up the rope and tucked the machine-pistol into the front of his coat. He put a finger to his lips, grinned at the woman and went quietly up the stairs.

The woman took off her veil and hat, revealing a young, surprisingly pretty face and elaborately coiffured, metallic blonde hair. She unbuttoned her black maxi-coat and slipped out of it. Underneath she wore a trim, dark-green uniform skirt and jacket, with metal lapel badges, and a white blouse. She took a small green forage cap out of her handbag and put it on, rolled hat and veil in the maxi-coat and dropped them in the suitcase and slung the black satchel over her shoulder.

Up on the first floor the commando looped the rope round the handle of the radar-room door, pulled it tight and made the other end fast to the iron handrail at the turn of the stairs. He tested it, ducked under it and came back down.

Sitting in the back of the Land-Rover Bruchman saw the woman come out of the tower door in her uniform and nod to him. He switched in the mobile radio telephone, adjusted the volume control of his hearing-aid and dialled the Duty Controller.

"Tower."

Bruchman said, "Civil Airways Authority here. Let me speak to Miss Rahav, will you?"

"Who?"

"Miss Rahav. She's one of our CAA inspectors."

"Not here, I'm afraid."

"No? She should be by now."

"Sorry. She's not."

"Ah," Bruchman said. "Well, look, she's due any minute. Will you ask her to ring Head Office when she gets there?"

"Will do."

"Thanks." Bruchman cut the connection and climbed out of the Land-Rover. He joined the woman and the commando in the tower and closed the door. "Right. They're expecting you now, Esther. Use the lift. I want them distracted long enough for us to get up the stairs. Shouldn't be difficult."

She nodded.

"Got the box of tricks for the panic button?"

"Yes." Esther patted her satchel.

Bruchman looked at the commando. He had taken off his long coat and was tucking the spare magazines into the pockets of his leather jacket. "Ready, then, Nick?" He pulled open the lift door and Esther stepped inside.

"One-and-a-half minutes. That's all we need," Bruchman said. Esther nodded and pressed the button.

The six-wheeled Romulus APC came out on to the parade ground travelling fast. From the open turret Tigal could see the other one outside the Armoury, its commander and crew standing beside it. He lifted his hand, acknowledging the lieutenant's salute, as they rolled past. Into the microphone he said, "Straight down to the main gate, Matt. Slow down a bit."

Matt changed down through the gears, letting the speed fall away. Tigal picked up the loud-hailer and switched it on. "*Stand to, the Guard.*" His voice cracked out, echoing off the walls of the buildings. "*Come on. Let's have you then.*"

Back on the parade ground the crew of the other Romulus heard his words and grinned at each other. "Good old Adj," one of them said. "Dead regimental, emergency or no bloody emergency."

The Romulus slowed to a walking-pace. As the Roman guards doubled out, pulling on their helmets and fastening their combat jackets, the six commandos on the superstructure dropped down and ran towards them, knives out and ready. Jumped by apparently friendly troops, the Romans never had a chance. In less than thirty seconds they were all dead.

Tigal switched off the loud-hailer and spoke on the intercom. "Everybody out. Swing her round, Matt."

The Romulus slewed round and stopped broadside-on to the road, blocking the gateway neatly. The commandos tumbled out of the back doors and ran to take up their positions. Matt climbed out of the driver's hatch and stood on the casing, rifle in hand, facing the little square outside the gates. Tigal unplugged the intercom lead and hoisted himself up out of the turret. "Get those bodies out of sight," he shouted. "Come on, shake it up a bit. We haven't got all day." He dropped to the ground and went up on to the guardroom veranda, watching his men drag the last of the bodies through the door of the cell-block and come running out again. "Right, lads." he said. "Up you get."

They swarmed up the veranda posts on to the roof and lay flat, sighting their automatic rifles up the camp road. There were others already lying on the roofs of the Stores and the NAAFI, and more down at ground level, crouched at the corners of the buildings. In the guardroom itself they were smashing the windows to give themselves a clear field of fire. Satisfied that the trap was set, Tigal turned and signalled to Matt.

Matt climbed down into the turret of the Romulus and traversed left, swinging the 7·62 mm. machine-gun to cover the camp road. Tigal went into the guardroom and pulled the switch of the klaxon.

The harsh panic note blared out for the second time that afternoon and he stood in the doorway, looking up the road, waiting for the other Romulus to come down.

Hearing the klaxon the people gathered in the little square outside the gates began to scatter. Up on the roofs the commandos tucked their rifle butts firmly into their shoulders and eased off the safety catches.

The stand-by Romulus came round the corner of the Armoury. The lieutenant in the turret saw the empty road and the Romulus blocking the exit, and reacted quickly. But not quite quickly enough. By the time he had relayed the order to halt, the Romulus, travelling close to its limit, had covered thirty yards. It rolled past the end of the NAAFI building, crabbing slightly as the driver hit the brakes. The commando lying with his legs straddling the roof ridge fired a short burst. The heavy-calibre bullets took the lieutenant in the base of the neck, almost decapitating him. The Romulus ran on ten more yards and stopped, well over on the right-hand side of the road, up against the wall of the Stores. The Romans came out of the rear doors in a crouching run and were caught in a lethal cross-fire from the commandos. The driver stood up, leaning forward to pull his hatch cover into place. Matt squeezed the trigger of the turret gun briefly and saw the driver lifted and hurled backwards as the bullets slammed into his chest.

Tigal cut the klaxon and picked up the phone. He dialled the Orderly Room. "OK, we've got the gate and the other APC. Now listen. Two of you stay on the switchboard. Anyone rings up, transfer to me here . . . Roger. The rest of you split into three groups and work your way through the camp and down to us here . . . no, no prisoners. And I want grenades in the messes and the barrack blocks. . . . Yep. If Seeker was right there won't be much opposition . . . Roger. We'll deal with the Armoury from this end. . . . OK. On your way."

He put the phone down and stepped out on to the veranda. The clock by the door said fourteen-twenty-seven.

The Lancia purred down the winding road between the tall cypresses that barred the smooth tarmac with shadows. The commando beside the driver had his pistol out of its holster and was screwing a silencer on to the barrel. The car swung left into the main drive. The commando cocked the pistol, held it in his right hand between the two front seats and wound down the window at his side. The road curved and straightened; through the windscreen they could see the open gate and a corporal of the Praetorian Guard standing outside the wooden sentry-box. Between the corporal and the car one of the Pebble 5 commandos, wearing dungarees and an old hat, was trimming the grass verge with long-handled shears.

The driver pressed the horn button briefly and began to brake. The corporal saw the pennant, stamped to attention and presented arms. Pilate sat forward, reaching for the window handle.

"I wouldn't if I were you," Rosh said quietly.

Pilate turned his head and saw the pistol in Rosh's hand. He sank back in the seat, the sweat shining on his face.

The Lancia drifted to a stop opposite the sentry-box. The corporal stood stiffly, eyes front, rifle held vertically against his chest. Rosh glanced back through the rear window and saw the commando had put down his shears and was walking unhurriedly towards the car.

The man beside the driver lifted the pistol into his lap. "Corporal."

"Sir." The corporal swung his rifle down and took a pace forward. The bullet from the silenced pistol thudded into his forehead. He dropped in mid stride, dead before he hit the ground.

The commando came up, hooked his hands under the corporal's armpits and dragged him into the sentry-box. He turned his head and looked towards the car, his fingers already busy on the buttons of the dead man's tunic. "OK. Take off," he said. "I can cope."

The man beside the driver grinned. "Hope it fits you, mate."

As the Lancia pulled away Pilate said in a shocked voice, "Murderers."

Rosh looked at him coldly. "This is war, my friend."

"It's murder," Pilate said. "Wanton, cold-blooded murder."

They forked right out of the Nablus road into the Rehov Shivtei Israel, moving down through the smart suburbs northwest of the city. The light afternoon traffic pulled over to let them pass as the drivers looked in their mirrors and saw the pennant flying above the Lancia's bonnet.

"There was no reason to kill that corporal," Pilate said. "He saw my pennant. He would have let us through."

Rosh nodded. "Right. But it's not quite so simple as that. Any minute now that aide of yours is going to start worrying. He'll ring up the gate and ask questions. We needed to put one of our men there to make sure he gets the right answers."

They crossed the Rehov Hanevi'im, where Tigal had waited earlier in the furniture van, and went on down towards Zahal Square, the old grey city crouched like a lion below them. There were more people in the streets now: pilgrims and their families up for the Feast, window-shopping in their best clothes. Pilate looked at them miserably. They stared at the car without expression and turned their heads away in a pointed gesture of rejection.

"They don't seem to like you much," Rosh said pleasantly.

"No."

"It doesn't worry you at all?"

Pilate licked his lips. "I've always considered it more important to be respected than to be popular."

Rosh heard the fear under the pompous words. "Don't kid yourself," he said brutally. "They don't respect you either. They hate your Roman guts."

Pilate's eyes flickered. "That is something men in my position must learn to live with."

"Live with," Rosh said. "And perhaps die for."

"Die for?"

Rosh nodded. "It's a possibility I think you should reckon with."

Pilate looked at him. Below the silver hair, the senatorial brow, his face had shrunk against the bones. The brown, myopic eyes were filmed with fear. "In God's name," he said. "What's this all about?"

Rosh made his voice casual. "You're on your way to abdicate. We've got our own king now."

6

Sitting left of centre at the long console in the control room, Cy Paxton put down the phone disgustedly. "That's all we need. A spot-check by CAA." He was in his shirt-sleeves; a compact, unflappable man with prematurely grey hair.

A yard to his right, Lex Vigo, the Ground Controller, young, laconic, unfashionably neat in charcoal grey slacks, white shirt and rather conservative tie, pushed the headphones back behind his ears. "You're joking, of course."

Paxton shook his head. "She's on her way up."

"She?" Vigo's eyebrows rose interestedly. "You mean it's a girl?"

"Female, anyway." Paxton grinned. "Don't get excited, son. She's probably flat-chested and wears bifocals." He watched the blip on the radar repeater scope slide over the threshold of the glide-path and pressed his microphone switch. "Alitalia 61. This is Kalandia Tower. Turn left two degrees on to one zero three. Clear for straight-in approach. Runway 24. Over."

"Roger, Kalandia." The Trident captain's voice was loud in his headphones. "Turning on to one zero three. Out."

Vigo said hopefully, "They're not all dragons in CAA. I remember one time at Lod they sent a little redhead. She . . ."

Out of the corner of his eye Paxton saw the warning light flash as the lift came up. "Bifocals," he said. "You'll see."

The lift door slid open. Cool and poised in her green uniform, Esther stepped out. Paxton slipped off his headphones and put them on the console. He stood up. "Miss Rahav?"

Esther nodded, unbuttoned the left breast-pocket of her jacket and took out a CAA pass. "CAA."

Paxton said, "I'm Paxton. This is my Ground Controller, Lex Vigo."

Vigo grinned. "Hi." He half rose, his headphones still in place. He muttered happily to Paxton, "What d'you mean, flat-chested?"

Esther said coolly, "Please sit down, gentlemen. I believe you have a Trident on finals." She walked forward as they settled back in their seats and put her satchel on the console in front of the red EMERGENCY button between the two controllers. "He's on the scope now, I take it?"

Paxton hooked on his headphones and nodded, pointing to the blip on the little screen. "Head Office want you to ring them, by the way," he said.

As if on cue the phone by his left hand began to ring. He pulled the headphone away from his ear and picked up the receiver. "Tower."

The Airport Manager's voice said, "This is an emergency, Cy. Divert 61 to Lod. He must not land here. Understood?"

Paxton glanced at the blip on the screen. "Bit late for that, sir. He's well down the glide-path already."

"You've got to stop him, Cy. There's a hostile reception committee waiting for Largo. It's vital he——" The voice stopped abruptly. Paxton heard a rattle, a series of clicks. Then the phone went dead. He put down the receiver and lifted his hand to his microphone switch.

The blunt, cold snout of the machine-pistol nudged the back of his neck. A voice behind him said, "Hands flat on the desk." The gun jabbed in under his ear. "Not tomorrow. Now!"

Esther said, "You too, please, Mr. Vigo."

Vigo turned his head and saw the small automatic in her hand less than two feet from his head.

"I hope you aren't going to be foolish," Esther said. She smiled charmingly, her eyes reflecting the green of her uniform; a pretty girl, fresh-faced, dangerous.

Vigo shrugged and let his hands lie on the console.

The little blip that was Alitalia 61 slid past the two-thousand-yard marker, coming in sweetly down the centre of the glide-path. Esther stepped back a pace, positioning herself to cover both controllers. The commando moved round the end of the console, his machine-pistol levelled at Paxton.

Bruchman walked from the head of the stairs, past Esther to the satchel; neat, almost dapper, in his black suit, the hearing-aid box hooked on his breast-pocket like a square, white plastic flower. He opened the satchel and took out a small metal-alloy box fitted with terminal wires. He crouched down under the console, took a screwdriver out of his pocket and unscrewed the plate below the red EMERGENCY button. It took him only a few seconds to wire-in the metal box, tape it to the underside of the console and replace the plate. He straightened up and smiled at Paxton. The Controller looked at the black olive eyes without pleasure.

"This little device", Bruchman said in his flat voice, "has an effective blast range of twenty-five yards. It also has a short-delay fuse. If one of you gentlemen is foolish enough to press the panic button there will be just time for us to get down round the bend of the stairs. We will not, of course, be in a position to cover you from there and you will doubtless make an attempt to escape." He shook his head. "A useless attempt, I'm afraid." He stepped round the back of Paxton's chair, walked down the length of the console and stood looking out of the window.

Paxton stared at his back. "Just one small question. What exactly do you hope to . . . ?"

"You're wasting your time, Mr. Paxton," Esther said. "He's switched-off his sound."

There was a flash of sunlight on metal and a muffled, beating roar as the big Series 2E Trident, with the Alitalia logo painted on its high, distinctive fin, dipped over the perimeter fence, the multiple wheels of its landing-gear reaching for the concrete.

"Here comes our VIP," Esther said.

The howl of jets in reverse thrust thundered against the windows. The Trident slowed on the runway. Esther leaned forward and flicked on the relay switch. Through the loud-speaker the captain's voice asked for taxi instructions.

Esther smiled at Vigo. "Answer him, please, Mr. Vigo. Strictly by the book. No tricks. No heroics." The automatic in her hand was very steady.

Tied to a chair in his office above the terminal building the Airport Manager watched the Trident swinging in towards Gate

One, and the whistle of its engines was like a voice in his head screaming at the captain to turn round quickly before it was too late. Through the window on his left he could see the passengers filing up the steps into the EL AL Caravelle at Gate Six, and at them too the voice was screaming. He saw it all happening with a kind of sick despair, like a man trapped in a nightmare, forced to watch ordinary people shuffling unknowingly towards some horrifying climax of which he was powerless to warn them. The commando sitting behind his desk, the sub-machine gun lying cocked on the blotter, the mute telephone he could no longer reach—all these were part of the nightmare. He looked at the commando, his eyes blazing in his white face. "For God's sake, man," he said hoarsely. "You can't wipe out a hundred and forty innocent people just like that."

"You'd better believe it," the commando said. "We can. And if we have to, we will."

The four funeral cars were lined up neatly on the tarmac outside Gate One. Twelve men of Pebble 3 commando, sub-machine guns held muzzles down under their long black coats, stood by the wheeled steps and watched the Trident coming down the taxi-path towards them. Grouped casually in the sunshine they looked calm and relaxed; a perfectly normal, if somewhat soberly dressed, reception committee for a man holding senatorial rank.

Behind them in the corridor that led from Gate One through Customs and Immigration to the Arrivals Hall there was blood on the tiled floor and half-a-dozen bodies sprawled inside the plate-glass doors starred by bullets. Four commandos—all that were left of the original ten set to hold the corridor—stood in a tight semi-circle behind the girl from the car-hire counter and faced the Roman security guards beyond the doors. One of the commandos had his right arm round the girl's waist. In his hand pressed against her stomach was a grenade from which the pin had been withdrawn. The girl sagged, eyes closed, face chalk-white, in the circle of his arm.

From the right-hand seat on the flight deck of the Caravelle the First Officer saw the last passenger come aboard and flipped a switch as the door shut. "Kalandia Tower, this is EL AL 632. Do you read me? Over."

In the control room of the tower Esther said, "Thank you, Mr. Vigo. Be careful, please."

Vigo pressed his microphone switch. "EL AL 632, this is Kalandia Tower. Reading you fives. Over."

"EL AL 632. Permission to start engines. Over."

Vigo looked at the machine-pistol resting on the wind-velocity indicator, pointed unwaveringly at his head. "Roger, EL AL 632. Out."

Julius Largo, wearing a dove-grey, light-weight suit, biscuit-coloured shirt and a broad-brimmed Panama hat, ran lightly down the steps to the tarmac. Sixty-one, lean, the tan on his face dark below white hair, Largo liked to be described as spry. Behind rimless glasses his eyes were coolly watchful; shrewd blue eyes unaffected by his smile.

"Gentlemen," he said, and put out his hand.

One of the commandos gripped it and held on, turning on the ball of his foot, slipping his left arm under Largo's elbow and clinching it tight. Another fell in on the senator's left. The rest bunched round, coats open now, guns levelled.

"This way, Senator." They began to march him towards the waiting cars. A crackle of shots sounded from the corridor beyond the gate. Clustered at the top of the steps by the Trident's doors, several passengers screamed and began to push back inside.

Largo said, "What's this? Trouble?"

"Spot of bother," the commando on his right said. "Sounds worse than it is."

They got into the back seat of the first car with him between them. The driver started the engine and slipped into gear. The commandos were tumbling into the other cars, running out of the corridor across the tarmac, covered by two of their number who walked slowly backwards, the guns jumping in their hands.

Largo sat back calmly as the cars began to move. "Some Jewish terrorist organization, I take it?"

The man on his right shrugged. "Something like that."

Largo nodded. "One had heard, of course, that things were a trifle—turbulent in this Province. Indeed one is here precisely for that reason." He took off his hat and rested it primly on his knees. "Even so, one hardly expected quite so—vigorous a reception." He leaned forward slightly, looking at himself in the driver's mirror and ran a hand lightly over his thick white hair, touched the knot of his tie. "I shall be interested to hear the Governor-General's explanation." He sat back, his eyes gleaming coldly behind his glasses. "As, I imagine, in due course His Imperial Majesty will."

"EL AL 632 to tower. Holding on runway 24. Over."

Vigo said, "Roger, 632. Take-off in one minute. Over."

"One minute. Roger." The First Officer's voice changed. "What's all the excitement by Gate One? Over."

Esther said warningly, "Careful, Mr. Vigo."

Vigo pressed his microphone switch and swallowed. "One of these stupid bomb hoaxes. No sweat. Out."

Esther nodded approvingly. "Very sensible."

Bruchman turned from the window and walked back towards the controllers. He stood between them and turned up the volume control on his hearing-aid. "Now listen to me," he said. "And listen very carefully."

The 84 mm. projectile sliced the turret off the third Romulus in Chain Street, killing the commander, exploding downwards among the men packed inside. Barabbas grabbed his automatic rifle and moved to the right of the window opening, pressing against the wall, peering down into the street below.

"Father to all Little Boys. All Little Boys. A riot has broken out in sector C Charlie figures 10. Big Boy 3 has been captured undamaged and fully operational." Locked into the Roman Armed Patrol frequency, Hodor crouched over the RT set, moving his coloured marker pins on the map, setting up one of the Roman armoured cars for an attack, creating a little private civil war in the northern suburbs. "All Little Boys proceed at once to Yisa Bracha and Yeheskiel. This Big Boy must be destroyed. Acknowledge. Over."

He flipped the switch, listened for a moment, grinned and put up his thumb to Barabbas as the patrol crews in the armed Land-Rovers began to call in.

Down in the smoke-filled street Macer was rallying the survivors from the APCs, deploying them behind the wrecked vehicles. Barabbas swung his rifle, firing short bursts to pin the Romans down. He shouted across to Hodor, "Get through to Jacobson. Tell him we need some action."

Hodor changed frequencies and switched to TRANSMIT. "Slingshot to Pebble 2. Come in, Pebble 2. Over."

"Pebble 2 here. Over." Something in Jacobson's voice—a hesitancy, a barely perceptible note of bitterness—touched Hodor like a cold finger.

"Andrew, for God's sake," he said. "What's Davidson up to down there? Over."

"Hold on, Ben. We're trying to locate him now. Out."

Barabbas saw one of the Romans climb up on the back of the leading Romulus and tilt the machine-gun up and round on its pintle mounting. He ducked away from the opening, back flat to the wall, as the heavy-calibre bullets ripped up through the ceiling. A cloud of plaster dust filled the room, powdering down on their heads, making up their sweating faces into grotesque grey masks.

"Trying to what?" Barabbas spat. He pulled the pin out of a grenade, let the spring-loaded lever fly off and hurled it through the window opening. The machine-gun stopped abruptly. Barabbas crossed to the table in two long strides and grabbed the microphone out of Hodor's hand. "Pebble 2," he said harshly. "This is Barabbas. Now hear me and hear me good. You get those men of yours over to these gates damn' quick and take some of the pressure off us. Right? Over."

"Roger, Slingshot. But——"

"No buts," Barabbas snarled. "Get 'em here now. And tell Davidson to stop dithering and get a bloody move on or we're all going for the chop. Him included. Out."

Tigal ran up the camp road, climbed into the Romulus by the Stores and swung it out to block the road. Between him and the Armoury several bodies lay on the concrete, each with a little cloud of black flies hovering over it. Some of his own men were among the corpses. But most were Roman.

He heard the thud of a heavy explosion and saw the Armoury roof puff up like a pie crust and a bright red flame shoot out of the window in the end wall. He pulled himself up through the turret, shouting to his men who came running back down the road, up over the Romulus and on down to the guardroom. He sat on the turret rim with a grenade in his hand and waited until they were all over and clear. Then he pulled the pin, dropped the grenade down between his feet and vaulted out, running round the corner of the Stores. The Romulus blew up. Bits of metal slammed into the brickwork and rattled on the concrete road. Tigal shouted to Matt to turn the other Romulus in the gateway and ran across the road to the guardroom.

His walkie-talkie was on the table by the door. He picked it up, thumbed the microphone switch. "Pebble 4 to Slingshot. Mission accomplished. Over."

Round him in the guardroom and out on the veranda his men stood breathing hard, their faces running with sweat below their helmets.

He grinned, looking at them with that special affection that exists only between soldiers who have faced death together; a strangely innocent love, compounded of pride and courage, generous, forgiving, inarticulate. "Well done, lads," he said.

They grinned back at him delightedly, teeth white in their dirty faces; a handful of irregulars in stolen uniforms who had taken on a crack Roman legion in their own backyard and won. One of them lit a cigarette and gave it to him. Tigal put it between his lips. A vague unease began to spread like a shadow across his mind; a sense of regret, of anticlimax. If all they said about Davidson and his kingdom was true he wouldn't be needed again. The Tigers had had their hour and now it was over. Tomorrow was empty, without promise.

He shook the walkie-talkie irritably. "Pebble 4 to Slingshot. Come in, Ben. Over." He pressed the speaker against his ear, heard

c 65

the muted rattle of rifle-fire and Hodor's voice suddenly loud, breathy.

"Hullo, Pebble 4. This is Slingshot. We need you here. I say again, we need you here. Over."

Tigal felt his heart thump. "They're in trouble. Ten of you in the Romulus. Move." He pressed the microphone switch. "Pebble 4 to Slingshot. On our way. Out."

From the shadow of the doorway under the iron fire-escape the bearded commando watched the Lancia come down the alley and across the private car park behind Radio House. He had the rear door open almost before the car had stopped. Rosh got out and they bundled Pilate between them into the building.

Sorek crossed the hall to meet them, stepping lightly, smiling. Rosh saw the excitement bright like fever in his eyes, took in the shattered lift door, the broken glass spiked in the window frames, the half-naked bodies of the two dead soldiers. "Fun and games?"

Sorek shrugged. "Bit uptight. Nothing we can't handle." He put his hands on his hips and stared at Pilate. "So this is our hero."

Pilate lifted his head a little, his shoulders squaring under the splendid tunic as his body went through the motions of facing a crisis his mind refused to recognise. Muddy brown in the pallor of his face, his eyes slithered from Sorek to the men crouched at the windows, flickered uneasily over the two corpses, settled with a gleam of hope on the two commandos wearing military uniforms. "You men," he said hoarsely. "Help me."

Sorek shook his head. "Bad luck, man," he said. "They're ours." He reached out his hand and touched the rows of ribbons on Pilate's tunic with the tips of his fingers. "Such gaudy, butterfly splendour," he said. "The colours of courage without the substance. I wonder if you'll survive the transformation."

"Transformation?" Pilate licked his lips. "What . . . ?"

"From butterfly back to chrysalis," Sorek said. "From glory to ignominy." He shook his head. "I doubt you'll stand the shock."

One of the commandos fired a brief burst out of the window. The quick hammering of the gun sounded unnaturally loud in the high-ceilinged hall. Sorek saw Pilate flinch. His fingers caressing

66

the medal ribbons stiffened and jabbed into Pilate's chest. His eyes lost their warmth. "You've fluttered and postured in the sun long enough," he said, and the rasp in his voice surprised even Rosh. "It's you for the dark now, my friend."

The commando fired again. Rosh moved quickly to stand, half crouching, behind him.

At the foot of the steps a Riot Squad half-track was parked on the pavement, backed up against the bonnet of the Land-Rover. The twin barrels of its water-cannon pointed up at the windows. The crowd had shifted to the far side of the road and packed into the shelter of the Jaffa Gate. Two police cars, slewed across the road, held back the traffic. On either side long lines of cars glittered in the sun through a blue haze of exhaust fumes.

The hose for the water-cannon lay limply across the bonnet of the Land-Rover. Watching, Rosh saw a soldier duck out from behind the half-track, grab the hose and begin to drag it towards the hydrant by the rear nearside wheel of the Land-Rover. The commando lifted his gun and sprayed bullets on the pavement just in front of him. He dropped the hose and scuttled back into cover.

Rosh turned. "Right. Let's have him out on the steps before somebody gets hurt."

Pilate said quickly, "You can't send me out there."

"But sir," Sorek said mockingly, "you *are* the Governor-General. One last little flutter in the sun for the butterfly of Rome."

"You don't understand," Pilate said, gabbling the words. "I can't just walk out and . . . there have to be precautions. A high balcony, police, my bullet-proof vest." His eyes darted pleadingly from Sorek to Rosh. "In my position I can't afford to . . ."

Rosh drew his pistol and cocked it. He stepped up to Pilate and jabbed the muzzle into his ribs. "You can't afford not to," he said. "We shoot you here, now. Or you take your chance out there with your loving subjects. Which?"

Hidden from the commandos on the far side of the half-track the sergeant unslung his automatic rifle and thumbed off the safety-catch. He edged along towards the rear of the vehicle and crouched, sighting over the metal tracks, settling the butt snugly into the hollow of his shoulder. Through the telescopic sight he

67

saw the doors open at the top of the steps and took first pressure on the trigger.

The silver-haired figure in Field Marshal's uniform filled the sight. The crossed wires bisected the gold button of the right breast pocket. The sergeant blinked, swore softly and eased his finger off the trigger with elaborate care.

Flanked by the two commandos in military uniform, Pilate stood just outside the doors, screwing up his eyes in the bright sunlight, his gold buttons gleaming, the coloured ribbons brave on the dark blue of his tunic. Standing a little behind him and to his left Rosh held the pistol against the small of his back. "Relax," he said. "I'll do the talking."

The crowd in the Jaffa Gate recognised the Governor-General and raised a ragged cheer. They spilled out across the road to cluster on the pavement by the half-track. Down the lines of cars caught in the traffic jam doors were opening. Drivers climbed out and stood, shading their eyes to get a better view. The smoke from the burning Romulus carriers in Chain Street drifted over the city to merge with that rising from the wrecked Armoury by the Damascus Gate. In the sudden silence the sound of the riot in the Temple courtyard came as a muted rumble across the rooftops.

Rosh raised his voice, a splendidly rakish figure with the cavalry cloak over his shoulder and the silver spurs on the heels of his high black boots. "It is the Governor-General's wish that you should all disperse quietly to your homes. There is no cause for alarm."

A voice in the crowd shouted, "You could've fooled me, mate," and was greeted with a burst of nervous laughter.

Rosh smiled. "All right. There has been some excitement. But it's all over now." Dropping his voice he said to Pilate, "Wave to them, man. Show the flag, for God's sake."

Pilate lifted his arm and waved it hesitantly. Below him the soldiers had climbed out of the half-track and stood ready with their rifles in their hands. He looked at them desperately, conscious of the gun in his back.

"Not a chance," Rosh said softly. "You'd be dead before they made the second step." He shouted, "His Excellency will be making a special broadcast to the nation at six o'clock this evening on radio and TV."

Pilate half turned his head. "What . . . ?"

"Eyes front," Rosh said sharply. And added more gently, "Don't worry about it. You'll be given a script. Rather a good one, in fact. Sorek's written it. He's very talented."

At the window behind them Sorek shouted, "Three cheers for His Excellency. Hip, hip . . ."

The commandos roared, "Hooray." The crowd joined in the second and third times.

"Another wave, perhaps?" Rosh said pleasantly. "Well done, sir. Thank you."

Down in the road the traffic was moving again. Encouraged by the police the crowd began to break up and move away. Pilate watched them hungrily, hopelessly, like a man on a desert island who sees his rescuers turn back half-way to the beach.

The sergeant got his men back into the half-track, stamped his right heel down hard on the pavement and presented arms. Pilate returned the salute sketchily.

"At least you'll have that to remember," Rosh said.

"You stop him half-way down the runway," Bruchman said. "Or he falls apart in the air thirty seconds after take-off."

Paxton looked at the UHF transmitter in the open suitcase on the console. Locked into the frequency of the receiver concealed in the coffin handle aboard the Caravelle, it needed only a flick of the switch to activate the firing mechanism and explode the bomb. A very big bomb. Bruchman had emphasised that.

At the holding-point at the end of runway 24 the Caravelle crouched for flight, trembling a little in the sunlight as the First Officer fed power into the jets.

"I could stop him now," Paxton said. "Where he is."

Bruchman shook his head. "My brief is to close this airport. And that means I want him half-way down the runway." The correct charge at the precise second in the exact place.

"Not easy," Paxton said. "Once he starts her rolling. He won't be expecting an abort order."

"And will ignore it from anyone but you," Bruchman said. "A voice he recognises and trusts."

Paxton said, "You've done your homework, I'll say that for you." He considered the little man in the black suit standing beside him. So small a man, so ordinary, to have so much power in his hands. "There are a hundred and forty people in that aircraft, Mr Bruchman. Innocent people."

Bruchman nodded. "A big responsibility for you. Of course, you have a choice. You could press the panic button." He smiled briefly, a cold, mechanical smile as impersonal as the metal face of the transmitter. "It would be a noble gesture. But useless."

"632 to Tower," the Caravelle captain's voice called in through the speaker. "Ready to go. Over."

"Well, Mr. Paxton?" Bruchman said flatly.

Paxton took a deep breath and nodded. "OK, Lex. Give him a green."

On the flight deck the First Officer opened the throttles and eased off the brakes. The vivid acceleration pushed him deeper into his seat. The runway rushed towards them, whipping back into the belly of the plane like a spring-loaded steel tape. Out of the corner of his eye he could see the control column vibrating under the captain's hands. He began to call the airspeed readings. "Seventy, eighty, ninety-five. Coming up to V One. V One . . . now."

"632. Abort. Abort. Abort." Paxton's voice slammed in through the headphones, rock-steady, authoritative. Like the punching of a fire-alarm knob it triggered off a pattern of instant reaction.

The First Officer yanked the throttles back. Dangerously close to flying speed the Caravelle faltered. He felt the long fuselage twitch as the weight teetered from wings to wheels and back again. The captain was calling for reverse thrust, braced stiff-armed, holding the nose-wheel down, fighting to keep the aircraft on the runway.

Up in the tower they saw the Caravelle flutter as the brakes dragged it back and down. Bulging out of shape under the tremendous pressure the heavy tyres clawed at the runway, throwing off puffs of smoke, leaving black streaks of burnt rubber on the concrete. The oleo-leg of the nose-wheel assembly dipped sharply. The Caravelle yawed to the right, threatened to ground-loop, recovered shakily, bounced, shuddered. They heard the engines shut down to a breathy whistle through which rose the high, thin squeal of the brakes.

Vigo checked that the commando with the machine-pistol was looking out through the windows at the Caravelle, braced his legs under the console, leaned back in his chair and thrust out his right hand, finger pointing. "Oh, no. My God, look at that!"

He saw Bruchman lean over the open suitcase, saw the automatic in Esther's hand jut into view in the corner of his left eye as she moved forward. He twisted in his seat, gripped her wrist, pulled her arm down and round and up behind her back. She gasped and jack-knifed and he snatched the gun out of her hand and held her forward with her face pressed against the metal top of the console. The commando turned sharply.

"Drop it, baby," Vigo said.

The commando saw the automatic pressed into Esther's neck, looked quickly at Bruchman and put his machine-pistol down on the console.

"Help yourself, Cy," Vigo said.

"I think not, Mr. Paxton." Bruchman's voice was undisturbed. The tip of the middle finger of his right hand caressed the firing switch on the transmitter with the gentle touch of a lover. Or the paw of a cat with a mouse.

Paxton sank back in his chair.

"Stand away from it, Bruchman," Vigo said. His left hand forced Esther's wrist up between her shoulders. His right hand was steady, holding the muzzle of the automatic against the white skin just below her ear.

Bruchman smiled coldly. "A hundred and forty to one. Reasonable odds, wouldn't you say?"

Down on the runway the Caravelle came safely to a stop just past the half-way mark. The captain's voice came through the speaker, throaty with anger. "Just what the oil-fired, super-heated hell is going on up there, Tower? Over."

"Gone?" Jacobson blinked the sweat out of his eyes. "What d'you mean, gone?"

Judas Simson shrugged his narrow shoulders. "He's run away,"

71

he said. "Again." Behind the heavy-rimmed glasses his eyes were as bleak as his voice.

Standing at the top of the portico steps Jacobson looked round wildly. The sweat was suddenly cold on his face. "But he can't've. Damn it, we've got this place sealed up tight."

"Not quite," Simson said. "There's a back way. Through the Temple into the High Priest's garden and out into the street by the Lion Gate." His lip curled. "Cousin John knows it well."

"Who?"

"John Zebedee. Caiaphas is his cousin."

Jacobson shook his head in bewilderment. "But why? We've got it sewn up, for God's sake. Look at 'em down there."

Below them in the courtyard the crowd seethed. The men had armed themselves with stones and lengths of jagged timber torn from the smashed stalls and were moving purposefully towards the iron gates, united now in their hatred of the Romans. Packed behind them in the corner by the Temple wall the women urged them on, their voices shrilling in a high, monotonous chant that scraped the nerves like a broken finger-nail. Crouched on the wall by the gates the Pebble 2 commandos were firing down into the troops in Chain Street.

Simson shook his head. "It'll be Zebedee's doing. He doesn't like violence."

"Now he tells me." Jacobson's voice shook with anger. "So what're we supposed to do about this lot?" He looked over the heads of the crowd as a heavy burst of firing swept two of his commandos off the wall. Their bodies twisted in the air and hit the cobbles just in front of the advancing men. What happened then was like the bursting of a dam. With a great shout of anger the mob rushed the gates, smashed through them and spilled out into the street beyond. Heedless of bullets they surged round the wrecked Romulus carriers and swamped the remnants of Macer's force. Within seconds the courtyard was empty except for a number of battered, unrecognisable corpses and the keening women.

"Dear God in heaven," Jacobson said softly.

With Davidson there to lead and control, it would have been the moment of victory; the fulfilment of the dream as the Messiah entered the city in triumph. Without him, it was a plunge into disaster.

A sentence remembered from his boyhood when he had stood with his father in the synagogue dropped like a stone into his mind: "They were scattered because there was no shepherd; and they became food for all the wild beasts."

He spoke urgently into his walkie-talkie. "Pebble 2 to Slingshot. Over."

"Hullo, Pebble 2. This is Slingshot." Hodor's voice was jubilant. "Many thanks for your help. Stand by to activate Phase 2. Out."

Phase 2—the procession through the streets of the Old City and the presentation of the Shepherd-King to his people on the steps of the Praetorium. Jacobson closed his eyes and squeezed the walkie-talkie in both hands, forcing himself to speak slowly. "Pebble 2 to Slingshot. Negative Phase 2. Davidson has backed down. I say again, Davidson has backed down. Over."

In the smoke-blackened Command Post Hodor stared at Barabbas, his eyes big with shock. "He's backed——"

"I heard." Barabbas snatched the microphone from him. "Andrew, this is Barabbas. Hold him there. Use force if you have to, but hold him. I'm coming down to knock some sense into his head. Out."

"Negative." The speaker amplified the hollowness in Jacobson's voice. "Davidson is not here. He's cut and run. Over."

"Cut and run?" It seemed to Barabbas that the floor of the room shifted under his feet, the walls cracking and tilting as his world began to crumble. "What about the others? Johnson, Levison, the Zebedee boys? Over."

"All gone," Jacobson said. "Except Judas Simson. He's still here. Over."

Barabbas thrust the microphone at Hodor. "Pull 'em out. All of 'em. Quick!"

Hodor hesitated, looking at his battle map. "Pull them out? But we're home and dry. Radio House, Army HQ, Pilate—we've got the lot. We can't . . ."

"Damn' right we can't," Barabbas said savagely. "Not without Davidson."

"But——"

C*

"Don't argue, damn you. Pull 'em out while there's still some left to pull out. We need a king. Davidson was it. Until we find someone else the people will follow we haven't got a prayer." He stood by the rocket launcher, fists bunched, eyes like black adamants, the sweat glistening in the red stubble of his hair, streaking his dust-caked face. "It's over, Ben. Finished. Kaput. Pull 'em out. That's an order."

Hodor punched the switch, his face bitter. "Slingshot to all Pebbles. All Pebbles. The sling is broken. Abort. Abort. Acknowledge. Over."

7

Hodor's signal to abort not only stopped SLINGSHOT. It destroyed it. The dream, the plan, the buoyant, reckless drive—that small, ugly word wiped them out.

Keyed up to accept violence and death, the commandos had no defence against betrayal. So long as Davidson was there, waiting in the wings, they were invincible. Without him they were lost.

It was as though David, having felled Goliath with a well-aimed stone, had run up the slope of the hill and drawn the giant's sword to cut off his head. And sensed, in that moment of triumph, that the God in whom he trusted did not exist. The sword was suddenly heavy in his hand so that he could no longer lift it. And the giant awoke and plucked the sword from him and killed him.

For Jack Tigal, approaching the junction of Chain and David streets in the captured Romulus, Hodor's signal was literally a death sentence, executed within minutes of being pronounced.

He acknowledged the order and saw the crowd burst out of the mouth of Chain Street, heard above the smooth beat of the carrier's engine the deep, animal growl of a street mob that had tasted blood. He ducked his head to the intercom microphone. "Turn right, Matt. Make for the Jaffa Gate. And get your foot down. It's all off."

He rammed the heel of his hand on the siren button, lurching against the rim of the open turret as the Romulus swung into David Street. The angry faces wheeled below him and he twisted round and saw the millrace of struggling men eddying round the wrecked APCs down by the Temple gates. A lump of limestone, sharp-edged, big as a man's fist, thudded against his helmet.

"Keep her going, Matt," he yelled. "The silly bastards think we're Romans."

The roaring mob poured after them down the funnel of the narrow street. Still looking back, Tigal called up his men in Army HQ on the walkie-talkie and ordered them out. The stones were flying thickly now, rattling on the superstructure, splintering against the walls on either side. He reached out to grab the pintle-mounted machine-gun and swung it round to fire over the heads of the running men.

The iron bracket of the ornamental lamp projecting from the wall above a house door caught him just below the rim of his helmet. His head snapped down as his neck broke. The edge of the turret chopped through his big hooked nose and bit deep into his face.

It was, as Hodor said later, a hell of a way to die.

Outwardly calm in spite of the sickness in his stomach, Rosh piloted the Governor-General down the steps of Radio House to the armed Land-Rover, preceded by the two uniformed commandos, their automatic rifles cocked and set to maximum rate of fire. He put Pilate in the front passenger seat and got in behind the wheel. The two commandos climbed in the back.

As they pulled away from the kerb the people queueing for country buses beside the Jaffa Gate stared and pointed.

"Smile, damn you," Rosh said. "You've got something to smile about now."

Pilate slumped in the bucket seat. "When you're taking me away to kill me?"

"Kill you?" Rosh said bitterly. "And have half the city shot in reprisal? Don't flatter yourself. You're not worth it." He turned right in Zahal Square and drove up past the Damascus Gate, heading for Shmuel Ben Adiya and the rough country beyond.

Sorek stood in the entrance-hall and watched the Land-Rover drive away. The sun gleamed on the white helmets of the commandos, picked out the rich colours in Pilate's tunic and Rosh's cavalry cloak. It was like watching a dream fade in the morning light.

Behind him, Farat said, "Coming, Peter?"

Sorek turned. "Everybody gone?"

Farat nodded. "All clear." The downward curve of his moustache echoed the disappointment in his eyes. "Time we were off, boy."

"Yes. OK," Sorek said.

"There's a couple of cars out the back. We can take our pick."

"In a minute," Sorek said. "You go ahead. I'll join you."

Farat looked at him uncertainly, worried by the dullness in his eyes. "Don't leave it too long."

Sorek nodded. "I won't."

When Farat had gone he closed the main doors and stood looking out through the glass panels. Implacable behind its grey walls the city crouched in the sunlight, its jagged skyline humped above the Jaffa Gate like the neck frill of a huge stone lizard. A hard, imprisoned city, heavy with ancient wrongs. What fools they had been to dare to believe they could set it free armed only with a dream and a handful of guns.

He pressed his forehead against the warm glass. His head ached with words—the abdication speech he had written for Pilate to deliver, the cues he had prepared for the interview on camera with Jesus Davidson. Good words, exact, subtle; words of truth and liberty to match the dawn of a new age of man. Words that were now meaningless; empty, foolish phrases floating in his brain. There was no new age. The country beyond the iron gates was no different from the world he knew and had rejected. He realised, too late, that to try to translate the dream into reality was to destroy it.

He saw the Romulus burst out of the Jaffa Gate, the lizard's scaly claw reaching out to crush. Tigal's body lay face down, folded over the turret rim, his right forearm hooked over the butt of the machine-gun. Sorek failed to recognise him, but he recognised the Tenth Legion insignia painted on the superstructure. He tensed and saw the machine-gun swing, pointing up towards him as the Romulus turned sharply to the left. It seemed to him, in that split second of fear, that a bullet from the angled barrel thudded into his forehead. But it was, in fact, a steel wrench which one of the forgotten maintenance engineers, coming soft-footed up the basement stairs, clubbed against his temple.

The four funeral cars came down Nablus Road in sedate convoy. As they turned right towards Zahal Square the walkie-talkie in the leading car picked up Hodor's abort signal. Sitting in the back Largo saw the stunned eyes of the commandos and smiled. "Back to the drawing-board, I fancy."

The man on his right snapped, "Shut your face, you."

"Charming," Largo said.

The driver glanced in his mirror. "Let's dump this old queen and go home."

"What about Tzev? He's still stuck in Kalandia control."

The man on Largo's left said, "Esther too. And Nick. We can't just leave them there."

"So?" the driver said.

"So we go back and get 'em."

They cut across the corner of the square into Shivtei Ysrael, travelling fast now, weaving through the traffic. A long, high, articulated delivery truck nosed out of an alley beside one of the departmental stores and blocked the street. The driver of the black car put his hand on the horn and braked hard. As the men on either side of him lurched forward, Largo grabbed the door handle and wrenched it down. The door flew open. He half jumped, half fell out of the car, stumbled, regained his balance and ran into the crowd on the pavement. One of the commandos made to follow him.

"Forget it," the driver said.

"But he——"

"The hell with him. It's Tzev we want now."

Andrew Jacobson ran along the base of the courtyard wall calling his men down. He felt his throat tighten and the bile was bitter in his mouth when he saw how few were left to answer.

They clustered round him in the shadow of the Golden Gate, sweating, dirty, clothes and hair thick with dust. He told them the news, his voice curt, and watched their grins fade. He kept two of them with him and sent the rest away. They went out through the gate, stumbling in their weariness, shoulders bowed, guns trailing loosely in their hands; a pathetic little group of beaten men who minutes before had been within sight of victory.

78

One of the men with him said, "Just let me get my hands on Davidson, that's all. Just let me get my hands on him."

"Amen to that," Jacobson said. He clipped a fresh magazine into his rifle and jerked his head towards the Command Post. "Let's go and get the boss."

They went with him willingly enough. But there was no bounce in their step, no eagerness in their eyes. They crossed the courtyard like three lonely ghosts, picking their way between the fly-shrouded bodies, dragging their feet in the dust of the dream.

Rosh drove round the long curve below Mount Scopus, pulled in to the side of the road and braked to a halt. The traffic was behind them now, the road empty, shimmering in the heat. To their right the ground fell away steeply into a deep ravine.

Rosh said, "Get out."

Pilate stared down into the ravine. The wings of hair, more grey now than silver, drooped over his temples, emphasising the weakness of his jawline. "You can't leave me here." He turned in the seat and saw the pistol in Rosh's hand. "No. Please. There's no need for that. I——"

"Out," Rosh said, his voice thick with disgust.

Pilate scrambled out awkwardly and began to walk back along the road, looking over his shoulder every few steps. One of the commandos set his rifle to single-shot and fired a couple of rounds into the air. Pilate broke into a shambling, rubber-legged trot.

Rosh watched him go. His eyes were slate-grey, bleak with thoughts of what might have been, what had so nearly been. Only the certain knowledge of reprisals, carried out with typical Roman callousness on women and children, prevented him from using his pistol.

Standing in the open lift Esther said, "Ready, Tzev."

Bruchman gave no sign that he had heard her. He had moved the suitcase to the end of the console and stood with it open under his hand. The two controllers sat in their places, hands in front of them, heads turned towards him. In the lift with Esther the commando kept his foot against the door and covered them with his machine-pistol. But they were not concerned with him. They were watching Bruchman's finger curled round the transmitter switch.

Down on runway 24 the Caravelle stood silent in the sunlight with the coffin bomb in its belly and a hundred and forty people strapped in their seats.

"Tzev." Esther's voice was pleading. Used as she was to Bruchman's detached calm there was something about him now that worried her: a remoteness frightening in its intensity.

"Tzev, come on. Let's go home." She shook her head. It was like talking to a robot. As if Bruchman, the man, shocked by Hodor's abort signal which had dropped like a spanner into his delicately balanced world, had withdrawn into some far, silent place and could no longer be reached. The slight figure in the black suit with the hearing-aid plugged into his ear was only a sort of after-image. The real Bruchman had already gone.

"It's over, Tzev," Esther said. "Finished."

Paxton sat rigid, his muscles aching, his mouth dry, watching that thin finger on the switch, aware of the struggle going on deep in Bruchman's mind. He compressed his lips, resisting the impulse to speak. He sensed the fine, tenuous thread that stretched between Bruchman and the girl; a thread that was their only hope of saving the Caravelle; a thread that could be broken by an unexpected voice, an incautious word.

"Not now, Tzev," Esther said gently. "There's no point now."

Something—the tone of her voice, her choice of words—got through. Bruchman nodded stiffly. His hand left the switch, felt in his pocket, took out a tiny pair of watchmaker's pliers. He snipped two wires in the transmitter, closed the suitcase and fastened the catches carefully. His movements were deft, economical. He lifted the case down and walked to the lift. The controllers turned slowly in their chairs, watching him.

At the door he said in his flat, mechanical voice, "The firing mechanism is housed in the handle of the coffin nearest the left foot. It can be unscrewed safely and withdrawn. It has a right-hand thread. Do not attempt to use your telephone. It is booby-trapped." He inclined his head briefly. "Shalom, gentlemen," he said and stepped into the lift. The door slid shut. There was a low whine of gears as the lift went on down.

Paxton swung back to face the console. "Get that thing off the panic button circuit. Quick." He pressed his microphone switch. "Tower to 632. Over."

Crouched under the console Vigo said, "I didn't see him fix the phone, did you?"

Paxton shook his head. "No. But I'm not taking any chances."

"632 to Tower. So what's new? Over." The strain in the captain's voice was wire-taut under the casual words.

"Tower here," Paxton said. "OK. The panic's over. You can start getting the pax off. Over."

"Will do. Over."

Paxton saw the black car swing out on to the perimeter road and head for the terminal buildings. "Tower here. My phone's on the blink. Can you get through to Security? There's a black car heading for the exit. I want it stopped. Over."

"Will do. Over and out."

Bruchman was driving; Esther and the commando were in the back.

They rounded the end of the terminal building and slowed for the check-point.

"Get down," Bruchman said.

Esther and the commando crouched on the floor in the back of the car. Bruchman wound down the window and held out his green card, letting the car roll slowly. The soldier stepped forward. As he did so the alarm klaxons burst into life. The soldier turned his head, startled. Bruchman dropped into first gear and accelerated away, off the perimeter road now, driving down towards the front of the terminal.

They were fifty yards from the corner when the long black bonnet of the first of the funeral cars came round, travelling fast towards them. Bruchman braked and pulled the car to the left, swerving off the road into the short-stay car park. He drove down the line of cars and rounded the end of it, braking hard. "Out," he said. "Separate and keep under cover."

Esther and the commando tumbled out of the car and ran up the line, crouching. Bruchman drove up the other side, doubled back round the top, drove down to the end, made to turn and found his way blocked by a badly parked car. He cut the engine and got out. The klaxons were still blaring. He ducked behind the parked car and looked up the line.

The four funeral cars which had come to rescue him made a U-turn, tyres squealing on the concrete, and headed back towards the exit. He saw the first one slow and the back door open. Esther and the commando clambered over the chain round the car park and were pulled into the car. The little convoy picked up speed, turned into the approach road and raced down to the main Nablus–Jerusalem highway.

Bruchman waited a minute or two and then stood up and began to walk up the line of cars towards the exit. The noise of the klaxons bothered him and he switched off his hearing-aid. He walked steadily, without haste, remote in his silent, private world, a small, neat figure in a black suit, reflected in the windows of the parked cars as he passed.

He heard neither the shouted order to halt nor the crack of the rifle that followed it. The bullet hit him in the left leg, just above the knee. He looked down in surprise, felt his leg buckle and pitched forward on to his face on the concrete.

The soldiers ran up and stood looking at him. He seemed so small a man to have caused so much trouble.

Lying under the wreck of the Romulus in Chain Street, Colonel Macer opened an eye slowly and saw Jacobson's boots walk past him in huge perspective. A stone had sliced into his left cheek, cutting deep. The dried blood glued his face to the cobbles. He lifted his head slightly and winced as the edges of the wound tore open again. He saw Jacobson turn at the gate into the yard and beckon. He let his head sink down, closing his eyes against the sudden dizziness, and heard the two commandos go by. His arms were doubled under him, cramped, lifeless. He flexed his biceps, digging the toes of his boots into a crack between the cobbles, easing himself back under the carrier. He heard Jacobson call, "Barabbas," and the rattle of the lock being turned. He squirmed round on his stomach and crawled out on the far side of the

Romulus, pulling himself up beside the middle wheel, legs trembling, head swimming. After a moment he edged along to the rear, fumbled his pistol out of its holster and peered round.

Barabbas stood in the gateway, his automatic rifle in his hand, the rocket launcher slung across his back. He had put on his shirt, leaving the front unbuttoned. The mat of red hair on his chest was dark with sweat and dirt. There was blood streaked on his face, a grey-white scum of dust and spittle rimming his mouth. Jacobson and the two commandos were with him, their backs to Macer.

The Roman colonel laid his pistol on the flat ledge above the rear wheel of the APC, took a couple of deep breaths to clear his head and hauled himself up on to the superstructure. Lying prone he was able to reach the machine-gun. He edged it slowly round on its mounting, lined the barrel up on the group in the gateway and squeezed the trigger.

The noise of the gun was like a trip-hammer. Great clouds of flies rose off the street in a black mist. Above the roofs the kite-hawks wheeled away in alarm.

Macer was shooting a little wide, the bullets gouging huge splinters out of the left-hand gate-post. He swung the barrel right and clenched his teeth as the shock of the recoil vibrated through shoulders and neck to his head. The two commandos went down. Barabbas was closing the gate as Jacobson dived through and rolled to his right behind the sheltering wall. The bullets thudded into the wooden gate and stopped abruptly when the magazine was empty.

Barabbas whipped the key round in the lock and heaved Jacobson to his feet. Hodor came limping out of the house and they hustled him across the yard to the back wall. Jacobson jumped, caught the top of the wall with both hands and pulled himself up. He sat astride it and leaned forward, reaching down to grab Hodor. Barabbas linked his hands under Hodor's good foot and boosted him up.

The little cripple was lying face down, like a sack across the wall, when Macer blew the lock with his pistol and kicked the gate open. Jacobson wrapped his arms round Hodor and rolled off the top of the wall on the far side. Barabbas swung round, his rifle coming up. A bullet from the pistol kicked it out of his hand. He looked into Macer's eyes, cold and steady in the torn, blood-smeared face, and had no doubt about where the next bullet would go.

Alone now, without his king, his little army scattered, his dream of freedom broken, Jesus Barabbas leaned his head back against the wall and waited for death.

8

(Excerpt from the script of a newscast televised at 9 p.m. on Tuesday 10th April from the Jerusalem studios of the Imperial Television Corporation.)

Video	*Audio*
CUT to Jack Daniels M/CU against back-projection still of Temple	Earlier today security forces in Jerusalem were called out to deal with a riot in the courtyard of the Temple there.
	A group of left-wing militants led by Jesus Barabbas staged a violent demonstration in protest against the alleged commercialisation of the Passover Feast. Shots were exchanged. There were some casualties.
MIX to still of Command Post	Master-minded from this rented room in a house at the end of Chain Street overlooking the Temple area, the demonstration was obviously designed to overspill into the surrounding streets. Had it been allowed to do so the consequences might have been very serious indeed.
MIX to telecine 1 Clip of street crowds	The city is packed with pilgrims up for the Passover.

Video	*Audio*
	This major religious festival commemorates the revolt of the Jewish slaves in Egypt more than a thousand years ago and their subsequent trek to freedom under Moses. It generates its own peculiar atmosphere of excitement and intense religious fervour—an atmosphere in which this afternoon's demonstration could well have triggered off an explosion of violence resulting in considerable loss of life and damage to property.
MIX to still of Saracen APC and crew	That it did not do so is due to the disciplined efficiency of the security forces—men of the Tenth Legion commanded by Colonel Titus Macer—who handled the situation firmly and with restraint to contain it and bring it quickly under control.
MIX to still of H.E.	They were supported in their actions by His Excellency, the Governor-General, who drove through the city at the height of the disturbance to make a personal appearance at the Jaffa Gate. A timely and courageous act which did much to ease the tension and restore calm.
MIX to telecine 2 Clip of Barabbas entering Antonia under heavy guard	A number of people were arrested—notably Barabbas himself and two of his gang, Tzev

Video	Audio
	Bruchman and Peter Sorek. All three are notorious terrorists long sought by the authorities. They are being held in the Antonia Fortress for interrogation on charges of insurrection and murder. It is understood that the Public Prosecutor will ask for the death penalty.
CUT to still of Caiaphas	His Grace the High Priest said earlier this evening that in common with all peace-loving people he deeply deplored this afternoon's incident. He denied allegations that the Passover was becoming increasingly commercialised and described the demonstration as "a wanton act of hooliganism, the work of an embittered minority group". He expressed admiration for the way in which the situation had been contained and confirmed that the Passover celebrations would continue normally.
CUT to still of Largo	Earlier this afternoon a distinguished visitor flew in from Rome.
	Senator Julius T. Largo is here as the personal guest of the Governor-General and will be staying at the Residency. He will be the guest of honour at a banquet tomorrow evening. Senator Largo is . . .

PART TWO: Wednesday

1

At ten minutes to ten on the morning of Wednesday 11th April Major Ajax Pallas, Military Intelligence, attached to the Tenth Legion, Jerusalem, turned right off the Jericho road and drove his white convertible up the steep slope, through the Lion Gate and into the courtyard of the Antonia Fortress.

A tall, spare man in his early forties, neat in newly pressed khaki drill shirt and slacks, a green and white polka-dot silk scarf knotted at his throat, Pallas crossed the cobbles, walked round the Post Office Telephone Service pick-up parked by the steps and went briskly up into the main guardroom, raising his swagger cane in response to the sentry's salute.

Gilder, his staff sergeant, stood up behind the trestle table. "Tenshun!"

"Morning, Staff." Pallas nodded to the two clerks and the orderly corporal and paused on his way through to his office. "Who's this?"

The man kneeling by the wall with a bag of tools open beside him looked up; a small, dark man, wearing a blue T-shirt and dungarees.

"Post Office engineer, sir." Gilder said. "Telephone maintenance."

"Morning," Pallas said.

Seeker nodded. "Shalom."

"Trouble?"

"Fault in the wiring somewhere, Guv," Seeker said and shook his head. "I dunno who put this lot in but he must've gone to school with Abraham."

"Long job?"

Seeker shrugged. "Depends. Sometimes you find it right off.

Then again, you might be scratching round half the effervescing morning."

"Yes," Pallas said. "Well, be as quick as you can. I'll have some calls to make directly."

"That's OK, Guv. Let me know when and I'll run you a temporary line through." He sucked his teeth, poking at the wires with his pliers. "Mind you, the whole bag of tricks needs ripping out and replacing. Patching up stuff as old as this is a waste of time. Added to which you've got your actual fire-risk, of course."

"Make a full report," Pallas said. He went through into his office, hung his cap on the hook by the door and sat down at his desk. Following him in, Gilder closed the door and stood waiting with a buff folder in his hands.

Pallas looked up at the staff sergeant's tanned face with its flat, grey eyes above the foam-padded surgical collar that came up under the chin and supported the back of his head.

"How's it coming, Staff?"

"Fine, sir, thank you."

"Neck still painful?"

"I'll live, sir," Gilder said. Five weeks earlier he had rolled out of a jeep when the brakes failed going down a one-in-six gradient in the hills north of Safad. The rim of his steel helmet had struck a small boulder, jerking the webbing strap up hard under his chin and breaking his neck. A desert veteran with a couple of good decorations, Gilder was not a man to enjoy sitting about in a hospital dressing-gown. When Pallas's assistant had finished his tour and been posted home, Gilder had jumped at the chance to take his place temporarily. Pallas found him helpful, if a touch regimental.

Gilder opened the folder, took out a sheet of paper and laid it on the desk.

"What's this?"

"Death certificate, sir. Bruchman."

Pallas raised his eyebrows. "Bruchman?"

"This morning, sir. O-two-fifty hours."

"From a leg wound?"

Gilder shook his head. "Suicide, sir. In his cell."

"Wasn't he searched when they brought him in?"

"Sir."

"Well?"

"It was that deaf-aid he wore, sir. He'd modified the ear-plug to carry a small explosive charge. Blew half his head off." Gilder grimaced. "Messy business."

Pallas nodded. "I can imagine. What about the youngster? Sorek, isn't it?"

"Concussed and delirious, sir." Gilder made it sound like an entry on a charge sheet; drunk and disorderly, concussed and delirious. He pointed to the multi-channel intercom on the desk. "Cell five, sir."

Pallas flipped the switch. Sorek's voice babbled into the room, high-pitched, erratic, the ancient Hebrew words spilling out of the intercom in a meaningless jumble of sounds.

Pallas listened. "Make any sense to you, Staff?"

"None, sir."

"How long's he been like this?"

"All night."

"MO's seen him, I take it?"

"Sir."

Pallas sighed. "And?"

"Suspected brain damage, sir."

Pallas cut the switch. "Which leaves us with Barabbas."

"Sir."

"And what sort of a state's he in?"

"Fit, sir. Few cuts and bruises. Minor stuff."

Pallas nodded. "Has he slept at all?"

"No, sir. Just lay on the bed with his hands behind his head and stared at the ceiling all night. We kept the light on, of course."

"Hm," Pallas said.

"He's a hard man, sir." There was a suspicion of admiration in Gilder's voice. "A very hard man."

Pallas said, "Troublesome?"

"No trouble, sir. Very quiet. The dangerous ones always are." Gilder put another piece of paper in front of Pallas, squaring it off regimentally two inches from the edge of the desk. "Casualty list, sir."

Pallas looked at the figures. "That many?"

"And that's not counting civilians, sir. Just our chaps." Gilder let his anger show for a moment. "Some damned good lads got the chop yesterday, sir."

And for what? Pallas thought. To keep a blunderer in the Residency and a quisling priest in the Palace. He said, "Odd, the way they faded out like that."

Gilder sniffed; a superb, parade-ground sniff redolent of contempt for the amateur. "Shot their bolt, sir, hadn't they? Nothing left."

"Bull," Pallas said bluntly. "They were home and dry when they quit. Had us cold and knew it."

"Caught us on the wrong foot, sir. That's all."

Pallas nodded. "Exactly. And why? Because of that dummy run last Sunday. We really were ready for them then. Reserves flown in from Haifa. Identity checks. Special security measures. And what happened? Nothing. Davidson comes ambling in on a donkey looking about as dangerous as a bank clerk on his day off. Bit of a reception committee, mainly women and kids. A couple of cheers for luck. Quick shufti round the Temple and home in time for tea. Leaving fifteen hundred men standing about armed to the teeth with egg all over their faces." He shook his head. "We thought that was it, didn't we? Another false alarm. All over till this time next year." He grinned ruefully. "The oldest trick in the book and we fell for it."

"Sir," Gilder said stiffly, his voice as cold as his eyes.

"All day Monday, nothing. No bomb hoaxes. No demos. Nothing. So Tuesday morning we stand down, send the reserves home, get back to the serious business of polishing buttons and blancoing belts. Then, Tuesday afternoon, out of the blue—bingo."

Gilder stood silent and angry, the sweat stains dark on his foam-rubber collar.

"HE's screaming for the name of the man behind it," Pallas said. "He's got Largo breathing down his neck and he wants to know p.d.q."

"That's easy, sir," Gilder said. "Barabbas is our man."

"I suspect not, Staff," Pallas said. "Barabbas is a terrorist and a saboteur. But I don't see him sitting in the Residency running the country. And that's what this is all about." He shook his head.

"There's somebody else. Somebody with brains and political ability, waiting in the wings to take over. He's the one we want." He looked up at Gilder. "This Davidson character . . ."

"Jesus Davidson, sir? Not a chance."

"I wonder. He keeps cropping up, y'know. He was there on Sunday and again yesterday."

"So were a lot of other people, sir," Gilder said. "Davidson's a nutter. Religious crank. Bit of a nuisance, but harmless."

"Which may be what we're meant to think," Pallas said. "What've we got on him, Staff?"

Gilder walked across to the filing cabinet and checked through one of the drawers. He pulled out a folder and opened it. "Not a lot here, sir. Apparently M.I. put a tail on him when he was first noticed, three years ago. Kept tabs on him for about a year."

"Anything?"

Gilder shook his head and winced as the pain gripped his neck. "One or two anti-Church speeches. Attacks on the Pharisees. Arguments about Jewish religious laws. That sort of stuff."

"Nothing political? Sedition? Refusal to pay taxes?"

"No, sir."

"Hm," Pallas said.

Gilder closed the file. "Like I said, sir, he's harmless."

Pallas nodded. He took out a pencil and wrote on the bottom of the casualty list. He turned the paper round, pushing it across the desk for Gilder to read. "Have a look at that, Staff."

Gilder read the two names. JESUS DAVIDSON. JESUS BARABBAS. He looked up at Pallas. "Sir?"

"Anything strike you?"

"Both called Jesus, sir."

"Yes. Know what it means? The Rescuer. The Conqueror. It's one of the Messianic names."

"Sir." Gilder made his voice politely bored. His neck was aching and the sweat-soaked collar was beginning to chafe.

Pallas said, a touch sharply, "It's part of the business of this department to understand local customs and beliefs, Staff. If you're to continue working with me you'll do well to bear that in mind."

"Sir."

"This Messiah," Pallas said. "He has many names. The Shepherd King. The Son of David. The Son of Man. The Son of the Father." He looked up. "How's your Hebrew, Staff?"

"Poorish, sir."

Pallas smiled. "Bokor tov. Shalom."

"That's about it, sir."

"Me too. But I know enough to translate Son of the Father. It's Bar Abbas. Barabbas. So—we have Jesus Davidson, the Son of David. And Jesus Barabbas, the Son of the Father. Two men, completely different in character, who both bear the Messianic name. Interesting, yes?"

He got up and went to the window, looking across the valley below the city wall to the green hump of the Mount of Olives. "This Messiah syndrome," he said then. "Extraordinary bit of folk-lore. They think he's God, you see. The Messiah. They've been waiting for centuries for him to come and set them free. That's what's kept them together through generations of occupation by foreign troops. Without it they'd've lost their identity as a nation." He swung round to face Gilder. "Without taking it too seriously we've always kept an eye open for likely candidates. Any young hothead who gets into the freedom and human rights bit— we watch him. Let him run a bit, just to make sure. And then clobber him. Hard."

Gilder watched him sit down again. "But what if Messiah isn't just one man? What if he's two? A dozen? A hundred? What if it's not a man at all, but an idea? An idea that lies dormant for centuries and then suddenly flares up and infects a nation?" He looked at the two names on the paper and up at Gilder. "You can hang one man, Staff. Or two. Or two dozen. God knows we've had to do it often enough. But you can't hang two and a half million." He sat back in his chair. "Suppose what happened yesterday was just for openers. A feeler. The curtain-raiser to something really big and ugly scheduled for later this week. Something they've already started the count-down on."

"Sir." Gilder looked pointedly at the clock on the wall. "We *have* got Barabbas. Perhaps he can answer your question."

"What? Oh yes. Yes, I expect he can. Whether he will or not's another matter." Pallas pressed a switch on the intercom.

"Cells. Duty sergeant."

"Major Pallas here, sar'nt. Bring Barabbas in to me will you?"

"Sir."

Pallas leaned back. "You know they've sent for SECPOL, Staff?"

"Sir?" Gilder's eyes hardened. There was no love lost between the Army and the Secret Police.

"Seems Largo insisted. Colonel Porteous is flying in from Rome tomorrow."

"Gives us a bit of time, sir."

"Yes," Pallas said. "But I doubt it'll be sufficient."

"All right," Hodor said. "So what went wrong this time?"

Simson shook his head. Behind his glasses his eyes were unhappy. "I'm sorry. I . . ."

"So are we, mate," Hodor said. "Very sorry." He shifted on his chair, easing his left foot. His face was grey with fatigue, the eyes dark-circled, the lines of pain cut deep at the corners of his mouth. "And bloody angry, too."

"I appreciate that," Simson said.

"That's nice," Hodor said bitterly. "Look, it was in the bag. We had Pilate, the airport, Army HQ, Radio House." He ticked them off on his fingers. "The mob was with us, hungry for blood. The army was running round in circles shooting each other up the arse. All he had to do, for God's sake, was be there and stay there."

"Yes."

Hodor blew out his cheeks in disgust. " 'Yes,' he says. Just like that."

"Easy, Ben," Jacobson said. Quiet-spoken, quietly dressed Andrew Jacobson.

Hodor turned on him angrily. "Tigal's dead, isn't he? And Bruchman. And God knows how many more. Sorek's flipped. Barabbas is in the Antonia being measured for a rope. Pilate's laughing his head off and Caiaphas's holding thanksgiving services for peace in our time. And all this smooth-talking priest's son can say is 'Yes'."

Simson's eyes narrowed. "How d'you know about Bruchman and Sorek?"

Opposite him Shad Rocci's moon-faced grin was sly, his voice like olive oil laced with whisky. "We keep in touch."

They were sitting round a table in the office of the Red Stocking: Ben Hodor, Rosh, Jacobson, Judas Simson and Rocci.

Fat, heavy-jowled, with black Italian eyes and black Jewish hair curling on the nape of his neck, Shadrach Rocci was the uncrowned king of the night-clubs and strip joints that clustered like gaudy flowers in the Old Quarter, a maze of narrow streets in the south-west corner of the city. A gross and sweaty sixteen stone, he wore silk shirts, eighty-guinea suits and a platinum Rolex Oyster strapped to his left wrist. He smoked hand-made, king-size black Balkan cigarettes, drank arak like water and was an expert with a flick-knife and a broken bottle.

The Red Stocking was his place; a cellar in Dag Street down near the Zion Gate, transformed by discreet lighting and soft carpets, patronised by the officers of the Tenth, city businessmen grown rich on Roman contracts, and the more discriminating members of the Diplomatic Corps on the Residency staff. Compared with clip-joints like the Tambour and the Pantie Club it had a certain raffish class. The strippers were young and inventive, the blue comic was sophisticated, the food and wine were outrageously priced and the hostesses topless.

The Magdala had given it its name, dancing twice nightly on the tiny stage, red hair flying, red-stockinged legs kicking, her nearly nude body the colour of magnolia blossom under the spotlights. That had been before she met Davidson, when she was still Barabbas's mistress.

More recently the star attraction had been Esther, flaunting an earthier brand of eroticism in black nylons, long black gloves and a jewelled G-string. But the memory of the Magdala still lingered around the white-and-gold-painted tables and her red stockings hung like a trophy above the bar.

Both girls in their turn had mingled with the customers between their acts, picking up snippets of information over glasses of vinegary champagne; not infrequently taking a high-ranking officer upstairs to one of the special bedrooms after the last cabaret at two in the morning. A surprising number of military convoys had been ambushed and bullion shipments hijacked because of an incautious word spoken around dawn between the black nylon sheets under the mirrored ceiling.

Hodor swallowed a mouthful of the harsh red wine that came from the coastal vineyards above Ashkelon. "Why?" he said, wincing as its rawness hit his stomach. "Why did Davidson cut and run?"

"I don't know," Simson said, the flat Kerioth vowels sad as a lament. "I honestly don't know." Lying all night in the barn, wide awake while the others slept, he had asked himself this question and found no convincing answer.

He touched his glass of orange juice with puritanical fingers. An intensely religious man, he was out of his element in the Red Stocking. He found it unclean, distasteful—the white and gold décor tawdry in the mid morning, the air rancid with stale cigar smoke and perfume, the cigarette burns in the stone-coloured carpet clustered round the table legs like beetles. He looked up at the nude photographs of the strippers on the wall above Rocci's head and averted his eyes quickly from the long, smooth thighs, the tilted breasts nippled with tinsel stars.

"I'm as disappointed as you are," he said.

Hodor spread his hands and looked round the table, his face bitter.

Rosh said, "Where is Davidson now?"

"Who the hell cares?" Hodor said.

"He's in Bethany," Simson said. "We all are."

"Mary Magdala's place?"

Simson nodded, seeing in his mind's eye the house at the end of the village, the little terraced vineyard, the white-walled barn hidden from the road.

"And what's he doing?" Rosh said patiently.

Simson hesitated, his eyes moving from face to face, looking for understanding, a willingness to believe. But from Rocci's cynical stare to Hodor's scowl he saw only rejection; the cold dislike he had seen so often in the last three years on the face of priest and Pharisee. "He's waiting," he said then. Even to him it sounded lame.

Hodor snorted angrily and pushed his glass across the table. Rocci lifted the wine bottle and refilled the glass. The big bloodstone set in his gold ring was like an eye, Simson thought. A dark, brooding eye shadowed with suffering.

He remembered the way Davidson had looked at him the night before. He had dropped off the bus in the village and dawdled along the road, making sure he was not being followed. It was early evening and the village was quiet. He went down through the vineyard and found Davidson alone, sitting on the wall behind the barn, staring down the great ravine that gaped like a wound torn through the mountains to the Dead Sea far below. The sun was dropping over the Negeb behind the Hebron hills. In the blood-red light of its setting the landscape was desolate beyond all believing.

Davidson had turned his head and Simson had stopped in mid-stride, appalled at what he saw in his eyes.

"What are you trying to do to me, Judas Ishkerioth?" Davidson's use of the nickname had sharpened the question, making it an accusation. But of what? Unbelief? A failure to understand? Or—and Simson felt his mind shy away from the word—betrayal?

Across the table Rosh saw the pallor creep across his smooth, intelligent face. "Waiting?" he said. "For what?"

Simson looked at him with a kind of despair. "The right time."

Hodor said brutally, "That was yesterday, mate. One-thirty p.m."

"No." It was said with sudden vehemence.

Jacobson said, "But you gave us the signal, damn it. You got off that bus and——"

"It was a mistake," Simson said flatly. "My mistake." He licked his lips. "On Monday evening, when he said he was going up to the city the next day, I naturally assumed he meant . . ." His voice faltered under their hard eyes; died.

Rosh said quietly, dangerously quietly, "So it was your decision?"

"Yes."

"And Davidson didn't know?"

Simson shook his head. "No."

"In a pig's eye," Hodor said. "Course he bloody knew." He leaned his elbows on the table, head thrust forward. "Look, mate, I dunno what goes on in that twisted little mind of yours, but if you're trying to whitewash Davidson, forget it. Because he's not worth it. He's a grade A, gold-plated, stove-enamelled coward, and that's all there is to it."

"No," Simson said urgently. "You don't understand him. He's not——"

"Damn' right I don't," Hodor said bitterly.

"But you do?" Rosh's voice was cool, deceptively casual.

I used to think so, Hodor thought. As much as anyone did, and more than most. Back in the early days, the country days, when they packed into the village synagogues to hear him speak and brought their invalids in faith for healing. There was understanding between us then. An empathy, a meeting of minds.

I knew who he was the first day I met him, long before Peter Johnson stumbled on the truth and blurted it out in his usual clumsy fashion. The things he said, the miracles, the shifting, agonising moods—I understood all that and shared it.

But not this weakness that saps his will now, he thought. Not this indecision, this pathetic, humiliating dependence on sycophants like John Zebedee. Not this growing obsession with, and fear of, death.

"Well?" Rosh said.

"He's a difficult man to know," Simson said. "It's not easy to get close to him." But it had been once, in the beginning. He remembered the private smiles they had exchanged, saying more than words could ever say; the quick look of pleasure when he grasped the meaning behind an event which had the others puzzled; the intimacy of the nickname which poked gentle fun at his Kerioth accent. For two years it had been like that, intuitive, deep, marked by a kind of splendid inevitability. As though, as his Arab cousins would say, it was written.

Then something had begun to go wrong; a tiny speck of decay, dormant for a while, suddenly mushrooming, spreading like a poisonous mould, eating the heart out of their relationship.

Rosh said, "I agree."

Simson looked at him, surprised by the sympathy in his voice. "You've met him?"

"Once," Rosh said, and stopped. It was like a door shutting.

"The women get close enough to him," Hodor said. "All over him, so I'm told."

Simson flushed, seeing the grin on Rocci's face, remembering with renewed disgust the embarrassing scene at the dinner party two weeks before. That brazen woman with her breasts exposed almost to the nipples and her skirt up round her thighs. A whore. A common street tart. Bursting in like that in front of all the guests and throwing herself at Davidson, mauling him about, drooling over him. And Davidson accepting it, enjoying it. Lying back in his chair and smiling as she bent over him, her hair tumbling into his face, her hands touching and stroking skilfully, shamelessly . . .

He remembered the shocked silence, the sniggers, the glib, unconvincing homily about love and forgiveness with its tasteless reference to embalming.

It was not as though she had been the only one.

"You'd think—" Hodor's voice was unpleasant—"with so many bints to choose from he could've left the Magdala alone. I mean, she was Barabbas's bird."

"And my bread and butter," Rocci said.

Simson said hotly, "It's not like that between them."

"Ah, for God's sake, man, we're not fools," Hodor snarled. "He's shacked-up with her now, isn't he? You said so yourself. While Barabbas is in the Antonia waiting to get his neck stretched." He picked up his glass, tipped the wine into his mouth, gulped it down. His face was flushed, his eyes hard and bright. "Make love not war," he said, his voice furry with hatred. "What a bloody marvellous slogan for the Messiah."

Simson pushed his chair back and stood up, a prim-lipped, oddly old-fashioned figure in his dark suit, white shirt, neatly knotted tie. "I don't have to sit here and listen to that kind of filth."

Hodor wiped his hand across his mouth, watching him walk to the door. "That's it, mate," he said coarsely. "Back to the love-nest. If he wants Mary Magdala all to himself—and who wouldn't? —maybe he'll let you have the use of her sister for half an hour."

Simson turned in the doorway, white-faced, eyes blazing.

Rocci grinned. "Poor Martha," he said. "She should be so lucky."

Rosh said, "OK, that's enough." He went out after Simson, round the little square stage and across the floor between the tables with the chairs upended on them. He caught up with Simson at the foot of the stairs.

"I'm sorry about that."

Simson said, "Yes. Thank you."

They began to climb together.

"We're all a bit uptight this morning," Rosh said. "Yesterday was rough."

"For me too, Mr. Rosh," Simson said coldly.

"Indeed." Rosh felt the anger like a piece of sheet iron between them. "You mustn't mind Ben Hodor," he said. "He's got a rough tongue but he's not as bad as he sometimes sounds."

"I'm glad to hear it."

"Worships Barabbas, of course," Rosh said. "Feels about him much as you do about Davidson."

It was a shrewd thrust and it went home. Simson stopped for a moment, the knuckles of his hand on the banisters showing white under the skin, and then continued.

"All that about the Magdala," Rosh said then. "You mustn't take it to heart."

"No?"

Rosh shook his head. "She belonged to Barabbas, you see. That's part of it. The other is this king-size inferiority complex Ben has about women. A sort of love–hate relationship. It's because of his damaged foot. He thinks women find him grotesque, physically repulsive. In his mind he tramples over them."

They reached the hallway at the top of the stairs and walked down towards the street door.

"The pity of it is," Rosh said, "underneath he's quite different. Gentle. Shy. Capable of real affection."

Simson said stiffly, "I find that very hard to believe."

Rosh nodded. "I know. But it shows through sometimes. Mainly when he's with Barabbas." He hesitated. "Don't misunderstand me, but you're not unlike each other, you and Ben."

"Thank you."

"No, I mean it," Rosh said. "You both tend to put people on pedestals and get hurt and angry when they disappoint you."

They stopped by the door at the end of the hall. On the wall behind Rosh was a gallery of big coloured photographs, one of them

103

of the Magdala taken a couple of years before when she had been queen of the Old Quarter. She was standing with her back to the camera, looking over her left shoulder, wearing white hot pants, white shoes and the famous red stockings. Simson's eyes traced the long, lovely line of her legs, the smooth curves of her buttocks thrust into prominence under the skin-tight pants by her high-heeled shoes; and turned up to her face framed in that astonishingly red hair. He read the frank invitation in her dark eyes, her full-lipped smile; and blushed.

Following his gaze, Rosh smiled. "Davidson certainly changed her."

Simson nodded. Or had she changed him? he thought. Not in the crude way Hodor had implied, but more subtly, more dangerously, feeding on his strength, diverting him from his purpose. In the last year or so there had been so many women; camp-followers, idolisers. Too many, he thought. Far too many. Neurotic, frustrated, battening on him, leeches draining him of power.

He stared at the photograph in fascinated disgust, remembering the Pharisees' jibes about the Davidson harem, and felt the shame and anger rise in him.

Rosh unlocked the door and turned. "About Davidson."

Simson looked at him. "What?"

"Davidson," Rosh said. "D'you think he's the Messiah?"

"Do you?" Simson said. How many times he had had this conversation over the last three years, and with how many people. Pharisees, lawyers, village priests, businessmen feeling the guilt of their wealth and looking for a righteous investment. Even, on one occasion, with Davidson himself. That was when Johnson had said his piece.

"You've met him," he said to Rosh. "Talked to him. What d'you think?"

Not that he expected a straight answer. Rosh was not Johnson.

"I don't know," Rosh said cautiously, his grey eyes uneasy. "Yes, I talked to him. But that was a long time ago . . ." He shook his head. "I found him—disturbing."

"Yes."

"I was rich then. Money to burn. He advised me to sell up and donate the proceeds to charity."

"And did you?"

Rosh smiled, a quick, rueful smile. "If you can call SLING-SHOT a charity."

"A worthy cause, perhaps," Simson said.

"But not the right one?"

"It would appear not." Simson looked at his watch. "I must get back. They'll be wondering——"

"You haven't answered my question," Rosh said.

Simson smiled, his face changing, losing its shuttered look. "You want me to put it into words? Yes, all right. Jesus Davidson is the Messiah," he said, and added in Hebrew the classic Messianic name, "He-who-shall-come."

Rosh nodded. "You said something earlier about the right time. When will that be?"

Simson hesitated. This too was a familiar conversation. "Exactly when I don't know," he said. "But within the next forty-eight hours."

"You sound very positive."

Simson nodded. "This is his Passover. The one we've been waiting for." It was said with total conviction; and something more. A hint of exultation, of fulfilment.

"A couple of hours' notice," Rosh said. "That's all we need. We took a pasting yesterday but there are still enough of us, down there at Masada, to make a show. Not the same without Barabbas, of course, but . . ." He met Simson's eyes and his voice tailed away. He shook his head, his smile apologetic. "He doesn't need us, does he?" he said. "He doesn't need that kind of help."

Jacobson's voice floated up the stairwell behind them. "Hey, Paul. Haven't you got rid of that creep yet?"

Rosh saw the angry flush on Simson's face. He opened the door quickly and offered his hand. "Shalom." He jerked his head towards the stairs. "I—I'm sorry."

"Shalom." Simson shook his hand and went out.

Standing in the doorway Rosh watched him go; a slim, narrow-shouldered figure, lonely in the sunlit street.

He doesn't need you, either, does he? he thought. And that's what hurts.

2

Just before eleven Seeker walked down the steps from the main guardroom, dropped his tool-bag into the back of the Telephone Service pick-up and got in behind the wheel. He drove out through the archway and turned left, threading his way down the narrow street past the Praetorium to the Damascus Gate. There was the usual queue of vehicles waiting to get out of the city. He lit a cigarette and sat patiently smoking, sandwiched between a fire-engine-red sherut minibus and an Army three-tonner.

Once through the gate he took the Nablus road, skirting the base of Skull Hill, driving north at a steady twenty-eight miles an hour as the traffic thinned. He took the left fork opposite the Mount Scopus Hotel and went up through the fashionable suburbs where the sprinklers spun in the sunlight on green lawns, past the Shmuel Hanavi gardens and the Sanhedrin cemetery, the marble tombs like huge white eggs under the trees, and into Bar Ilan.

He drove half a mile along the broad, curving boulevard, pulled on to the grass verge and stopped by a telegraph pole. He took a warning triangle out of the pick-up, walked back fifty yards and set it up on the soft shoulder. He returned to the pick-up, opened the nearside door and reached in for the metal box containing the portable telephone unit. He hung it round his neck by the leather strap, buckled on his safety belt, clipped the tool-bag to it and lifted a short aluminium ladder out of the back of the little truck. He propped the ladder against the pole and began to climb, small-boned and agile in his blue dungarees, his thick dark hair ruffled like a boy's.

At the top of the pole he hooked himself on, lying back comfortably against the leather safety belt, his feet braced on the steel rests driven into the wood. Thirty feet above the ground with the wires humming musically only inches above his head, he opened the tool-bag and studied the coded diagram pasted on the inside surface, tracing the route with a thin, broken-nailed finger. Satisfied, he unscrewed the cap of the circular terminal block and dropped it into his bag. He attached the telephone jumper leads, checking the connections against the diagram, took the receiver out of the metal box and dialled a number. He heard the bell ringing at the other end of the line and, a moment later, Shad Rocci's voice.

"Rocci."

"Seeker. They've sent for SECPOL."

"That figures. When?"

"Tomorrow morning. Early flight from Rome."

"Into Lod?"

"Yes."

"How many?"

"Three. Porteous plus two."

"That bastard?"

"Yes. Can you set it up?"

"Have to, won't we?"

"Rosh?"

"Yup. Maybe. We'll need more details."

"Tonight."

"Liz?"

"Who else?"

"Will she?"

"She always does."

"OK. How's the man?"

"Alive," Seeker said and broke the connection.

He referred to the diagram and reset the jumper leads on different terminals. Below him a Roman patrol in an armed Land-Rover came round the curve, cruising slowly. He saw the steel-helmeted trooper sitting in the back with his arm hooked casually over the machine-gun on its pintle mounting. The trooper glanced at the parked pick-up and tilted his head to look up. Seeker looked at the sunburned face below the white helmet and raised his hand. The trooper grinned and waved back.

He waited a couple of minutes until the Land-Rover was out of sight and then dialled another number.

"Inter-Med Exports. Shalom."

"Liz."

"David." He heard the welcoming warmth in her voice and pictured her pushing her blonde hair away from her face with the back of her hand, sitting cool and poised in the outer office that was the front for SECPOL's Jerusalem headquarters in King Solomon's Street.

"Mahar—tomorrow," he said in Hebrew. "You know about it?"

"Yes."

"We need details, Liz. Route, timing schedule, size of escort."

"Yes. I see." The voice in his ear was cold now, and small.

"I'm sorry, love. It's important."

"I understand."

"He's available tonight?"

"Oh yes, he's available."

He visualised the black-uniformed man in the inner office; the corseted waist, the bullet head, the hard, button eyes. "I hate to ask you to do this, Liz."

"It's just a game," she said.

Swinging gently on his high perch, the pressure of the safety belt like a reassuring hand supporting his back, Seeker heard the revulsion in her voice. It was a game Esther and her kind would play willingly enough. But they would not do for the man in the black uniform with the effeminate hands and curious tastes. It had to be Elizabeth for him: shy, sensitive Liz whose outraged modesty gave him his kicks. And loosened his tongue. That was the point, Seeker told himself fiercely.

"Liz," he said. "I wish . . ." As always on these occasions there were no words.

"I know," she said. "It's OK, David. Really."

"I'll tell you this, love. He's number one on my private, personal list when the day comes."

"We should live that long," the girl said. And then, brisk, matter-of-fact, "Half eleven be OK?"

"Earlier if you can."

"I'll try. He doesn't like to be hurried when he's—gift-wrapping."

"Thanks, Liz," Seeker said. "You're a sabra."

"L'hitra'ot."

He heard the click as she put the phone down, yanked off the leads with unnecessary violence and began to pack up.

"Let's try it again, shall we?" Pallas said. "From the top."

The first session had ended just before one and he had gone to lunch, leaving Barabbas standing in front of the desk with an armed corporal to keep him on his feet. Now it was two-fifteen.

"I'm trying to make it easy for you," Pallas said.

Barabbas set his feet apart, folded his arms across his chest and tried not to think about the ache that started somewhere down in his calves and spread up his thighs, across the small of his back to his shoulders. Below the cropped red hair his eyes were wary, waiting for the thud of a pickaxe handle in his kidneys, the smack of a rifle butt against the side of his head. He had been standing for more than three hours, had not slept for thirty. Pallas's face was beginning to slip out of focus.

"Why did you pull out?" Pallas said. It was where they had begun at ten-thirty that morning.

Barabbas shook his head.

Pallas nodded towards Gilder sitting by the door. "My staff sergeant says you ran out of steam. Blew it all in the first hour and had nothing left when the crunch came."

"Then he's a bloody fool."

"So why did you stop?" Pallas said. He waited a moment. "All right. Put it this way. Who ordered you to pull out?"

"Nobody. It was my decision."

"You were in command?"

"You know damned well I was."

"And you called it off?"

Barabbas looked at him wearily. "I told you. It was my decision."

"Why?"

There was the briefest of pauses, like a faulty round in a magazine subtly changing the rhythm of the firing. "Because I had to," Barabbas said then.

"But you were winning."

"Winning?" Barabbas glowered at him. "We'd won, mate."

Pallas shook his head. "I'm sorry, but it doesn't add up. No commander stops short like that on the brink of success. Unless, of course, somebody in the Top Brass pulls rank on him and orders him out." He leaned forward, his hands flat on the desk. "So who was it?"

Barabbas looked at him, hating the freshly laundered uniform, the clean hands with their well-kept nails, the educated Roman drawl that snagged in his mind, barbing every question with a threat.

"Who was it?" Pallas said again.

It was the same question the SECPOL major had asked, in exactly the same tone, that June morning in the square ten years before. Lying in the gutter that rimmed the domed roof of the synagogue, Barabbas had looked down through the interstices in the stone Star of David and seen the row of hostages lined up. Twenty men of the town, picked at random, his father among them.

"I shall ask you once more, and only once more," the major had said. "Somebody destroyed an Imperial Army truck and killed the driver. Who was it?"

Nobody had answered him. The people of the town had stood silent, stony-faced, penned along one side of the square by the sub-machine guns of the black-uniformed SECPOL troopers. Barabbas remembered how their shadows had reached across the sunlit cobbles, like comforting arms, to touch the hostages standing bare-headed in the sweet morning air. And how the rattle of the guns that scythed them down had sounded strangely innocuous, echoing off the white-walled houses, innocent as a tinsmith's hammer.

He had shouted at them then, as he had shouted three days earlier at the corporal driver when he reversed the big eight-wheeler too fast along the narrow street and crushed Barabbas's thirteen-year-old sister to a pulp against the house wall. "Murderers. Bloody, stinking murderers." His voice lost in the stammer of the guns, his tears creating rainbow colours around the crumpled heap of clothing on the cobbles that moments before had been his father . . .

"Well?" Pallas said patiently.

Barabbas shook his head. "Nobody."

He had left the town the next morning. Taken off his black-smith's leather apron for the last time, kissed his weeping mother and given her to his brothers to comfort, and hitched a ride down through Nazareth and Nablus to Jerusalem. Twenty-five years old, built like a bull, nothing in his heart but hatred . . .

"Nobody?" Pallas said.

"No. I pulled 'em out myself."

Through the open window he could hear the growl of the traffic in the street outside, voices talking, a girl's laughter. All the sounds of freedom. The scent of the oranges piled high on the stalls by the Lion Gate drifted into the room. A clean, sharp smell freshening the sultry afternoon.

Like a good after-shave, he thought. The sort Rosh would use. He rubbed his hand over his face, feeling the rasp of stubble.

Pallas smiled apologetically. "I'm sorry about that. Regulations, I'm afraid. Damn' silly of course. You're obviously not one to anticipate the hangman with a razor blade. Still, that's the Army for you. No imagination." He opened a packet of cigarettes, took one out, lit it. "I'd offer you one but the Staff Sergeant wouldn't approve." He leaned back in his chair, comfortable, easy. "Not that it need necessarily come to that. A hanging, I mean. If you should decide to co-operate . . ."

Barabbas shook his head. "No dice."

Pallas looked at the tilt of his chin and nodded. "In your position I like to think I'd have the guts to say the same." He stretched his legs out under the desk. "I wonder if Davidson would?"

"Davidson?" Barabbas said quickly; a shade too quickly. "What's he got to do with it?"

Pallas looked surprised. "Isn't he the brains behind it? You do the fighting. He does the planning. Isn't that right?"

"Planning? Jesus Davidson? He couldn't plan a church outing and get it on the right day."

"Know him well, do you?"

Tired and angry, Barabbas saw the trap too late. "I know of him."

Pallas nodded. "So he is involved." He said it quietly, a statement not a question.

"No he's bloody not," Barabbas said. "He's bad news. A Jonah. Moody. Sees things. Hears voices. Doesn't know who the hell he is half the time. You can't work with a man like that." He could see it now, as Ben Hodor had seen it from the beginning.

"So it wasn't Davidson who gave the order to pull out?"

"For God's sake. I told you. It was my decision."

"So you did," Pallas said mildly. "So you did."

"But you don't believe me?"

"I might," Pallas said, "if I knew why." He drew on his cigarette and let the smoke trickle out of his nostrils. "What were you hoping to achieve, anyway? If things had worked out."

"Freedom," Barabbas said simply, as though it were a new word, freshly-minted, bright with meaning.

Pallas looked at him, eyebrows raised. "You're not serious?"

Barabbas's face reddened. "Damn' right I'm serious." This at least remained. Davidson had dropped out and SLINGSHOT had failed. But the dream was still there, intact, its glory untarnished.

Pallas sighed. "You disappoint me. If you'd said power, now. Or money. But freedom . . ." He made it sound like a joke in bad taste.

Tiredness momentarily forgotten as his temper quickened, Barabbas said, "What's so funny about freedom, then?"

Pallas shrugged. "It doesn't exist. It's a myth. A politician's gimmick. Sounds magnificent. Means nothing."

"It means something to us."

"Us?"

"Jews," Barabbas said savagely. "Yids. Sheenies. The scum of your Empire. We know what freedom means."

"Rome in ruins and Israel on top?"

"That's part of it." The New Jerusalem. The Messiah on his throne, crowned with glory and majesty. The world on its knees before the Son of God.

"Good God, man, don't be so damned naïve. Use your head for once. Supposing you'd won yesterday . . ."

"We did bloody win," Barabbas snarled. Inside his jump boots his feet burned and ached. He seemed to have been standing for ever, scummy with his own sweat, teased by the words of this sly, smiling Roman as a bull is teased by flies.

"And backed off," Pallas said brutally. "All right. But if you'd pressed on . . ."

"We'd be free now."

"Oh, please," Pallas said. "Free? Somebody would still be Big Brother. Issuing orders. Grabbing power for himself. Signing the death warrants of anyone rash enough to get in his way."

"He'd be one of us," Barabbas said. "Not your lousy lot."

"So what? The name of the game'd still be tyranny. All you'd have'd be a different boss." He smiled grimly. "A different one every few months, most likely. Each more ruthless than the one before. Until finally the daddy of 'em all showed up. Your actual, archetypal Big Brother, brutal enough and cunning enough to claw his way to the top of the heap and stay there. And when he comes, God help you. You and all like you who dream of freedom."

Barabbas said doggedly, "When we take over it won't be like that."

"It'll always be like that," Pallas said. "You should know. You in this God-haunted, priest-ridden, fly-blown apology for a country." His eyes narrowed, watching the weariness and doubt struggling in Barabbas's face. He spoke slowly, without mercy, his words lancing the tired brain, infecting the wound with the virus of confusion. "You talk about men being free. Hell, we're not even men, let alone free men. We're shadows, ghosts. Reflections in the mind of a mad, sadistic giant you call God, products of his diseased imagination. Doomed to be moved around in the twisted patterns of his fantasy until he gets bored and puts us out of his mind." He looked straight into Barabbas's eyes. "Death, that's the only freedom we'll ever know."

Barabbas closed his eyes, fighting to stay on his feet. The images Pallas had thrust into his head merged with others already there. The crumpled bodies of the hostages in the square; the smear of blood and mucus on the wall where his sister had died; the tears on the face of his mother that no words could comfort. Ten-year-old images infused now with renewed horror as he remembered the carnage in Chain Street, the mob howling in the Temple court-yard, the betrayal of trust that had wounded deeper than bullet or knife.

But there were also images of life floating up through his memory.

The laughter in the eyes of the red-haired girl who had danced for other men but given herself only to him; the hands of Jesus Davidson, hardened by the hammer, skilled with the chisel, giving bread to the hungry and sight to the blind, sharing with the poor a foretaste of the Kingdom; Sorek's voice weaving the dream into a reality on the loom of words; the love of Ben Hodor that no words could ever clothe. Good images, these, and enduring; feeding on pain and disappointment, rooted in suffering, rising out of it. Evidence that one day the dream would come true.

"Our King," he said then, opening his eyes, swaying a little on legs the trembling of which he could no longer fully control. "Our King, when he comes . . ."

"Will be doomed like any other man," Pallas said flatly. "Oh, you'll dress him in the trappings of freedom, of course. But he'll bear in his hands the symbols of tyranny. He may not want to. But he'll have no choice."

"He will be free," Barabbas said, his voice detached, a monotone. "And because he is free we will be free too."

Pallas heard the changed intonation, the mechanical singsong quality in the confident words. Now who's that talking? he thought. Not you, my lad, that's for sure. Davidson, perhaps?

He said, "Free? Free to do what? That's the crunch question. What happens when you've won your freedom? You should've asked yourself that yesterday morning before you went for the jackpot."

"Free to live." The desperation in Barabbas's voice was like a cry for help. The cry of a man out of his depth and drowning in a sea of words.

Pallas nodded, measuring his man like a boxer. You poor, bewildered bastard, he thought. And threw the low punch. "Try telling Bruchman that," he said levelly. "He's dead."

Barabbas's head sank down. He peered at Pallas through half-closed, gummy eyelids. "Tzev Bruchman?" It was no more than a whisper.

"Afraid so. Lost his cool at the end and blew his head off." Pallas saw Barabbas's chest swell as he sucked air into his lungs, saw the knuckles gleam white on the bunched fists.

You're out on your feet, laddie, he thought. And no bell to save you.

114

"You've been conned, Barabbas," he said cruelly. "Shoved out on a limb and left to dangle. Somebody in this town doesn't like you much. Somebody you trusted. It wasn't Bruchman he was after. It was you. When he gave that order to pull out he expected——"

"God damn you," Barabbas croaked. "I gave the bloody order. As soon as I heard he'd gone I knew we——"

"Gone?" Pallas pounced on the word. "Who? Who'd gone?"

Barabbas shut his mouth and stared at the wall.

"His name," Pallas said urgently. "Just tell me his name, damn it."

Barabbas shook his head. He was swaying perceptibly now, the room tilting round him, the white walls searing his eyes.

"Good God, man," Pallas said. "Don't you want to eat? Lie down? Sleep?" He waited a moment and then shrugged. "As you wish. If you won't tell me . . ."

Barabbas made one last effort. "There's nothing to tell."

"I don't think the SECPOL boys will accept that," Pallas said. "In fact I'm damned sure they won't." He looked at Barabbas with a kind of compassion. "It could be—unpleasant." He sighed. "OK, Staff. Take him down."

Barabbas turned stiffly and walked to the door, weaving slightly.

Pallas looked at his massive shoulders, his thick, muscular legs. God help you, he thought, when those cruel bastards get at you tomorrow.

Gilder opened the door and Barabbas blundered through. Pallas heard the stamp of feet, the voice of the guard. "Get a grip, you dozy man."

He said, "Staff."

"Sir?" Gilder turned in the doorway.

"I want him starved. And kept awake. All night, understand? No food. No sleep. Right?"

"Sir, is that necessary? He's——"

"Damn it man, I'm doing him a kindness. The weaker he is when Porteous starts on him the sooner he'll be out of his misery."

3

"Darling," the Lady Claudia said. "You're not eating a thing."

Pilate shook his head irritably, his eyes pricking in the dazzle of crystal and silver on the long, white-clothed tables under the chandeliers. "I'm not hungry."

The phenobarbitone his doctor had prescribed as a steadier to help him through the evening had dulled his appetite. He had refused the hors d'oeuvres, morosely sipping a glass of iced grapefruit juice while his guests ate quantities of techina, dipping pieces of warm pita bread into the aromatic paste of creamed sesame seeds and parsley. He had accepted a small portion of the fish course—a whole baked carp stuffed with eggs, breadcrumbs and spices—but had done no more than push it round his plate with a fork. Now he stared without enthusiasm at the shishlik and pilaf in front of him, drained his glass of red wine and tapped it impatiently on the table for a refill.

Claudia looked at the shine of sweat on his flushed face. "Just thirsty?" she said pointedly.

The daughter of one of Rome's noblest families, she sat erect deside her husband, poised and cool in a black lace dress, a double rope of fine pearls round her neck, diamonds in the gleaming black hair piled on top of her head.

Sitting on her left at the top table, Julius Largo dabbed his lips with his napkin and admired the almost Grecian perfection of her profile. He saw her nod and smile as Colonel Macer, half-way down one of the tables, caught her eye and raised his glass. On neck and shoulders and over the classic bone-structure of her face Claudia's skin was flawless. The curve of her mouth as she smiled, the dark, lustrous eyes, the unlined forehead—all these could have graced a woman fifteen years her junior. Watching her, Largo marvelled, not for the first time, that such a woman could love a man like Pilate.

He touched the carnation in the lapel of his white dinner jacket and sighed, remembering the withered skin and thin-lipped mouth of his wife in Rome.

Pilate pushed his plate away and tapped his glass for more wine. A burst of laughter erupted above the dinner-table chatter of sixty people. The laughter came from a group of young officers and under-secretaries at the far end of the room and went on a fraction too long. Pilate glared at them peevishly, suspecting that they were laughing at him.

Largo sat back. "An excellent meal." He bowed to Claudia. "In charming company, ma'am."

She smiled. "I'm glad you're enjoying it."

Pilate grunted. "That damned chef. When's he going to learn how to cook pilaf?"

The liveried waiters removed the plates, brought thin crystal bowls of cold fruit soup, poured Karl Netter White Label into the champagne glasses.

Pilate spooned the cinnamon-spiced soup into his mouth, gulping it down between mouthfuls of champagne, aware that he was behaving badly, unable to help himself. The alcohol was beginning to mix with the phenobarbitone in his bloodstream, affecting his co-ordination. His spoon clinked against the side of the bowl. Splashes of fruit soup stained the napkin tucked under his chin.

Largo watched him covertly, remembering his interview with Hallum, the Foreign Secretary, in Rome.

"In his own curious way the man is a kind of genius," Hallum had said in his thin, affected drawl. A fastidious, old-school aristocrat, hawk-faced, tall, he had sat with his head tilted back, looking down his long nose at Largo. "Anyone who can demoralise the Tenth has to be—well, special. Those men are hand-picked. Only a very unusual talent could blunt the cutting-edge Macer has honed on them. It's not a talent we can afford to indulge indefinitely. Especially in so potentially dangerous a place as the Middle East." He had smiled his wintry smile that had frosted the hopes of his opponents in a hundred diplomatic encounters. "The damage Pontius Pilate has contrived to do in seven short years of office is quite unbelievable."

"He's been warned, of course?" Largo had said.

"Oh yes, he's been warned. But it's a waste of time. Any advice, however diplomatically phrased, he takes as a personal insult. He sees treachery in every smile, a threat in every letter. His confidential reports read like a bad script for one of those second-rate spy films."

"Why not recall him?" Largo had said. "Pension him off."

"Something safe and agricultural north of the Po?" Hallum had nodded. "Yes, indeed. It's the obvious answer. Unfortunately there are certain delicate matters to be taken into consideration."

"Yes?"

"The Lady Claudia's father, principally. You know his standing and influence in—ah—high places. We would be ill-advised to offend him, however indirectly."

"I shouldn't have thought Pilate would cut much ice with him."

"Oh, none at all. As a man, that is. But as a son-in-law . . ."

"Yes."

"He is said to be very fond of his daughter. His only child, of course."

"I understand," Largo had said. "Of course, he's no longer a young man . . ."

"And very far from well. He has not been out of his house for months. Another year—less, perhaps—and the picture may well have changed dramatically."

"Meanwhile, what d'you want me to do about Pilate?"

"Oh, prop him up. You know the form. Get him through this Passover business with the minimum of fuss."

"It'll be a pleasure, Minister."

Hallum had looked at him shrewdly. "Yes. I rather thought it might. I can't, of course, make any promises at this stage. But I've known men be given a peerage for less."

Largo had said, "My only concern, Minister, is to serve the Empire in whatever way I can."

"My dear fellow," Hallum had said. "Isn't that what we all try to do?"

Largo finished the fruit soup, sipped his champagne, said casually, "I had hoped to see Herod here tonight."

"What?" Pilate's eyes focused uncertainly.

"Herod. I thought you'd have invited . . ."

"Can't stand him," Pilate said. "Never could. Puts grease on his hair. Picks his nose in public. Plays around with little boys."

Claudia flushed. "Darling, please."

Largo said, "Oh, he's unpleasant. I agree. But politically useful to us."

"I can manage without him," Pilate said. "Screaming little pervert."

"But does that matter? The point is, he keeps things running smoothly in Galilee, and that's worth a couple of legions to us."

Pilate grunted, running his finger round the inside of his high tunic collar. "Is that what they think back in Rome?" He emptied his glass. "Waiter."

"Steady, darling," Claudia said quietly. "I'm sure people are beginning to count the glasses."

"Let 'em. They spy on everything else I do. If they want to check on my drinking, they're welcome."

"Caiaphas too," Largo said. "Shouldn't he be here?"

"No he damned well shouldn't," Pilate said angrily. "I wouldn't invite him to the funeral of my worst enemy."

"Oh, quite. But we need him even more than we need Herod. Let's not fool ourselves. We may make the laws but its Caiaphas who persuades the peasants to respect them."

"Only so long as it suits his book."

"Precisely. All the more reason for making him feel wanted."

Pilate glowered at him. "So. That's it, is it? That's the grand strategy of the Pax Romana. I wear the uniform and take the salute at the Empire Day parade. Open a new sewage farm now and again. Present the degrees at the University on Graduation Day. All that rubbish. But the country's run by a puppet king who'd murder his own mother for the gold in her teeth and a psalm-singing hypocrite of a priest more at home in a shareholders' meeting than in his temple." He drained his glass and set it down clumsily. "Where's that waiter? Here, bring me some brandy, will you? This damned fizz's no drink for a man." Along the tables heads were turning now, the conversation faltering. "Herod and Caiaphas," Pilate said thickly. "Where were they yesterday afternoon, eh? Tell me that. Standing with me at the barricades where people were being shot at? No." He gulped down some brandy. "Thieves and cowards, that's what they are. Plenty to say for themselves until the trouble starts. Then where are they?" He glared round the room. "Invite them to dinner?" he said loudly. "No, Senator. That may be the way of your friends in Rome. But it's not mine. By God it's not."

There were three Jewish bankers sitting together less than ten feet from him; sober, respectable men, dignified, powerful. Claudia saw the affront on their faces. One of them pushed back his chair and began to rise. Claudia caught Macer's eye and nodded urgently.

Colonel Macer rose to the occasion, glass in hand. "Your Excellencies, Senator Largo, my lords, ladies and gentlemen." His voice rang out like a parade-ground command. "I give you the toast of His Imperial Majesty, the Emperor Tiberius."

"Tiberius," Pilate said loudly, struggling to his feet and slopping brandy on the cloth. "God save him from his friends."

Oh, man, Largo thought. Father-in-law or no father-in-law, you'll have to go.

In his villa off the Jaffa road Captain Leo Zax was absorbed in the initial stages of his ritual of pleasure. He had taken off his black SECPOL tunic, positioned the dining-table, fully extended, in the exact centre of the room and spread a green baize cloth over it. Six foot one in his boots and breeches, the ridge of his corset plainly visible under his white shirt, he moved with surprising, almost feminine, grace; a bony, bloodless man, ugly, with small, black eyes and a curiously prim mouth.

He opened a drawer in the sideboard and took out several pieces of pink ribbon and a large paper bag. The ribbon was freshly ironed, an inch-and-a-half wide, cut into eighteen-inch lengths. He pulled a chair up to the head of the table, put the paper bag on the seat and arranged the lengths of ribbon over the back with exaggerated care, stroking each piece into place with his thin, white fingers.

From the bottom drawer of the sideboard he took a roll of thin, transparent plastic sheeting twenty-four inches wide, a small stapler, a pair of dressmaker's scissors, a box of pins and a black felt pen. The ritual was as formal and as esoteric as the laying-out of a theatre trolley in a hospital: everything in its right place and in correct sequence. The pen, stapler and pins went on to the seat of the chair beside the paper bag; pins first, then stapler, then pen, neatly in line, not quite touching.

He unrolled a length of plastic sheeting, cut it off with the scissors and spread it neatly over the baize cloth. He cut off another length and laid it alongside the first, the edges overlapping. He put the scissors on the chair at right angles to the pen, returned the roll of sheeting to the drawer, closed it carefully and came back to the table.

He picked up the stapler and clipped the overlapping edges of the plastic sheeting together, put the stapler back in its proper place on the chair and turned to the blonde girl sitting in the corner of the room.

Unsmiling, button eyes coldly excited, he said, "Now."

Liz stood up, took off her cotton housecoat and walked naked to the table.

A little before nine o'clock the Reverend Jacob Nicodemus, member of the Sanhedrin, eased his dark-green estate car out through the Jaffa Gate, swung left under the towering wall of the Citadel and drove down past Mount Zion and the tomb of David.

The evening was sultry under an overcast that trapped the warm, exhausted air and held it down over the city. He leaned forward and switched on the fresh-air ventilation fan. In the white glare of the headlights the road was empty.

Glancing in the mirror to make sure he was not being followed, he cut across the mouth of the Hinnon valley to join the Silwan road just south of Siloam. He checked the mirror again, turned north of Kidron to the junction with the Jericho road below the Mount of Olives.

He stopped on the double white line, waiting until a Roman Land-Rover patrol had passed, and then turned sharp right. The headlights swung like a scythe and he saw Judas Simson standing by the bus stop outside Gethsemane. He flashed his lights twice, drove slowly past and pulled in to the verge. Simson came up, opened the passenger door and got in beside him. Nicodemus let in the clutch and began the long climb up to Bethany.

In the office at the Red Stocking Hodor looked at Rosh and Jacobson. "You two and Matt, then. OK?"

They nodded.

Hodor turned to Rocci. "We'll need SECPOL uniforms. Badges of rank. Three."

"And one for the driver," Jacobson said.

Hodor shook his head. "Matt can drive." He looked at Rocci. "Well?"

"No problem."

"Tonight?"

"Tonight. Sure."

Hodor nodded and looked at the map spread out on the table. The sound of applause came muted through the closed door as one of the strippers finished her act. Rocci cocked his head, listening, and grinned. "That's Hannah. She always gets 'em going."

Hodor said, "The bint with straight hair and glasses?"

Rocci nodded. "Dressed, she looks like a schoolmarm. But when she takes her clothes off . . ." He puckered his lips and made a kissing sound.

Jacobson said, "How're we going to stop 'em? Road block?"

"We'll use the Romulus," Hodor said. "Slewed broadside-on across the road. Simulated breakdown."

"Why not mines?" Seeker said. "Quickest way."

Hodor shook his head. "Three reasons. One, we haven't got Bruchman. Two, the time factor's too tight. And three, we want the bikes and the car."

"Right," Rosh said. "The Romulus then. Where?"

They bent their heads over the map spread out on the table. "Latrun, if they use the direct route. Janiya if they box clever and come round through Ramallah." Hodor looked at his watch and up at Seeker. "When's this Liz girl going to show?"

Seeker shrugged. "Hour and a half."

Rocci grinned slyly. "Kinky and slow with it, eh?"

Seeker flushed angrily. "Look, she doesn't exactly enjoy it y'know, having that damned queer maul her . . ."

"OK, Dave," Hodor said. "So long as she gets Zax to talk."

"She'll do that."

Jacobson shook his head. "Doesn't give us a lot of time."

"Enough," Hodor said. "You got that plan of the Antonia, Dave?"

Seeker pulled the drawing out of his pocket and unfolded it on the table over the map.

Hodor said, "Which is Pallas's room?"

"Here." Seeker pointed. "Off the main guardroom."

"OK?" Hodor said.

Rosh nodded. "How high's the window?"

"Above the street?" Seeker said. "Say twenty feet."

"So we need a truck," Hodor said. "High sides. Half a load of hay in the back. Rocci?"

Rocci shook his head. "Not a chance."

Rosh said, "There's that fifteen-hundredweight Jack Tigal collected in January when he knocked out the IAF weather unit west of Eilat. Slit the roof canvas, pile half a dozen mattresses inside. No bother."

"OK," Hodor said. "Get that laid on, will you, Andrew?"

Jacobson made a note.

"Pity Jack's not here to drive it," Seeker said.

Hodor scowled at him. His head ached and the pain in his left foot was stabbing through the codeine like a needle. "For God's sake, Dave. We're here to spring Barabbas out of the Antonia, not hold a wake for Jack Tigal."

Seeker said angrily, "I only meant——"

"I don't give a damn what you meant," Hodor said.

"Steady, Ben," Rosh said.

"Steady be damned," Hodor said. "We've got about six hours to mount a high-risk operation, most of it by guesswork. Being maudlin about Tigal doesn't bloody well help."

Rosh said, "Coffee might, perhaps."

Rocci leaned back and pressed a bell-push.

"I'm as anxious as you are to get Barabbas out," Seeker said, niggling at it, not leaving it alone.

"That's nice," Hodor said bitterly.

Jacobson said, "There are other drivers, besides Tigal."

"Brilliant," Hodor said. "So let's decide on one, shall we? Just for the hell of it."

The door opened to a burst of music; the brassy coarseness of a slide trombone slurring above the heavy beat of drums. One of the Red Stocking hostesses came in. Young, dark-haired, in a red mini-skirt; topless, with small, pointed breasts.

"Coffee, love," Rocci said. "Black and strong. And a bottle of arak. Like now, eh?"

As she turned to go Hodor said, "And put some clothes on before you come back."

Liz lay on her back on the table in the harsh white glare of the fluorescent light, feet together, hands clasped behind her head. The plastic sheeting clung to her, stapled down the front from throat to feet, decorated with elaborately tied bows of pink ribbon. She closed her eyes as Zax completed the tying of another bow, picked a pin out of the box on the chair and bent over her.

"You will please smile," he said.

She opened her eyes and smiled stiffly. That was part of the ritual. Whilst being gift-wrapped a girl must at all times smile.

"Thank you," Zax said in his cold, light voice.

Her skin crawled with sweat under the clinging plastic. The pitted lunar surface of his face hovered over her, the lips drawn back in a grin of concentration. She let her eyes go out of focus, retreating from the nightmare into the sanity of her own mind.

The ritual was well advanced now, the climax close. The flower would come next, then the label, neatly printed with the felt pen, addressed to himself, tied round her neck with the last piece of pink ribbon. There would be a pause while he walked round the table, adjusting a bow here, smoothing out a crease there. Then the finale. The tearing, crumpling horror as his fingers hooked into the plastic and ripped it away. The tears streaking his face. The terrible animal sobbing. The impotence. The sick, degrading nothingness . . .

124

And afterwards, when the reaction set in, the information she needed.

She heard the rustle of the paper bag and knew he was taking out the large white artificial flower. She felt his hand slide over the plastic covering her stomach and closed her eyes in revulsion.

"Please," Zax said petulantly, a pin between his teeth, "you will smile."

"Bazaar Street?" Nicodemus said.

"Number fourteen. I've just come from there now," Simson said.

"And he's planning to go there tomorrow evening?"

"That's right."

"Right?" Nicodemus gripped the wheel, holding the big car in a long left-hand curve. "It's madness. Utter madness. He might just as well walk into the Antonia and give himself up."

Simson looked at him, his face patterned with light reflected from the instrument panel.

"I've just come from a meeting of the Sanhedrin," Nicodemus said. "You know Pilate's bringing one of the top SECPOL men in tomorrow to break Barabbas? When he starts talking—and it won't take long once they get to work on him—he'll name Jesus Davidson as the man behind yesterday's attempted coup. By this time tomorrow there'll be a warrant out for his arrest. Every Roman patrol from Safad to Beer Sheba'll be looking for him." He pulled out round a farm cart parked on the verge. "It's exactly what Caiaphas has been waiting for. The chance to nail him on a capital charge. Not just blasphemy, treason." He saw the lights of a car in the mirror and eased his foot off the throttle, slowing to let the other car overtake. Watching its tail-lights disappear round the next bend he said, "He's determined to see Davidson hanged. Nothing less will satisfy him now. He's got a file full of evidence against him. Damning and conclusive, according to him."

"Evidence of what?"

"Blasphemy. False, of course, every word of it. Wouldn't begin to stand up in one of our courts."

"Which is why he's never issued a warrant himself."

Nicodemus nodded. "Yes. He's been waiting for something like this. Something big enough to carry the death penalty. As soon as he hears Davidson's involved he'll have that file of evidence in Pilate's hands within the hour."

"Will Pilate accept it?"

"Oh, yes. It won't mean anything to him, but he'll accept it. Constructive co-operation by the Church, helping to bring an enemy of the State to justice. That's how he'll see it."

Simson stared through the windscreen. The bitterness in Nicodemus's voice matched his own mood of despair. SLINGSHOT aborted. Barabbas in prison. Davidson betrayed. Caiaphas triumphant. He saw the pattern building up with a kind of relentless inevitability and felt the hope drain out of his mind.

"What are you going to do, Rabbi?" he said.

"Get him away. Now. Tonight."

"Where?" Foxes had holes. Birds, their nests. But where could Messiah hide? His destiny was a throne. If he refused that . . .

"Up north," Nicodemus said. "There's a small community of scholar-priests out on the edge of the desert east of Galilee. Good men. Recluses. Not impressed by Caiaphas. Davidson will be welcome there—you'll all be—until this blows over." He pointed to the petrol gauge. "I've got a full tank. I can have him there in five hours."

Simson thought about it. It was a chance, a way out. Risky, full of question marks, but possible. And wrong, he thought. Hopelessly, shamefully wrong. "If he'll go," he said then.

"Oh, I think he will. He's really got no choice now, has he? If he stays here he'll be dead within forty-eight hours."

A throne or a grave, Simson thought. And either one better than holing-up for the rest of your life in some off-the-map hovel on the edge of nowhere. "Dead," he said. "Or crowned."

The note of the engine changed as the houses of Bethany rose up on either side of the car, their white walls gleaming in the headlights. Nicodemus flicked on the right flasher. "Do you seriously think that's still a possibility?"

"Yes, I do," Simson said firmly, and felt something stir inside him. He thought of Barabbas sleepless in his cell and remembered how Davidson had spoken of betrayal. Not once but many times. A recurring theme of treachery that had shaken their confidence in him and in each other, eroded their trust, haunted them through these last difficult months. But if the traitor were Barabbas . . .

He felt the relief flood into his tired brain. Could the gasping out of a name under torture really be condemned as an act of betrayal?

"I think the time has come," he said then. "The crisis he's been waiting for. A confrontation not just with Caiaphas but with Pilate as well. Church and State. I think tomorrow, when Barabbas betrays him to SECPOL, Jesus Davidson will declare himself Messiah."

"I don't know," Nicodemus said. He changed down and turned the car in through the gateway of the house. "I've always hoped, of course. Until yesterday." He swung the car round the side of the house, braked, switched off engine and lights.

Sitting in the sudden darkness Simson said, "It's not a question of hope, Rabbi. Not now. Now it's a question of faith."

"You don't think he'll come with me?"

"I pray to God he won't," Simson said.

4

Major Max Sciotto, DSO, aide to the Governor-General, was not
having a good evening. The heat of the room had made his feet
swell and his shoes were pinching. His indigestion was playing him
up, his tongue was coated with what felt like nylon fur, and his
neighbour at the top table, an Army veterinary surgeon who had
apparently never heard of deodorant, talked incessantly and with
disgusting detail about the diseases to which polo ponies were
prone. On top of which, four places to his right, Pilate was now
maudlin drunk and due to turn nasty after another three or four
brandies.

Sciotto glanced covertly at his watch and looked down the room.
At the far end, just inside the door, the ITC camera-crew stood
waiting beneath their portable lighting gantry. Sciotto raised his
eyebrows questioningly. The crew chief nodded and put up a
thumb.

Sciotto cut into a particularly revolting description by the vet of
the way in which maggots cleaned an open wound. "Excuse me,
Colonel." He picked up a spoon and rapped the table. As the
conversation died he heaved his overweight body out of the chair
and managed a rather weary smile. "Your Excellencies, my lords,
ladies and gentlemen," he said in his vintage port, Staff College
drawl. "Pray silence for our distinguished Guest of Honour, the
Right Honourable, the Senator Julius T. Largo, Member of the
Most Noble Order of the Empire, Fellow of the Imperial Society."

As the television lights flicked on and Largo rose to speak,
Pallas slipped quietly out of his place, nodded to the Security
Officer by the door and went out into the hall. He collected his cap,
gloves and swagger cane, lit a cigarette and stood smoking by the
main door while the duty sergeant phoned for his car.

Fifteen minutes later he got out at the gate of the Antonia Fortress, told his driver to go on home, and walked through the archway into the courtyard.

Under the glare of a couple of arc lights Barabbas stumbled towards him across the cobbles, handcuffed between two guards. Naked to the waist, his face and chest running with sweat, the big man was out on his feet. His head rolled heavily from side to side. His eyes were half closed, red-rimmed, with black smudges like bruises under them. His mouth was open, sucking in air.

On either side of him, holding him up, the guards bellowed in his ears. "Left, left, left-right-left. Head up, damn you. Shoulders back. Left-right-left. Left-right-left . . ."

Watching that lolling head Pallas doubted if Barabbas was hearing them. They came to within six feet of him, swung Barabbas round and started back across the courtyard. "Left-right-left. Pick your feet up, man. Up, up, up. Left-right-left . . ."

Pallas shook his head and went up the steps into the guard-room.

"Evening, sar'nt."

"Sir." The sergeant of the guard stood stiffly.

Pallas said, "At ease, sar'nt." He jerked his head towards the courtyard. "How's he doing?"

"He's still awake, sir. Just."

"How long's he been out there?"

The sergeant looked up at the clock on the wall. "Twenty minutes, sir. We're walking him half an hour in every three hours."

"Make it fifteen minutes every two hours."

"Sir."

"Somebody with him all the time in the cell?"

"Sir. We've taken out the mattress and blankets. Put in a 200 watt bulb."

Pallas nodded.

"D'you reckon he'll last out, sir?" the sergeant said.

"What? Oh yes. He'll last. Strong as a bull."

"Sir."

"He'll get his second wind around o-three-hundred hours. Go for another twenty-four after that. No bother." He made his voice cool, professional. "He's had no food?"

"No, sir."

"Right. Put him under a cold shower when he comes in. Ten minutes. OK?"

"Sir."

"And give him a pint of black coffee afterwards. Strong. Plenty of sugar."

"Sir."

Pallas felt in his pocket for a small envelope. He took out three white pills and put them on the table. "Give him these in the coffee." He handed the envelope to the sergeant. "And another three at o-six-hundred."

"Sir." The sergeant looked at the chemist's name stamped on the envelope. "Pep pills?"

Pallas nodded gloomily. He felt like a crooked doctor, dedicated to taking life scientifically, by calculated degrees. "He hasn't said anything?"

The sergeant grinned. "Nothing printable."

"Pity. He could save himself a lot of grief tomorrow."

"We'll keep trying, sir."

"Trying?"

"Asking him for the name of the man in charge. If he gets tired enough he might . . ."

Pallas shook his head. "He won't talk to us."

The sergeant hesitated. "We could rough him up a bit, sir. Just enough to——"

"No!" Pallas's voice was sharp. "Let SECPOL do their own dirty work."

Seeker brought Liz down the back stairs into Rocci's office. She looked tired and strained, the skin of her face waxy, her eyes smudged, unnaturally bright. As though she needed a good cry to wash the shock out of her system and put some colour back into her cheeks.

But there was no time for tears. Hodor made that plain. Sitting at the table with the others, among them yet somehow apart from them, a biro in his hand, a pad of paper in front of him, he said impatiently, "What kept you?"

Liz sat down opposite him and pulled her coat around her, hugging her arms across her breasts. She felt their eyes on her, curious, speculative, like the eyes of a jury in a rape trial. It was as though she were still sitting naked on the table with Zax kneeling in front of her in the torn litter of pink ribbon and plastic sheeting, tears in his eyes, his hands reaching . . .

She licked her lips.

"Well, come on, girl," Hodor said. "Did he talk or didn't he?"

"Give her a chance for God's sake." Seeker poured a cup of coffee, added sugar and gave it to her.

Hodor glared at him. "I know, I know. She met a fate worse than death. OK, so I'm bleeding for her. We all are." This was Hodor at his worst, raw-nerved, bullying. Hodor without Barabbas, over-reacting, goaded by the pain in his foot, his imagined inferiority; snarling at any man who walked without a limp, any woman who pitied him.

Liz cradled the cup in her hands, warming them.

Seeker said, "When you're ready, love."

"They're using the northern route," she said, reciting the words in a monotone.

"Through Ramallah?" Hodor said.

"Yes."

"How big's the convoy?"

"One staff car, six outriders on motor-bikes, a five-ton troop carrier."

Hodor nodded, writing it down. "How many men in the carrier?"

"Twenty. Plus the driver and an NCO in the cab with him."

"Twenty-two. Plus the six on the bikes. Twenty-eight." Hodor looked up at Jacobson. "OK?"

"No problem."

Hodor nodded. "Timing?"

Liz said, "He's due in Lod at nine-forty tomorrow morning. They reckon to be in Jerusalem at quarter past eleven."

"Eleven-fifteen. At the Antonia?"

"Yes. They're routed down the Nablus road, through the Damascus Gate."

Hodor wrote it down. "What else?"

"Zax will be waiting at the Antonia. They're keeping Barabbas in his cell until Porteous arrives." She looked at the plan of the fortress spread out on the table and pointed. "Then they'll bring him to this room for interrogation."

Hodor looked at the plan. "Damn. That's no good. It's the other side of the courtyard from Pallas's room."

"That's no problem," Rosh said. "Porteous is a full colonel. I imagine he's used to having his own way, even if it means other people changing their plans."

"What about Pallas?" Hodor said. "Will he be there?"

Liz shook his head, relaxing a little now, the hot sweet coffee doing its work. "Not when Porteous arrives. He doesn't like SECPOL."

"That's a point in his favour," Jacobson said.

"Maybe," Hodor said. "But he still makes use of the bastards, doesn't he?"

"Pallas will hand over Barabbas to Zax at nine o'clock," Liz said.

"So," Hodor said, looking at his notes. "Zax meets Porteous at eleven-fifteen. Has he met him before?"

"No." Liz hesitated, seeing again the button eyes, feeling the cold white hands. "He—he's looking forward to it."

"I'll bet," Hodor said. "Hoping for promotion, damn him."

"Largo knows him well," Liz said. "Porteous, I mean."

"Largo?" Rosh said quickly. "Is he going to be there?"

She shook her head. "Porteous is to phone him as soon as Barabbas talks."

"At the Residency?"

"Yes. He'll be waiting there."

"Then he'll have a long wait," Hodor said. He folded the plan of the fortress and bent over the map underneath. "OK. Let's get down to cases. Now—"his finger jabbed at the map—"here's where we'll set it up. Approaching Janiya. There's a——"

Liz stood up. "D'you want me for anything else?"

"What?" Hodor looked up, frowning. "Oh. No. That's all. Seeker'll take you home." He watched her walk to the door. "You did a good job, girl," he said grudgingly.

She looked at him. "It wasn't a pleasure."

The guard corporal chalked a cross on the concrete floor of the cell. "Just there," he said. And at the top of his voice, "*Come on, you idle man. Move your bloody self!*"

Barabbas finished tying his bootlace, his fingers clumsy with fatigue. He lifted his head with an effort, forced himself to his feet and shuffled into position.

They had doubled him out of the shower, down the stone steps into the cell and given him black coffee in an enamel mug. But no towel. Naked and shivering, the water running off his back and legs to form little puddles on the floor, he had gulped the coffee greedily, the metal rim of the mug chattering against his teeth.

Afterwards they had thrown his shirt and trousers at him and told him to dress, watching him struggle to pull the clothes over his wet skin, force his feet into the socks; keeping up a continuous barrage of shouted orders.

"Still," the corporal said. He hit the cell door with his hand. "OK. Play the music."

Stereo pop with the volume turned up high exploded out of the twin speakers set against the ceiling in opposite corners of the cell. The corporal winced and wadded cotton wool into his ears.

Positioned to get the full effect, Barabbas swayed as the sound rushed at him, hammering into his head with terrible force. His mouth dropped open in shock, his stomach griped. Bile-bitter coffee rose into his throat, sweat broke out of his scalp and ran down his face. He clenched his fists, staring drunkenly at the whitewashed wall four feet in front of him. He felt as though an axe had dropped out of the roof, splitting him open from skull to navel.

Then his brain reacted defensively, curling in on itself, cauterised into isolation as the nerve-ends shrivelled. The white wall lost its solidity, rippled like milk over a cooler, faded and disappeared. In its place there was darkness; hollow, infinite; a long black tunnel through which his mind burrowed frantically to escape from the noise . . .

The girl with the red hair beckoned him across the flower-starred slope of the Galilean hillside. She wore a blue dress, the colour of hope, and her eyes were smiling. Below her the green grass curved steeply to the lake, lute-shaped and lovely in the spring sunshine. A long way away she was, yet he saw her face in close-up—the red lips parted in laughing invitation, the small white teeth, the flawless, honey-gold skin.

He began to run down the hill, light-footed, long-striding, opening his mouth to drink the wine-sweet air. But as he ran his bare feet were suddenly imprisoned in heavy, military-type boots. A helmet was rammed down on his head, its strap pulled tight under his chin. Grenades bulged in the thigh pockets of his trousers, webbing straps cut into his waist and chest, the weight of an anti-tank rifle dropped across his shoulders. The grass turned into soft sand and he laboured through it, grunting, gasping for breath.

When he reached the girl, Davidson was already there. A tall, smiling Davidson wearing a crown and a long, white cloak, his hands full of flowers.

Barabbas fell on his knees, groped about, found a flower and thrust it up at the girl. He saw her eyes widen in terror as the flower became a knife in his hand. He threw it away and staggered to his feet, lunging towards her. Davidson pulled her into his arms and Barabbas went plunging down the slope and into the lake.

The sun went in and the water turned black; black and cold and deep. He floundered helplessly, the weight of his equipment dragging him down. He shouted hoarsely for help, arms flailing, feet kicking desperately in waterlogged boots.

But Davidson and the girl were walking away along the shore, laughing and talking together, leaving behind them on the sand a trail of flowers.

He heard a voice screaming as he thrashed and struggled in the freezing water. He only recognised it as his own in the last split second of consciousness as the water rose over his mouth and nose and the scream died in a bubbling choke . . .

They cut the music, threw a bucket of water over him, picked him off the floor of the cell and propped him on the plank bed against the wall.

"Mary," he whispered. "Mary."

"Quite contrary," the corporal said and slapped his face briskly, left-right-left, until the weary eyelids opened.

134

5

(Excerpt from the script of the late news bulletin televised at 11.30 p.m. on Wednesday 11th April, from the Jerusalem studios of the Imperial Television Corporation.)

Video	*Audio*
	. . . expected shortly. Meanwhile the search by mobile patrol units of the Tenth Legion for pockets of terrorists believed to be hiding in the Judean hills continues.
CUT to Daniels M/CU	Speaking earlier this evening at a banquet given in his honour at the Residency by Their Excellencies the Governor-General and Lady Claudia, Senator Julius Largo expressed admiration for the way in which yesterday's demonstration had been brought under control.
MIX to telecine Clip of Largo speech M/CU	BRING UP Largo I have been particularly impressed by the devotion to duty shown by the men of the Tenth Legion under the command of Colonel Titus Macer. Their cool courage and magnificent disci-

Video	Audio

pline under extreme provocation were in the highest traditions of the Imperial Army. My only regret is that such action was necessary.

In an Empire as great as ours many different cultures find their place. This is as it should be. The Pax Romana is specifically designed to make it possible for men of different races and customs to live together in peace and harmony. The Passover celebrations currently taking place in this ancient city emphasise this. But let me stress one thing. The flexibility of our Constitution must not be construed as being a sign of weakness. Any individual who rejects the constitutional channels provided for the redress of grievances and presumes to take the law into his own hands—let that man beware. We will not tolerate subversive groups dedicated to violence. We will not tolerate terrorist gangs pledged to anarchy.

We desire that all men should live in peace. But if that peace is threatened we will not hesitate to act.

Make no mistake. We have the power to do this. If we have to use that power, we will.

CUT to Daniels
M/CU

Meanwhile, preparations for the

Video	*Audio*
	Passover continue. During the day traffic has been heavy on all the main routes into the capital as the big build-up of visitors reaches its climax.
	At one time this afternoon two-mile-long queues of cars were reported on . . .

PART THREE: Thursday

1

They left the caves below Masada just before first light, feeling their way out of the narrow ravine on to the shore road; half a hundred men, hastily briefed, heavily armed, tense and silent in the chilly dark.

Rosh led in the Land-Rover, wearing overalls to cover his black SECPOL uniform, a woollen cap comforter pulled down over his ears. Beside him, Hodor, in a leather sheepskin-lined jeep coat, sat huddled in the passenger seat.

Behind came the Romulus, Matt driving, Jacobson in the turret, both of them dressed as SECPOL officers under khaki overalls. The ten men in the back of the Saracen and the thirty in the five-tonner that brought up the rear wore battledress with the Tenth Legion flash on their sleeves, para helmets and jump boots.

They drove north up the west shore of the great salt lake, through Ein Gedi and Ein Feshha, the road empty, the water black under the drifting mist. Just beyond Ein Feshha where the road forked, the first rays of the morning sun topped the Moab mountains across the lake and lit the naked, yellow peaks that lifted out of the desert towards the Jerusalem plateau.

They took the left fork, leaving the lake behind, rolled through Jericho, still shadowed and sleeping, and began the long slogging climb up through the hairpin bends to Taiyba.

Half a mile beyond the village they pulled off the road into a wadi and stopped for breakfast: cold felafel stuffed into flat, round loaves of pita bread, washed down with coffee.

Two hours later, skirting Ramallah, they drove through the village of Janiya in a smother of white dust and came to the Dei Nidham turn-off which marked the eastern limit of the mile-long section of road Hodor had chosen for the ambush.

It was ten minutes to nine in the morning of Thursday 12th April.

"Nothing?" Pallas said, without hope.

"No, sir," Gilder said.

Pallas took off his cap and put it on the desk. "How is he?"

"Not too bad. A bit light-headed, but he knows what it's all about."

Pallas nodded. The pills had done their work. "What about Sorek?"

"No change, sir. Except that he's run out of steam and gone quiet."

"Sleeping?"

"More like a coma, actually."

Pallas looked at his watch. "Where's that Zax character, then? Time he was here."

They heard a car drive into the courtyard, and a moment later the slam of a door.

"Talk of the devil," Pallas said.

Gilder opened the office door. Zax came in through the guard-room, stopped just inside the office and saluted. "Good morning, Major."

Pallas nodded curtly. Saluting me when I'm not wearing my hat, for God's sake, he thought. Don't they teach these butchers anything?

He stood up and reached for his cap. "Captain Zax?"

"Yes."

Pallas pushed a slip of paper across the desk. "If you'll sign here, please."

Zax stepped forward, looked at the paper. "What's this?"

Pallas raised his eyebrows. "The usual form. Receipt for the prisoner Barabbas."

Zax smiled unpleasantly, eyes stony under the peak of his black cap. "I don't see any prisoner, Major."

Pallas looked at him, hating the gaunt face, the cold, sarcastic voice. "He's in the cells."

Zax nodded. "I'm sure he is, Major. And when I've been down to the cells and seen him, I'll be happy to sign for him."

Pallas said, "Is that really necessary?"

"I'm afraid so, Major. Yes. Nothing personal, of course. But in SECPOL we like to do things properly."

"Oh, very well." Pallas put on his cap and walked to the door.

They went down the steps, across the courtyard, through a steel door into the cell-block. The guard corporal stiffened to attention outside Barabbas's cell.

"Captain Zax wants to see the prisoner, corporal," Pallas said.

"Sir." The corporal slid open the shutter in the cell door. "In there, sir."

Zax said peevishly, "Well, open the door, man. Open the door. I'm not accustomed to peeping through holes."

The corporal looked at Pallas who nodded wearily. He slid back the bolts and swung the door open.

Barabbas was standing with his back to the wall. There were dark circles under his eyes and a greyish tinge to his skin beneath the tan and the stubble. Zax looked at him speculatively, his eyes noting the thick legs, the deep chest under the half-buttoned shirt, the massive cropped head above the heavy shoulders. He licked his lips. "Name?"

Barabbas pressed his mouth tight shut.

The corporal said, "He's Jesus Barabbas, sir."

Zax rounded on him angrily. "When I want information from you, corporal, I'll ask for it."

"Sir."

"Are you Barabbas?" Zax said.

"Yes," Barabbas said. "I'm Barabbas."

"So," Zax said gently. "The pig has a voice. Do you know who I am, pig?"

"Who you are," Barabbas said. "And what you are."

"Indeed? And what am I?"

Barabbas grinned. "A screaming queer, kinky as a plastic hose-pipe."

Zax flushed darkly, whipped his pistol out of its holster, gripped it by the barrel and took a step forward.

Pallas said quickly, "If you're ready to sign that receipt now, Captain? One prisoner. In good order."

Zax heard the emphasis on the last three words, hesitated and stepped back out of the cell.

"Thank you, corporal," Pallas said. "Lock him up."

Back in the office Zax signed the receipt, the ridge of his corset showing under his tunic as he bent stiffly over the desk.

Pallas nodded and put the slip of paper in his pocket. "All yours," he said.

"Thank you."

"If you'd care for some coffee while you're waiting . . . ?"

Zax shook his head. "Thank you, no."

"I understand," Pallas said. "With the sort of work you've got in front of you I couldn't stomach it either."

Where the B class road came down from Dei Nidham they dropped off a man with a diversion sign and left him to set it up and police it, closing the main road ahead. Since the opening of the Tel-Aviv/Jerusalem motorway through Ramla and Abu Ghosh, traffic on this northern route that wound up through a series of narrow passes in the hills had dwindled dramatically. But they could not afford to take chances.

Two hundred yards farther on, round a fairly tight right-hand bend cut under the steep shoulder of the hill, they ran the Romulus in under a clump of sycamores, swinging it at an angle, ready to reverse across the road when Hodor gave the signal. Standing up in the turret, his face and hair powdered with dust, Andrew Jacobson put up his thumb and grinned as the Land-Rover moved off with the five-tonner behind.

In three-quarters of a mile they began to run out of the pass. The down gradient here was about one in twelve as they swung left and stopped at the Beit Sira turn-off. A second diversion sign was erected there to seal off the section of the main road through the pass once the SECPOL staff car and its escort had gone through the junction.

The five-tonner turned left down the Beit Sira road for half a mile, executed a classic three-point turn and came back to within a hundred yards of the junction, pulling off the road into deep shadow under an overhang of rock.

Rosh turned the Land-Rover and headed back into the pass. A sheep track came down the hillside on the left and he changed into low gear, engaged the four-wheel drive and put the Land-Rover at the rough, one-in-four slope. They lurched up round the shoulder of the hill and parked out of sight of the road. The two men took their automatic rifles and the walkie-talkie set out of the Land-Rover and walked back down the track to the remains of an old stone-walled sheep pen about a hundred feet above the road.

They sat on the grass, backs to the broken wall, and lit cigarettes. Away to the west the road came out from between the flat-roofed houses of Kharbata, empty of traffic in the clear morning sunlight. Down in the pass to their left the blunt snout of the Romulus protruded from under the trees. Below them, to the right, by the diversion sign at the Beit Sira junction, the commando crouched ready in the ditch.

Hodor pulled up the aerial of the walkie-talkie and checked the network. Satisfied, he switched off and looked at his watch. It was just coming up to nine-thirty-eight. Twenty miles to the west, in the coastal haze over Lod, the early Trident from Rome would be on finals.

The fifteen-hundredweight truck, painted navy blue, with JERUSALEM CITY COUNCIL WATER BOARD stencilled in white on its sides, topped the long ascent from the Dead Sea and drove sedately through Bethany. The back flap of its bleached canvas tilt was tied down firmly. The newly cut slit in the roof, from cab to tailboard, was invisible from the road.

Sitting behind the wheel in a grimy suit of white overalls, Sabal watched the grey walls of Jerusalem growing up out of Kidron as the bonnet of the truck dipped to the hill. A big, calm man who on Tuesday had driven the hearse for Bruchman, he was humming to himself, comfortably aware of the knife tucked into the side of his right boot. Beside him, similarly clad, Falk slipped his hand into the cutaway pocket of his overall trousers and touched the butt of the pistol strapped to his thigh. One of Sorek's Pebble 1 commandos, he was slighter than Sabal but no less resourceful in

145

a crisis. Which was why Hodor had chosen them to take care of the getaway.

Sabal double-declutched neatly, changing down into second for the sharp left-hander opposite the gate of Gethsemane. "D'you reckon Rosh can pull it off?"

"Why not?" Falk said. "He got Pilate out, didn't he?"

Sabal nodded. "I dunno, though. The Antonia's going to be crawling with troops. Could be very dicey in there this morning."

"That's how Rosh likes it."

"Yup. That's true."

"Cold-blooded bastard."

Sabal grinned. "But nicely spoken with it."

The truck dropped down the Derech Ophel past Absalom's Pillar and rounded the south-east corner of the city under the towering walls. The sulphurous fumes from the Hinnon Valley tip wafted through the open windows of the cab as they forked left to Siloam and right towards Mount Zion.

"How're we for time?" Sabal said.

Falk looked at his watch. "Just gone ten."

Sabal nodded.

"Leave early," Hodor had said at the briefing eight hours before. "Don't risk getting stuck behind a convoy coming up that Jericho road. I want you in the suburbs by ten."

"Ten?" Falk had said. "What're we supposed to do for an hour and a half? Drive round looking spare?"

It had been cold in the cave at two in the morning. Nobody's temper had been too sweet.

"For God's sake," Hodor had snarled. "You can have a bloody puncture, can't you?"

Sabal checked the mirror, saw the road behind was empty. "Along here, then. OK?"

"As good a place as any."

Sabal pulled the truck off the road, braked, cut the engine. He put the walkie-talkie on top of the dashboard, switched it to RE-CEIVE and poked the aerial out of the window. "Right. Let's get that wheel off, then."

"The Praetorium?" The Telephone Service Manager looked worried; a thin-thatched, stringy man in a creased blue suit and dull shoes.

Seeker nodded. "The girl on their switchboard reports about a third of their lines are out."

"Oh, great. When was this?"

Seeker shrugged. "Ten minutes ago. Bit more, perhaps."

"And why wasn't I informed?"

"I'm informing you now," Seeker said. And added, "Sir."

The Service Manager ruffled the litter of papers on his desk. "That's not good enough. I'm supposed to have it in writing the minute it comes in. Top copy and two carbons. It's all laid down in the standard procedure schedule."

"Want me to go?" Seeker said.

"You chaps, you're all the same. No sense of responsibility. Wandering in here half-way through the morning and casually announcing that one of the major networks is——"

"I am on stand-by, actually."

"What?"

"Stand-by linesman," Seeker said. "I'm it."

The Service Manager looked at him balefully. "Don't hurry yourself, then, will you?" he said.

"You want me to go?"

"If it's not too much trouble."

Seeker grinned. "I'll need a pass. You know what they're like over there. Nerve-centre of the Empire and all that bull."

The Service Manager opened a drawer in his desk, took out a pre-signed special pass, date-stamped it and handed it to Seeker. "Anything else?" he said bitterly. "Clean handkerchief? Packed lunch?"

"You're a good, kind man, sir," Seeker said, putting the pass in his pocket. "It's a privilege to work for you."

He went out into the yard behind the Central Post Office, started the pick-up and drove out into the stream of traffic moving down past Herod's Gate and the bus station. He eased the pick-up over to the left for the turn in through the Damascus Gate, crawled down King Solomon's Street, showed his pass to the sentry and took the pick-up round into the car park behind the Praetorium building where the marble facing gave way to plain brick.

He parked neatly, collected his tool-bag, portable telephone unit and a coil of wire from the back of the pick-up and walked across to the fire escape.

Four storeys up on the roof he worked his way round to the front of the building, located the entry point of the telephone cables and squatted comfortably with his back against an air-vent serving the main administrative suite. He had a panoramic view of the city from Radio House to the Mount of Olives and across the Temple courtyard to the green terraced fields below Bethany. Immediately below, less than a hundred yards to his left, the arched gateway of the Antonia Fortress looked close enough to touch.

He opened his portable telephone unit and clamped the jumper leads on to a couple of the cables. Out of the tool-bag he took a pair of pliers and cut four wires in the complex, bunched them in his hand and secured them with the coil he had brought. He dropped the pliers back into the bag and dialled the Praetorium switchboard.

"Praetorium. Good morning." The girl's voice was clipped, professional.

"Telephone Service here," Seeker said. "I'm afraid a couple of your lines are on the blink. We're doing our best to trace the fault. Shouldn't take too long."

"How long?"

"Not more than an hour. Less if we get lucky."

"An hour? Look, this——"

"Sorry, miss. We'll get it right as soon as we can."

He broke the connection before she could reply, took his walkie-talkie out of the tool bag and extended the aerial.

"Watchman to Getaway. Do you read me? Over."

He flicked the switch to RECEIVE. After a moment Sabal's voice came through. "Hullo, Watchman. This is Getaway. Reading you fives. Over."

"Watchman here. I am in position. Are you? Over."

"Roger. We are two miles from target and holding. Over."

"OK, Getaway. Time check coming up." Seeker looked at his watch. "It is ten-twenty-seven . . . now."

2

A tall, coarsely handsome man in his black and silver SECPOL uniform, Colonel Victor Porteous sat stiffly upright in the back seat of the black 3-litre Mercedes and reached for his handkerchief for the tenth time since leaving Lod. Disturbed by the changing air pressures during the flight from Rome, further aggravated by the grey-white dust seeping in through the closed windows of the car, his sinuses were acting up again. His ears buzzed and crackled, his pale blue eyes watered as the thick mucus moved sluggishly through the swollen tubes around his eye sockets. He blew his nose hard and swallowed.

The SECPOL captain beside him said, "All right, sir?"

Porteous nodded, blinking the tears out of his eyes to look at the houses by the roadside. "Where's this dump?"

"Kharbata, sir," the driver said. "Almost half-way."

"Thank God for that," Porteous said. The catarrh clogged his voice. He sucked it up into his throat noisily, lowered the window for a moment and spat phlegm into the roadway.

The captain's mouth twisted in disgust.

Propped against the sheep-pen wall, elbows on drawn-up knees, Rosh focused the binoculars on the point where the road emerged from the village and saw the two leading motor-cyclists suddenly appear between the houses, their big six-fifty bikes filling the lenses. "Stand by," he said, keeping his voice cool.

Hodor flicked the walkie-talkie switch. "Father to all units. Stand by. Stand by. Number Four, get rid of that sign. Out."

The commando by the Beit Sira junction grabbed the diversion sign and pulled it back into the ditch with him. "Four here. Sign gone. Out."

At the eastern end of the pass the commando shouted above the noise of the tractor engine. "Sorry, mate."

The farmer on the tractor's iron saddle shouted back. "But I've got to get to Beit Sira."

"Not now. Later. An hour."

"What's up, then?"

"Faulty mine. Dangerous. Squad's on it now."

Grumbling, the farmer slammed the tractor into gear and turned it back towards Janiya.

Down the Beit Sira road the driver of the five-tonner started the engine and sat tensely, hands locked on the wheel, staring up towards the main road. Beside him in the cab his mate had the walkie-talkie set on RECEIVE and the volume turned high.

Three-quarters of a mile to the east the Romulus backed slowly out from under the trees and stopped broadside on across the road, blocking the pass. Its two heavy machine-guns were trained down towards the corner round which the convoy would come. Jacobson stood down out of the turret for a moment to let two commandos swing themselves up and out on to the casing. They whipped open one of the steel lockers bolted on the superstructure, pulled out a box of tools and jumped down to the road with it. They opened the box and spilled the tools out. One of them lay down on his back and edged his way under the Romulus. The other picked up a sixteen-inch wrench and crouched by the rear wheel. In the back, behind steel doors already unlocked and set slightly ajar, the commandos slipped off their safety catches and waited.

The black Mercedes with its six motor-cycle escorts was less than half a mile from the Beit Sira turn-off now. The five-ton troop carrier, identical to the one parked below the junction, had lost a little ground coming through Kharbata and was a couple of hundred yards farther back than the regulation quarter of a mile.

All to the good, Rosh thought. He waited until the leading pair of motor-cyclists disappeared from view under the hump of the hill and then said, "Now!"

Hodor spoke into the microphone. "Father to Three. *Go! Go! Go!* Out."

The five-tonner pulled out and moved up towards the junction, arriving just as the leading motor-cyclists rounded the curve to

enter the pass. The driver braked hard, stopping the truck with its
squat bonnet pushed out a couple of feet into the main road. The
motor-cyclists swept by, horns blaring; grotesque figures in their
high-domed white helmets and tinted visors. Ten yards behind
them, the Mercedes boxed in by two more outriders. Ten yards
behind the Mercedes, the rear pair of motor-cyclists. The seven
vehicles were travelling at forty miles an hour, like one unit, as
though tied together.

The driver of the five-tonner revved the engine and let in the
clutch, swinging hard right into the gradient to slot into place
behind the rear escorts already out of sight round the next curve.
As he accelerated away up the pass, the commando in the ditch
heaved the diversion sign up and pulled it across the road. He
stood beside it, left arm extended, pointing to the Beit Sira road.

The five-ton troop carrier bringing up the rear of the convoy
came thrashing round the bend, working hard to pick up its
correct distance. The driver saw the diversion sign and the man
in battledress with the Tenth Legion flash on his sleeve, hit the
brakes fiercely and changed down into second. The commando
stood his ground, waving the truck down to his left, saw the big,
square radiator grille loom up over him and veer away sharply as
the driver wrestled the wheel round. The five-tonner lurched away
down towards Beit Sira, its heavy-duty tyres churning up a spray of
dust and small stones.

The commando spoke into his walkie-talkie. "Four to Father.
Troop carrier diverted. Out."

Dwarfed by the steep walls of the pass the Mercedes and its
escorts braked hard and rolled to a stop ten yards from the Romulus.
Up in the turret Jacobson waved his arms. The commando crouching with the big steel wrench stood up uncertainly, keeping close
to the side of the vehicle. The man underneath rolled over on to
his stomach, squirmed in behind the front wheel and pulled a
Mauser HSc pistol out of his overalls.

The right-hand leading motor-cyclist pushed up the visor on
his helmet and shouted, "Get that bloody thing off the road."

The beat of the six six-fifty engines bounced back off the walls of
the pass. Jacobson put a hand behind his ear and shook his head.
The motor-cyclist cut his engine and signalled to the others to do

the same. In the sudden quiet they could hear Porteous blowing his nose.

The two leading motor-cyclists kicked down the stands of their bikes, got off and walked up to the Romulus. "What the hell's going on here?"

"Sorry about this," Jacobson called down. "Bit of trouble with——"

The rear doors swung wide and the commandos doubled out, automatic rifles cocked and ready. The motor-cyclists by the Romulus half turned towards them, reaching for their pistols. The man with the Mauser shot one in the groin. The other crumpled in agony as the crouching commando swung the big wrench up into the fork of his legs.

The bewildered escorts straddled their bikes helplessly as the commandos surrounded them, snatching the pistols out of their belts, poking their rifles into the open windows of the Mercedes. Only one man made a break for it: the left-hand rear escort. He was farthest from the commandos and managed to kick his bike into life, swing it round and jerk the throttle open. The back wheel spun and gripped the road. He shot away, crouched over the tank, swerved across the road and lay over for the corner. The five-tonner thundered round the bend and met him not quite head-on. The offside front mudguard plucked him out of the saddle and threw him twelve feet into the air. He turned slowly, describing a brief, lethal parabola, smashed into a tree and was killed instantly. The bike reared up, fell on its back, slid down the bank below the road and piled up against an outcrop of rock.

In the turret of the Romulus Jacobson thumbed the switch of his walkie-talkie. "Two to Father. OK, Ben. We've got 'em. Out."

Sabal and Falk pulled the wheel of the fifteen-hundredweight off the studs and let it drop. Falk bowled it along the side of the truck, propped it against the cab, reached in through the open window for the walkie-talkie. "Getaway to Watchman. Any news from Kharbata? Over."

"Hullo, Getaway. This is Watchman. Negative. Over."

"OK, Watchman. Listening out."

As he put the set back on the seat a voice behind him said, "Who're you talking to?"

Falk turned smoothly, not too quickly; balanced, knees slightly bent, right hand sliding into the cutaway pocket, gripping the butt of the pistol, pulling it free. By the time he was round the gun was out, pointing a good ten inches above the head of the small boy.

The boy was about eight; sturdy, freckled. He looked at the gun and up at Falk. "You the sheriff, mister?"

"Sheriff?"

"Like on the telly."

"Oh." Falk grinned and dropped the gun back into the holster on his thigh. "Yup. Sort of."

"Who were you talking to, Sheriff?"

"My boss, son."

The boy frowned. "Would he be the marshal?"

"Yup."

"Get rid of him," Sabal said.

"He's all right," Falk said. "Just a kid."

"I don't like kids. They talk too much." Sabal reached up behind the cab and pulled the spare wheel off its mounting. "Get lost, kid. We're busy."

"He's not doing us any harm," Falk said.

"No good, either." Sabal ran the spare wheel back, squatted, hoisted it in to the studs. "Next thing, his mother'll be here looking for him, with half the street for company." He scowled over his shoulder at the boy, his fingers busy with the wheel nuts. "Go on, shove off."

The boy looked at Falk. "You taking him in, Sheriff?"

"Yup."

"For God's sake, man," Sabal said. "Get shut of him, will you?"

"He's real mean, isn't he?" the boy said.

Falk grinned. "Better be moseying along, son."

"Do you need any help?"

"Thanks," Falk said. "But I reckon I can handle him."

"Sure." The boy nodded seriously. "The way you drew your gun. Real fast."

Sabal picked up the wheel brace. "Are you going to send him packing? Or d'you want me to do it?"

"OK," Falk said. "So long, son."

The boy looked at him, hesitating.

"Hit the trail," Falk said. "I've got things to do here." He winked and grinned.

"Yeh," the boy said. "OK. See ya, Sheriff." He went off down the road, running with a curious up and down step, clicking his tongue to an imaginary horse.

Crouched over the wheel Sabal said, "So what did Seeker say?"

"What?" Falk turned from watching the boy. "Oh, nothing doing yet." He looked at his watch. "Time enough still."

"Too much bloody time," Sabal said, spinning the brace.

"So slow down," Falk said. "Make it last."

Sabal spun the last nut tight and began to go round them again, using his heel on the brace. "Oh yes," he said bitterly. "Hang about here while that square-eyed little yob spreads the word there's a Water Board engineer out on the Silwan road with a dirty great pistol stuck in his fist." He threw the brace into the tool locker and began to let down the jack. "Why don't you do the job properly while you're at it? Get Seeker to ring up the editor of *Post* and tell him the whole story? Just be in time to catch the early edition."

"So what was I supposed to do? Shoot the kid?"

Sabal stowed the jack in the locker, slammed the lid and padlocked it. "Ah, the hell with it," he said. "Let's go for a ride."

Coming into Ramallah the leading motor-cyclists hit their horn buttons. The traffic parted to let them through.

Holding the Mercedes a length-and-a-half behind them Matt checked the mirror and saw the other three escorts riding abreast and the big five-tonner on station in the rear. In the back seat, Jacobson and Rosh sat side by side, looking older and thinner in the black SECPOL uniforms, their faces set below the peaked caps.

The convoy came down to the traffic lights in the town centre and swung right on to the Nablus/Jerusalem road.

Rosh looked at his watch. "Push it along, Matt. We're running six minutes late."

Matt flashed the headlights two or three times. The twin exhausts of the big six-fifty bikes howled as the riders saw the flashes in their mirrors and twisted the throttles open.

Fifteen minutes later they breasted the long rise into Neve Yatakov and saw the towers of Jerusalem on the skyline.

Jacobson lowered the window and poked the aerial of the walkie-talkie out. "Jacob to Watchman. Do you read me? Over."

"Hullo, Jacob. This is Watchman. Reading you good. Over."

"Watchman. Esau has lost his birthright," Jacobson said, and grinned, remembering how Porteous had looked, propped in a sitting position in the back of the Romulus, feet and hands tied, Elastoplast taped over his mouth; remembering the fury in those pale, watery eyes. "We estimate arrival in twelve minutes. Over."

"Roger, Jacob. Standing by. Out."

Twenty-one miles to the west Hodor sat on the sheep-pen wall and watched the troop carrier come racing up the Beit Sira road and turn right into the pass. "Father to Two," he said into the walkie-talkie. "OK. Here he comes. Out."

In the turret of the Romulus, parked facing west beside the trees, one of the commandos settled the anti-tank rifle on his shoulder and braced himself. On the hillside above him, lying behind the rocks with their rifles trained on the road, eight more commandos waited to pick off any survivors.

Crouched on the roof of the Praetorium Seeker saw the convoy come down past the Girls' College at the bottom of the Nablus road, heard the blare of their horns as they cut across to the Damascus Gate and entered the city. He lost them then for a couple of minutes until they turned into the street below him, slowed to a crawl now, and drove down to the archway of the Antonia Fortress. He saw the sentry present arms as the Mercedes turned into the courtyard. The motor-cycles and the troop carrier went on through the Lion Gate and down towards the Jericho road. They would be back in Masada within the hour.

Seeker pressed the switch of his walkie-talkie. "Watchman to Getaway. What is your position? Over."

"Hullo, Watchman," Falk's voice came thinly through the tiny speaker. "We are coming south down Ha-ayin Chet, fifty yards in from Paratroopers Road. Over."

"OK, Getaway. Jacob is here. You can come in now. Out."

In the cab of the fifteen-hundredweight Falk lowered the walkie-talkie. "They made it. Let's go."

He looked at his watch as Sabal swung the truck left into Paratroopers Road. It was eleven-nineteen.

3

Matt stopped the Mercedes at the foot of the steps leading up to the main guardroom and slid out from behind the wheel as Jacobson and Rosh got out of the back. Zax came down the steps to greet them.

"Zax." He saluted. "Good morning, Colonel."

Rosh nodded curtly, dabbing at his nose with a handkerchief.

"Good trip, sir?" Zax said.

"Lousy." Rosh began to climb the steps, Jacobson beside him, Matt just behind.

"Not that way, excuse me, Colonel," Zax said.

Rosh ignored him, paused on the top step for Matt to open the door for him, and went on in. Zax ran up the steps and followed the three of them into Pallas's room.

"I've arranged for coffee in a room across the courtyard, sir," Zax said. "Directly above the cells."

"Now he tells us," Matt said.

"This one will do," Rosh said. He walked round the desk and sat down.

"But, sir, I——"

"You heard the Colonel," Jacobson said. "He likes it here."

"So shut up," Matt said.

Zax swallowed and nodded. "Of course, I'll have the coffee sent——"

"For God's sake stop babbling about your damned coffee," Rosh said. "You sound like a Yid waiter."

"Looks like one, too," Matt said.

"I'm sorry, sir," Zax said. "After your journey I assumed you——"

"Never assume," Jacobson said.

157

"No coffee," Matt said.

"Well?" Rosh said bleakly.

Zax looked at him. He felt like a football being kicked round the room. "Sir?"

"Good God Almighty, look at him," Jacobson said. "Clueless as next week's crossword. The prisoners, man. The prisoners."

"You want him now?" Zax licked his lips. He was sweating hard and his mouth was dry.

"Them," Jacobson said. "Not him. Them. Barabbas and Sorek. Right?"

"If you haven't lost 'em," Matt said.

"And that's on the cards," Jacobson said. "The security here's unbelievably bad."

Zax's little button eyes blinked unhappily. "We pride ourselves on our security in the Antonia."

"Then you're a bigger fool than you look," Rosh said. "We've been here all of ten minutes and nobody's checked us out yet."

Zax flushed. "I'm sorry, sir. I naturally assumed——"

"There you go again," Jacobson said. "Never assume, Zax."

Rosh unbuttoned his tunic pocket, took out the identity card filched from Porteous and laid it on the desk. Jacobson and Matt did the same.

Zax smiled uncertainly, anxious to do the right thing. "Please, gentlemen. It's really not necessary."

"Have you ever met Colonel Porteous?" Rosh said.

Zax shook his head.

"Then look at the cards, damn you. We might be anyone, just walking in here."

Zax stepped forward, studied the cards, nodded. "Thank you, gentlemen. All in order."

"The prisoners," Matt said.

"Both of them," Jacobson said.

"Now," Rosh said.

Zax saluted. "At once, gentlemen. At once."

Following the tired old truck piled high with timber through the Damascus Gate, Sabal saw the load shift and slide.

158

"Any minute now," Falk said, "he's going to lose that lot."

"Silly bastard," Sabal said, and blew the horn of the fifteen-hundredweight.

The driver of the timber truck let in the clutch with a jerk. The truck lunged through the gateway, slewing a little to the left. The pile of timber leaned out dangerously. Two of the ropes snapped. Sixty twelve-foot-long planks slid off the truck and built an instant barricade across the narrow street.

Sabal braked hard and leaned out of the cab, bellowing curses at the truck driver.

"Back up," Falk said. "Quick. We can cut down to Herod's Gate and in through that way."

But it was too late. Sabal looking in the mirror saw the queue of cars piling up behind, boxing him in. He yanked on the handbrake and whipped the cab door open. "Well, come on," he shouted to Falk. "Don't just sit there. That stuff won't move itself, y'know."

Rosh looked at the two men standing in front of the desk and hid his dismay.

Swaying on his feet, Barabbas stared drunkenly at the wall. His eyes were slitted and bloodshot, the skin of his face puffy with fatigue, ragged with stubble. His knees were bent, his big hands hung limply at his sides.

Standing on his left Peter Sorek had a vacant, almost idiotic look. His mouth hung open. Tears had streaked the dirt on his face.

"So which is which?" Rosh said.

"Barabbas is the big one," Zax said.

Rosh nodded. "Jesus Barabbas, can you hear me?" He saw the eyes move down and focus on his face; saw the sudden incredulous gleam of hope. He nodded. "Yes, it's me. Colonel Porteous of the Secret Police. For once in your miserable life you're a VIP, Barabbas. I've come a long way to talk to you. Or rather, to listen to you talk." He noticed with relief that his words were getting through. Barabbas's back straightened a little. The limp hands began to curl into fists.

Leaning against the wall Jacobson saw the recognition in Barabbas's eyes and nodded to Matt who was standing just inside the door, his thumb hooked into his belt beside the holster.

Zax said, "I think you'll find him co-operative, Colonel. We've been softening him up a little overnight."

Rosh nodded. "This one too?"

Sorek stared back at him with dull eyes. A trickle of saliva ran out of the corner of his mouth and dribbled slowly down his chin and on to the damp patch on the front of his shirt.

Zax shook his head. "Not too bright, I'm afraid. If I might suggest, Colonel, you'll get more out of Barabbas."

Rosh said, "We'll see. You still got that coffee ready?"

"Colonel?"

"Coffee, man, coffee. God damn it, five minutes ago you were practically begging us to drink it."

"But I understood you to say you didn't want it."

"I don't. It's for him." Rosh pointed to Barabbas.

Zax looked shocked. "The prisoner? You want coffee for him?"

"Lots of it. Hot, black, with as much sugar as you can cram into it." Rosh pulled a small perspex tube of pills out of his pocket and set it on the table. "Whatever crude, old-fashioned methods you use in this fly-blown sewer of a town, Zax, in Rome we have developed subtler techniques. Two of these in a mug of hot coffee and a man begins to relax. Treble the dose and he becomes positively loquacious. Do you follow me?"

Zax nodded eagerly. "Of course. Coffee, Colonel. At once."

Matt let him out, closed the door and locked it. Rosh stood up, grinning, and gripped Barabbas's hand. "Think we'd forgotten you?"

"Come on, Peter," Jacobson was saying to Sorek. "Get a grip, laddie. It's me. Andrew."

Sorek looked at him with the same vacant, unblinking stare.

At the window Matt said, "What time d'you make it?"

Rosh turned quickly. "Eleven-forty-one. Why?"

Matt shook his head. "They aren't here yet."

"Get up on the truck," Sabal gasped. "Go on, damn you. Move."

The driver of the timber truck climbed up with agonising slowness; a thin, worried little man, easily panicked.

Sabal and Falk picked up one of the heavy planks and swung it up to him. The driver scrabbled for it, off balance, and let it slide back on to the road.

"You clumsy, bloody twit," Sabal snarled. "Get up there with him, mate. I'll bung the blasted things up myself."

The heat was fierce in the narrow street. The sweat ran off them in rivers. Clouds of flies buzzed round their heads.

Falk got up on the truck and Sabal began heaving the planks up to him, working desperately against the clock, his boiler suit soaked with sweat.

Seeker moved round the edge of the Praetorium roof and leaned out to look down towards the Damascus Gate. He saw the timber spilled across the street and the queue of cars jammed in behind the fifteen-hundredweight. He watched Sabal manhandling the planks, estimated how long it would take to clear a way through, looked at his watch and shook his head. He went back to his vantage point overlooking the Antonia, repositioned the jumper leads and dialled.

Rosh picked up the phone immediately. "Yes?"

"And Isaac said, 'The hands are the hands of Esau, but the voice is the voice of Jacob.' "

"OK, Seeker. This is Rosh."

"You ready to go?"

"Damn' right we are. Where's that fifteen-hundredweight?"

"They're trapped in a snarl-up."

"What? Where?"

"Just inside the Damascus Gate."

Rosh groaned. "That close, for God's sake. How long're they likely to be?"

"Ten minutes. Could be more."

"Hell's teeth. That's no good to us."

Seeker said, "Can you stall a bit?"

"For ten minutes?"

"I know it's dicey but . . ."

"Bloody dicey."

"I'm sorry," Seeker said. "You'll just have to play it by ear."

In the main guardroom Zax said, "What?"

"That colonel in there, sir," the sergeant said. "He's not Colonel Porteous."

Zax looked at him suspiciously. "You're sure of that?"

The sergeant nodded. "Sir. I was i/c guard on that Starfighter wreckage down at Gaza last October. Suspected sabotage."

"And?"

"Colonel Porteous was in charge of the investigation, sir."

"You saw him?"

"Every day for a week. Close as I am to you now, sir."

Zax's eyes gleamed with excitement as twelve hours earlier they had gleamed at the girl swathed in plastic sheeting. "So who's the officer in there now?"

The sergeant shook his head. "I dunno, sir. But he's not Colonel Porteous."

"He claims to be."

"No, sir. He's not. Definitely."

A corporal came up the steps with a tray. "Coffee, sir. Shall I take it in?"

Zax was beginning to enjoy himself. "One moment. Sergeant, I want six of your best men in here. At the double."

"Sir."

Zax heard the doubt in the sergeant's voice. "Well?"

"I was just thinking, sir. The window in that room opens on to . . ."

"As you were," Zax said. "Get those six men outside. Quick, now."

"Sir." The sergeant snatched up his cap and turned to the outer door.

"And Sergeant. I don't give a damn about Sorek or the others. But I want Barabbas alive. Understand?"

"Sir."

As the sergeant ran down the steps Zax nodded to the corporal and unbuttoned the flap of his holster. "Right. In you go."

The corporal balanced the tray on one hand and tried the door. "It's locked, sir."

Zax paled and then grinned with relief as Rosh's voice called, "Who is it?"

"Zax."

The key rattled in the lock and Matt opened the door.

Zax followed the corporal in and closed the door behind him. "What were you doing with the door locked?" he said, and paused. "Colonel."

"Waiting for you," Rosh said coolly. "What kept you?"

Zax smiled. "A little matter of identification." He watched Jacobson pour two mugs of coffee, give one to Barabbas and hold the other up to Sorek's lips.

Rosh looked at him warily, not liking the smile. Liking even less the sudden, almost jaunty, confidence. "Still worrying about security?"

"Should I be?" Zax said.

We've been rumbled, Rosh thought. Somebody's tipped him off. He knows we're phony and he's licking his lips over us, damn him. Well, I'm not playing mouse to his cat.

He put his foot casually on the seat of the chair and rested an elbow on his knee. "A good officer of SECPOL should always be suspicious, Zax. It's part of his stock-in-trade." He pressed the ball of his foot firmly on the chair, watching Zax's eyes.

Zax nodded. "Exactly so, Colonel. That's why I'm wondering why you neglected to put the pills in the prisoners' coffee." He smiled; the bright, feverish smile Liz had seen before the tears streaked his face. "An oversight, no doubt. But likely to prove a fatal one, Colonel." He tilted his head to one side. "Colonel—who, I wonder? Not Porteous. But . . . ?"

The chair slammed back against the wall as Rosh came over the desk in a single, smooth bound and grabbed Zax by the lapels of his tunic.

Matt locked the door and put the key in his pocket.

Zax opened his mouth to shout and Rosh hit him hard with the back of his hand and shoved him backwards. "Take him, Matt. Up against the door."

The corporal went for the pistol in his belt. Barabbas jerked the contents of the coffee jug into his eyes, kicked him in the groin and kneed him brutally as he doubled over. The corporal's head snapped back and he crumpled like an empty bag.

Rosh had his pistol out pointing at Zax. "OK, Matt. You'll be taking Sorek."

Sorek was standing limply by the desk, staring at the corporal's body. Matt went across to him and slid an arm round his waist, ready to hoist him over his shoulder.

Pressed against the door, white-faced, Zax licked his torn lips. "If I'm not out of here in five minutes the sergeant will take action."

"Shoot the door down, you mean?" Rosh said. "Unpleasant for you." He looked at Zax coldly. "Not that it matters. In five minutes you'll be dead anyway."

Sabal threw the last of the planks under the truck, blinked the sweat out of his eyes, shouted, "Come on. Let's have you," and ran for the cab.

Falk jumped down and scrambled in beside him. He looked at the narrow gap between the truck and the wall. "You'll never get her through there."

Sabal shoved the gear lever into first, gunned the engine and let in the clutch. "Oh yes I will, mate."

The fifteen-hundredweight edged through the gap, the side of the canvas tilt scraping along the wall, snagging on a projecting stone, tearing slightly as the truck broke free. Sabal put his hand flat on the horn button, whipped up into second and barged down the street. Shoppers and tourists scattered in front of him, seeming to fall away like corn under a scythe as he put the wheel hard over and hauled the truck round past the portico of the Praetorium, down towards the Antonia.

Standing by the window Jacobson saw the slit in the canvas roof gape and close again as the truck buckled over the uneven cobbles of the street. "OK," he said. "Here they come now."

Rosh levelled his pistol at the man pressed against the door. Arms and legs spread, head back, little eyes beady with fear, Zax looked curiously insubstantial; a two-dimensional cardboard cut-out of a man, bloodless, without bone, held upright only by the jack boots and the corset.

"You've wrapped your last parcel, Zax," Rosh said and shot him twice in the chest.

He heard the squeal of the fifteen-hundredweight's brakes right under the window. "Out you go, Matt."

Jacobson stepped back as Matt carried Sorek to the window, sat him on the sill facing into the room, gripped his legs below the knees and toppled him out. He somersaulted backwards, dropped neatly through the slit in the canvas and landed on the mattresses.

Kneeling on the sill Matt turned his head and put up his thumb.

In the doorway of the house across the street the sergeant said, "Let's have him, then."

Down on one knee beside him the soldier squeezed the trigger.

The grin on Matt's face froze as the bullets smashed into the side of his head. He fell forward out of the window; a big, brave man in an alien uniform, loyal to his friends and to the dream; dead before he hit the truck.

Sabal felt the springs bounce twice, heard the quick-firing stammer of the automatic rifles, pushed the gear lever into first and waited, riding the clutch, sweating.

A sustained burst of firing from several doorways down the street plugged a row of holes along the side of the fifteen-hundred-weight, killed Sorek crouching over Matt in the half darkness, shattered the cab window and bored into Sabal's neck. He fell on the wheel and the truck jumped as his foot slipped off the clutch. It lurched across the street, swung to the right and crashed into an orange stall by the Lion Gate. Falk kicked the cab door open and rolled out into a crossfire of bullets.

The six men with the sergeant stepped out into the open, hosing the window in the Antonia wall with their rifles.

"Hold it," the sergeant shouted. He pulled the pin out of a grenade and lobbed it neatly up through the window.

Jacobson, Barabbas and Rosh ducked as the glass flew in splinters out of the window frame and threw themselves down behind the desk. The grenade thudded on to the floor beside Jacobson. He grabbed it and hurled it back out of the window. It exploded three feet above the ground, killing the sergeant and two of the men.

Rosh pushed himself up on to his knees and looked at Barabbas. "OK?"

Barabbas nodded. The coffee or the excitement or both seemed to have given him new strength. His eyes were bright, his hands steady. He was living on his nerves, way out beyond the limit with probably less than an hour to go before he crumpled up. But for the moment, while the tension lasted, he was right on the ball.

"Andrew?"

"Yes. OK."

Rosh straightened his back, rested his forearm on the desk top and levelled his pistol. "Let's see who's at home," he said and shot the lock off the door into the main guardroom.

They waited for the guards to come running in. Five seconds. Ten. But nothing happened. No sound came from the guardroom. Down in the streets outside somebody shouted hoarsely, but the firing had stopped.

"Make for the Merc," Rosh said. "I'll drive. Let's go."

They jumped up, ran across the room, threw the door open and stopped short.

The three sub-machine guns lifted slightly to point at their chests. Standing behind the guards, Staff Sergeant Gilder managed a stiff little smile. "It's the end of the line, gentlemen, I'm afraid," he said.

The Land-Rover led the Romulus out of the pass and crossed over the Dei Nidham junction. Hodor held up his hand and they stopped briefly to let the commando drag the diversion sign back into place behind them, then moved on through Janiya towards Ramallah.

In the sealed-off section of the pass the smoke from the burning troop carrier rose up between the steep hillsides and curled away westwards, an insubstantial memorial to the Romans killed that day.

Beyond Ramallah the two vehicles parted company. The Romulus took the minor road going east through Beitin and Taiyba to drop down into Jericho and back along the lakeside to the caves below Masada. The Land-Rover turned right on to the Jerusalem road.

At the top of the rise before Neve Yatakov they pulled into a lay-by and Hodor called up Seeker on the walkie-talkie.

"Hullo, Father." The range was extreme and Seeker's voice faint. "This is Watchman. Over."

Hodor put his mouth close to the microphone and spoke slowly. "Father to Watchman. Have they sprung him? Over."

"Negative." The word hit Hodor like a hammer blow. "I say again, negative. Over."

Hodor sat silent, staring at the spare wheel strapped on the bonnet. Printed on his mind was a picture of Barabbas's dirt-streaked face looking up to him from the yard behind the house in Chain Street; that last vivid glimpse as he and Jacobson had rolled off the top of the wall to freedom.

"Watchman to Father." The urgency in Seeker's voice brought him back to the present. "Are you still there? Over."

Hodor flipped the switch. "Roger, Watchman. I'm coming in. Over and out."

He pulled the stopper out of his water-bottle, moistened his handkerchief and wiped the dust and sweat from his face. He slid a fresh clip into his pistol and tucked it into the waistband of his trousers under his faded plaid shirt, swallowed two codeine tablets with a mouthful of water and nodded to the driver. "Drop me off this side of the village. Work your way back to base through Hizma."

He stood at the corner of the Hizma road and watched the Land-Rover go down the hill in a flurry of dust. Then he limped into Neve Yatakov to the bus stop by the Post Office and waited there, a lonely, tired man, crippled now in spirit as well as in body.

The Romulus picked up the lakeside road at Nahal Kalya and rolled south down the western shore. The black tarmac surface was spongy in the afternoon heat, dragging at the six huge tyres. Along the white salt beach the skeletons of dead trees lifted bleached grey arms in curiously human attitudes of suffering. Under the evaporation mist the water of the lake, sluggish with salt, supporting no living creature, had a dull, metallic sheen, like a great, grey sheet of unpolished pewter.

Inside the Romulus the heat was appalling. The driver had his hatch open but the draught of tired air that came in was sucked out again through the open turret and never reached the rear compartment. The commandos took it in turns to stand up in the turret with their heads out, but for the prisoners there was no relief. They lay bound and gagged in the half darkness like animals trussed for roasting in some giant oven, slathered in sweat and struggling for air.

Porteous, lying on his back a little apart from the other two, was snoring heavily. One of the commandos wiped his streaming face with the back of his hand and said, "How in hell he can sleep in this lot beats me."

But Porteous was not asleep. He was fighting for his life. The intense, humid heat pouring out of the steel sides penetrated his swollen sinuses, loosening the mucus which oozed down his nose and clotted in the back of his throat. With his mouth sealed by the elastoplast gag he was forced to breathe through his nose. Eyes closed, his face scarlet, his chest heaving under the tight-fitting tunic, he sucked desperately at the stale air, pulling it up through his blocked nostrils and down into his lungs in slow, snoring breaths. Tears and sweat mingled saltily on his cheeks stinging the raw graze on the left side of his face where he had rubbed it against the steel floor in a desperate effort to peel away at least one corner of the gag. His head throbbed viciously. Trapped under the small of his back his bound wrists ground into the floor, sending agonising stabs of pain up his arms.

But none of these things—the headache splitting his skull, the grazed cheek, the bruised wrists—none of these mattered. What did matter—the only thing, the one remaining reality in his nightmare of slow suffocation—was the iron band encircling his chest, gripping, squeezing, crushing, collapsing his lungs, strangling his labouring heart.

Alone in the hot red darkness behind his eyelids, Colonel Victor Porteous, inventor of a dozen subtle ways to kill a man slowly and with maximum pain, was himself dying an agonising, unhurried death by heart failure brought on, quite simply, by a gradually declining ability to breathe.

Twenty-five miles west of the Romulus and a little over three and a half thousand feet above it, Simson got off the bus by the Jaffa Gate and began to walk up David Street.

It was, he decided, a magnificent afternoon. The sun shone in a cloudless sky above the city. The flints in the stone walls glittered. Like diamonds, Simson thought, and felt the excitement catch in his throat.

He was like a man with failing sight who for months has been groping through a world of vague outlines and muted colours, and who, one glorious morning, wakens to find his sight not simply restored, but enhanced and extended; able to discern, below the surface reality, the timeless shapes of truth. He understood now what a meaningful world Bartimaeus, the blind beggar of Jericho, had discovered when Davidson had given him back his sight.

The striped awnings along the street were the banners of a royal procession, the painted signs above the shops the heraldic emblems of some divine order of knighthood. The tourists in their brightly coloured shirts and dresses moved in the white-gold light like exotic flowers floating on a stream. He gazed over their heads along the length of the narrow street and saw the gates of the Temple standing open in welcome and the great pinnacles like golden spears lifted against the sky. The multilingual jabber of voices all round him was the sound of a people at prayer, the hooting of the traffic a fanfare of trumpets.

Jerusalem that Thursday afternoon in April was filled, it seemed to him, with peace and hope; her sins forgiven, her warfare accomplished; waiting in the sunshine, a bride adorned for her husband.

His feet quickened on the cobbles as he came to the end of the street and turned down right towards the Zion Gate. Ever since Davidson had refused Nicodemus's offer of escape the previous evening he had known in his heart that this was to be the day for which they had waited so long. The conviction had grown steadily through the morning and nothing had been able to shake it. Not the tactless coarseness of the Johnson brothers wolfing their food like animals at breakfast and conjecturing morbidly on the fate of Barabbas in the hands of SECPOL. Not the black pessimism of Thomas Didymus, nor John Zebedee's fawning, nor the veiled anxiety like unshed tears in the eyes of Mary Magdala.

Not even the withdrawn, brooding silence that cloaked Davidson himself, hollowing the young, bearded face, darkening the skin beneath the eyes, so that he sat like a stranger unspeaking among them. Gripped by a kind of controlled exultation, Simson had been able to dismiss even this as being no more than nerves. Coronation nerves.

He slipped into an alley near the Zion Gate and stood behind a pile of empty packing-cases, waiting a full two minutes to be sure he was not being followed. Satisfied, he ran down the steps to the back door of the Red Stocking.

In the office behind the stage Shad Rocci put the phone down and shook his head. "He's dead."

Seeker said, "Not Porteous?"

Rocci nodded.

"God damn it," Hodor said angrily. "What'd they go and kill him for?"

"They didn't," Rocci said. "It was his heart. Just packed up on him. He was dead when they got to Masada."

Hodor sat back and blew out his cheeks. "That's that, then."

It was the final blow; the last little bit of insurance against Rosh's failure to get Barabbas out. Tricky and full of pitfalls—the exchanging of a terrorist leader for a SECPOL officer of Porteous's standing—but possible, just. Now even that was gone.

"Nobody's going to swap Barabbas for a dead colonel," Hodor said.

Rocci uncorked the arak bottle and filled three glasses. "We've done all we could, Ben. It's just not our day."

Hodor tipped the arak into his mouth and swallowed. "Our day was Tuesday, mate. We had it made then. Turn your back on a chance like that and you don't deserve to win." He pushed his glass across for a refill. "They'll hang him tomorrow. Rosh and Jacobson too."

Seeker said, "So soon?"

Hodor nodded. "They won't take any more chances."

"We've still got the Romulus," Seeker said. "Maybe we could——"

"No," Hodor said. "Enough's enough. We've had it now."

His hand went to the pistol in his waistband as the door opened and Simson stepped inside.

"So you've heard, have you?" Hodor said bitterly.

Simson smiled and shook his head. "No. But I can guess." He pulled out a chair and sat down opposite Seeker. "14 Bazaar Street, that's where he'll be. Six o'clock this evening."

They looked at him, puzzled as much by his smiling confidence as by his words.

"Now," he said briskly. "What's the best way to go about it? We must get Pilate down there in person, of course. And the TV boys too. Shouldn't be difficult once they know Pilate's involved."

Hodor said harshly, "Just what in hell are you on about?"

Simson looked at him and licked his lips, shocked by the defeat on Hodor's face. "I'm very sorry," he said quietly. "I should've asked. I . . ." He looked at Seeker and then at Rocci. They met his gaze coldly. "Is he—he's dead, then?"

Hodor said, "Who?"

"Barabbas."

"As good as," Seeker said. "It didn't work."

Simson said, "But has he told them?"

"Told them what?"

"About Davidson. When Porteous questioned him—he did give them Davidson's name?"

Hodor's lip curled. "Don't worry, mate. Your precious Davidson's safe. Porteous never got to Barabbas. We saw to that."

Simson's face went white. He closed his eyes for a moment, giddy as the confidence oozed out of him. "You mean he hasn't talked? Not to anybody?"

"No."

"But that's impossible." Simson stared at them wildly, feeling the walls of the room close round him like a trap. "I don't understand. It was all fixed. Inevitable. Part of the pattern. What's happened? What's gone wrong?" The questions were like a call for help as the dream of the King shifted in his mind and began to totter.

Hodor said wearily, "Everything. Every damned thing. Beginning with a little matter of a badly loaded truck."

"What?" The words were meaningless to Simson; absurdly irrelevant.

"We were all set to spring him this morning," Seeker said. "And we damn' near did it, too. And then this dim bastard of a truck driver sheds his load and the whole flaming option goes for a chop."

"So Barabbas is still there? In the Antonia?"

"Yes," Hodor said. "Until tomorrow. Then they'll hang him."

"When he's talked to Porteous?"

"For God's sake, man, get a grip," Hodor said. "Porteous is dead."

Over the first shock, Simson's brain tripped into top gear, racing round the crumbling edifice of the dream, shoring it up, holding it together, searching desperately for a way to save it from total destruction.

He looked at the three men with him round the table, saw their faces stony in defeat and read it as desperation. Dangerous men. Reckless. The basic mistake had been to use them at all. He could see that now. The para-military coup had looked right. But it had been wrong. Hopelessly, clumsily wrong. Life, that was what the Messiah's kingdom was about. Not death, life. Freedom and healing and love.

He knew he could never hope to get that through to them now. There were two separate dreams of freedom—his and theirs. Davidson's and Barabbas's. Tuesday's disaster had been the result of trying to weld the two together.

But this they would never accept. At the end of the day their loyalty was to Barabbas, not to Davidson. No longer interested in the Messianic kingdom, they wanted only to set their leader free. And to do that they would stop at nothing.

Yet somehow they must be stopped. This was the Messiah's night. Nothing must be allowed to interfere with that.

He understood now why Davidson had surrounded himself with such a collection of nonentities. Men of spirit and nerve got in his way, thwarted his will. He was the Messiah, and the Messiah stood alone, before all men, above all men. Yet needing, in the final crisis, one good friend with nerve and spirit to do what must be done.

Simson took a deep breath as the plan slotted, complete and perfect, into his mind. The panic faded as quickly as the euphoria it had shattered. In its place he felt a great sense of purpose; a calculating, ice-cold calm.

He said quietly, "So we've got about twelve hours to get Barabbas out."

Hodor looked at him sharply, hearing the new note of authority in his voice. "Get him out? It's too late for that."

"Perhaps," Simson said. "Perhaps not." He smiled, a grave, reassuring smile that showed no trace of the madness in his mind. "As I recall, it is a tradition for the Governor-General to make a gesture at this time of the year—a sort of vicarious sharing in the Passover celebrations—by granting a free pardon to a prisoner in the Antonia."

There was a little silence. Then Seeker said, "Not Barabbas?"

173

"Why not?"

"With the record he's got?" Hodor said wearily. "And after last Tuesday?" He shook his head. "Forget it. Pilate's been gunning for him for years. He's not going to let him go now."

Simson nodded. "As things stand, no. But suppose Pilate finds himself with another prisoner on his hands. More important than Barabbas. More dangerous. A man he dare not release. And suppose he's manoeuvred into a position where he has to make a choice. A straight choice. Barabbas or . . ."

"Or who?" Hodor said.

"The King of the Jews," Simson said.

"Hang them?" Largo said.

Pilate nodded. "Tomorrow morning. Nine o'clock. I'm having the necessary orders drafted now."

Largo put a spoonful of black cherry jam into his mouth, savoured its sweetness for a moment, swallowed and took a sip of coffee. The cloth on the table laid at one end of the Residency terrace was dazzlingly white in the afternoon sun and he was wearing tinted anti-glare shields clipped on to his glasses. In a cream sharkskin suit worn with a midnight blue shirt and two-tone, slip-on shoes he looked like a distinguished, slightly raffish, film producer.

"It's your decision, of course," he said politely, injecting just the right amount of doubt into his voice.

Pilate scowled. He disliked people who hid their eyes behind dark glasses. "You don't agree?"

Largo sighed. "I agree Barabbas must hang, yes."

"And the other two?"

"Oh, yes. And the other two."

"Well then?" Pilate said peevishly.

"It's a question of timing, really, isn't it?"

Pilate blinked at him unhappily. Rattled by that morning's incident at the Antonia and the disappearance of Porteous, he was in no mood for Largo's confidence-pricking questions. "Look, we've had a difficult week so far and——"

"That's certainly true."

And will go down in your report, Pilate thought. All the juicy, damning little details. He remembered his behaviour at the banquet the previous evening and winced. "All right. So let's clamp down hard. Show 'em who's boss." He intended it to be a firm, authoritative statement, but even to him the words sounded unconvincing, like the punch-line in a tough western spoken in error not by the hero but by the cowardly saloon-keeper.

"The iron fist of Rome?" Largo said. "Oh, quite."

"Have to use it sometimes."

"Yes. It's just that . . ."

"What?"

"As I understand it, tomorrow's the big day. Eve of the Passover Sabbath."

"So?"

Largo grinned. "Better the day, better the deed? Is that it?"

"It'll give them something to think about while they're singing those awful dirges in the Temple tomorrow night."

"You don't think it's perhaps a trifle unwise to hang three Freedom Fighters at the height of a freedom festival?"

"Freedom Fighters be damned," Pilate said. "They're common thugs. Murderers."

Largo nodded. "To you and me, yes. But to the Jews they're Freedom Fighters. Heroes in the struggle against Rome. And if you hang them tomorrow they could well become martyrs." He finished his coffee and put down his cup. "I'd be inclined to wait a few days, if I were you. Let the dust settle a bit."

Pilate shook his head. "I can't afford to do that. You saw what happened at the Antonia this morning. As long as Barabbas is in there they'll try to get him out. It's just asking for trouble."

Largo shrugged. "That's a risk you'll have to take, of course. To my mind, not a serious one."

Not for you, Pilate thought, chewing the nail of his left forefinger. But damned serious for me if anything goes wrong.

He stared morosely at the security guards patrolling the grounds. Whatever he decided to do, Largo would discredit him in his report. If he hanged Barabbas it would go down as a panic measure, badly timed and ill advised. If he didn't, he'd be accused yet again of indecision. Either way, if things turned awkward, he'd be for the high jump.

He dabbed at his forehead with his handkerchief. Under his arms his white shirt clung damply to his skin.

Largo watched him, smiling. "As I said, it's your decision." He waited a moment and then added, "There is also the question of Colonel Porteous. I take it you have that in hand?"

"I've got people out looking for him," Pilate said.

"And?"

Pilate shook his head. "Nothing, so far."

"I see." It was an accusation.

Pilate flushed angrily. "Well, give them a chance. He's only been missing since——"

"Oh, quite."

"I can only work with the forces at my disposal," Pilate said waspishly. "It's a question of priorities. The safety of the city is more important than the life of one man."

"And him most probably dead," Largo said cruelly. "Yes." He watched the indecision in Pilate's face. "Still, I think you should make some sort of statement."

"Statement?"

Largo sighed. "Oh, you know. Something vaguely optimistic with an underlying note of determination. And just a suggestion of outrage." He smiled behind his dark glasses. "Just so you're covered."

Pilate nodded doubtfully. "If you think it wise."

"I do," Largo said. He made his voice suddenly warm. "Another two days and it'll be all over. The Passover finished. Everything back to normal." He leaned forward and patted Pilate's arm. "Come Sunday you'll have nothing whatever to worry about."

5

In his study overlooking the walled garden behind the Palace, His Grace the Lord Caiaphas, High Priest of Jewry, sat at his desk and looked up at Simson. He was wearing a black cassock and skull-cap which emphasised the pallor of his face, austere and finely boned above the neatly trimmed beard. Under arched eyebrows his eyes were cold, like black ice.

"14 Bazaar Street," he said, his precise, cultured voice as cold as his eyes. "Isn't that the Rabbi Joseph's house?"

Standing in front of the desk Simson said, "Yes, Your Grace, his town house." Getting in to see Caiaphas without an appointment had not been easy. Until he had mentioned the name of Jesus Davidson.

"And the blasphemer Davidson will be dining there tonight?"

"At six o'clock, Your Grace. Rabbi Joseph will not be there himself. But he has put his house at our disposal for the evening."

Caiaphas compressed his lips. "You realise the implications of what you are saying? The inference is that Rabbi Joseph is one of Davidson's supporters."

"Not quite a supporter, Your Grace. A sympathiser and a friend."

Caiaphas shook his head. "I cannot accept that. Rabbi Joseph is one of the Sanhedrin's most senior and distinguished members."

"I'm sorry, Your Grace," Simson said. He paused, timing it carefully, and added, "Nor is he the only one."

"In the Sanhedrin?"

Simson nodded. "I'm afraid so."

"Who?" The voice was razor-edged now, incisive, like a scalpel.

Simson hesitated.

"I'm waiting, Simson."

"Jacob Nicodemus, Your Grace."

Caiaphas nodded, his face bleak. "So. Nicodemus too. That does not altogether surprise me. I have for some time entertained certain misgivings about him. But Joseph . . ."

"Davidson has a considerable appeal, Your Grace. A charisma. He——"

"Davidson is a blasphemer and a heretic. One expects such a man to have some passing influence on simple country peasants. But to discover that he has also seduced members of the Church's highest court with his doctrines . . ." He shook his head.

"I'm sorry, Your Grace," Simson said calmly. "But it seemed right that you should be made aware of the danger."

Caiaphas nodded and got up. He went to stand at the window, a black silhouette in the fading sunlight. "You are Rabbi Simon's son, are you not? From Kerioth?"

"Yes, Your Grace."

"Your father and I were students together in the old days."

Hearing the softer note in his voice Simson relaxed. "He always spoke highly of you, Your Grace."

"Did he? Did he indeed? That was kind. Typical of him, of course." Caiaphas turned, smiling. "A fine scholar, your father. And a good rabbi. His death at so comparatively early an age was a great loss to Israel and to the Church."

"It is good of you to say so."

Caiaphas nodded, walked back to his desk and sat down. "It must have been—what? Two years ago, now?"

"Three, Your Grace. Three years this coming July."

"So long? Ah yes, I remember. It was just about the time you took up with this illiterate know-all from Galilee, was it not?" And the ice was back in his eyes, the voice ribbed with steel.

Simson's face paled a little. "Yes, Your Grace."

"It must have been a great shock to your father."

"It was not easy for either of us," Simson said stiffly.

"No," Caiaphas said. "I don't suppose it was."

"A man must follow his conscience, Your Grace."

"However mistaken. And whatever the cost. To himself and to others." Caiaphas sat back and folded his arms. "And now you have come to make amends, is that right? Three years later—three

178

years too late, one might almost say—you have come to undo the damage."

Simson flushed. Behind his glasses his eyes flashed angrily. "I see now that he is mistaken, Your Grace."

Caiaphas inclined his head gravely. "That, at least, is to your credit." The scorn in his voice was not lost on Simson. "And in what, precisely, is he mistaken, do you think?"

Simson hesitated. As the minutes ticked by he was increasingly aware of the leashed power in this cold, quiet-spoken man who sat like a spider and spun a web of questions to trap the unwary. The outlines of his plan to force Davidson's hand, so clear-cut half an hour before, were beginning to blur. He had not expected it to take so long, nor to be so emotionally disturbing. In an effort to regain his composure he lifted his eyes to look at the blue and gold ceramic Star of David on the wall above Caiaphas; the Messianic symbol in the colours of hope and royalty.

Seeing him look up, the High Priest said, "Is it, perhaps, his claim to be the Messiah? Is that what troubles your conscience, Judas Simson?"

"You know about that, Your Grace?"

"I do indeed."

A tiny flame of hope flickered for a moment in Simson's mind. Even at this late hour, if Caiaphas should throw in his lot with Davidson . . .

He said, "You don't think . . . ?"

The High Priest drew the corners of his mouth down in disgust. His words quenched the hope decisively. "He breaks the Sabbath, consorts with prostitutes and calls the riff-raff of the streets his friends. Are these the qualities and attributes of the Messiah?"

Simson nodded. "I see that now, Your Grace." He paused for a moment and then played his trump card. "As I see the danger of his other claim."

"What other claim?"

"That he is the King of the Jews." Simson saw the High Priest's eyes glint with sudden interest. "In recent months, Your Grace, he has become increasingly politically motivated. The early idealism which——"

Caiaphas broke in sharply. "The King of the Jews, you say?"

"Yes, Your Grace. That is his latest claim."

"I see." Caiaphas leaned forward, elbows on the desk. "Now listen to me, and listen carefully. This is most important. A blasphemy charge we can substantiate without difficulty. We have had witnesses standing by for weeks now prepared to swear to that. But blasphemy is not enough, d'you see? It doesn't impress Rome. And only Rome can rid us of this pest from Galilee." He was speaking more quickly now, hands clasped on the desk, his face intent. "The death penalty. That's what we need. It's the only way to silence him. He is like a cancer in the nation and must be cut out. Cut out and destroyed before he destroys us all. And that means asking the Governor-General for a death warrant." He sat back, his face bitter. "There was a time when we could have dealt with him in our own courts. But now this right, together with so many more, is denied us. Now only Rome can execute a man. And Rome will demand evidence not of blasphemy but of treason." He smiled, a twisted, ironic smile. "Odd, is it not, that a crime against God is considered by our masters to be less serious than a crime against the Emperor?" He pointed a finger at Simson. "Judas Simson, God is giving you the opportunity to redeem your folly. Can I rely on you, if necessary, to swear before the Governor-General that Davidson claims to be the King of the Jews?"

Simson breathed deeply, savouring already the climactic moment before Pilate when he would be the herald of the Messiah's declaration of his kingdom. "It will be a privilege, Your Grace."

Caiaphas looked at him sharply. "Yes. Quite so. Good. Very good." He got up and began to pace the study. The power unleashed now, crackling and sparking like a high-voltage charge. Watching his restless energy Simson found it difficult to believe this was the same man who stood with such dignity day by day in the high place of the Temple, who, only moments before, had been sitting at his desk, cold and austere.

"Now," Caiaphas said. "When? Tonight, of course. It must be tonight."

Simson looked at his watch. "He'll be in the house in Bazaar Street in less than an hour."

"That won't do," Caiaphas said. "Far too central. Too many people about. Country folk up for the Feast. Arrest him there and we could be in real difficulties." He turned towards Simson. "What about later? After the meal?"

Simson shook his head. He had not thought beyond six o'clock. There had been no reason to do so. "I'm not sure. We usually go for a walk after we've eaten."

"A walk? Where?"

"Somewhere quiet where we can talk." Simson swallowed, remembering how often he had sat with the others by the lakeside in the evening, or on the grassy slope of the Mount of Olives, with the stars shining and the air pleasantly cool; the calm water and the sleeping city and that quiet, magical voice speaking of the Kingdom, the words as nourishing and satisfying as the supper already eaten. He looked at the High Priest and forced himself to continue. "Mount Zion, perhaps. Or along the Bethany road. Or in Gethsemane. That's a favourite place with him."

"In the olive groves?"

"Yes, Your Grace."

"That's better. That's much better. Lonely. Not too far out." Caiaphas nodded. "Oh, yes, Simson. I like the sound of Gethsemane."

"I'm not sure, of course," Simson said.

"But you can find out? Let me know?"

Simson nodded.

"Excellent. Downstairs in the library. Say, seven-thirty. Earlier if you can, of course. I'll put all the necessary preparations in hand. Have the deposition drawn up for you to sign. Get the Sanhedrin together for an emergency session." He went to his desk and sat down, rubbing his hands. "We'll use the Temple Guards. Two platoons should suffice. Sanballet to command, I think. Major Sanballet. Cool. Reliable. Absolutely loyal." He pulled a pad of paper towards him, picked up his pen and looked up, seeming slightly surprised to find Simson still there. "Yes?"

Simson said, "You'll have him brought back here, will you, Your Grace?" He saw Caiaphas's eyebrows rise and added quickly, "I mean, a bunch of soldiers milling about in the dark. We don't want an accident . . ."

Caiaphas smiled briefly. "There'll be no accident. Major San-ballet will see to that. Davidson will be properly arrested, brought back here under guard and given a fair hearing. He will be remembered briefly, if indeed at all, as a traitor executed for plotting against the Emperor, not revered as a martyr done to death secretly in some dark and lonely place." He looked at Simson shrewdly. "Does that satisfy you?"

Simson nodded, seeing the plan leap clearly into focus again in his mind. "Completely, Your Grace. Thank you."

Major Pallas had been playing squash at the Officers' Club and was sitting in the bar, still in T-shirt and shorts, when he was called to the phone.

"Gilder here, sir."

"Yes, Staff?"

"Sorry to bother you, sir, but something's come up I think you should know about."

"Yes?"

"From the Residency, sir. Execution orders for Barabbas, Rosh and Jacobson."

"When?"

"Tomorrow morning. O–nine-hundred hours." Gilder hesitated. "On Skull Hill."

"Skull Hill?" Pallas's voice rose. "You mean it's to be public?"

"Semi-public, yes, sir. Nobody'll be able to get all that close. The area's to be roped off and two full companies of the Tenth will be there. Parade at o-seven-thirty at HQ. March out o- . . ."

"A public hanging," Pallas said, almost to himself. "He must be mad."

"It's not all that unusual, sir," Gilder said. "For armed insurrection. It's been done often enough before."

"On Passover Friday?"

"Well, no, sir. Never in Passover week, as a matter of fact."

"Look, Staff," Pallas said. "I want those orders checked and double-checked."

"Already been done, sir."

"And?"

"The orders stand. The Governor-General's signed them himself."

"Has he, by God? What's he trying to do? Start a revolution?"

"As I understand it, sir, it's because of Colonel Porteous."

"Instead of hostages?"

"Or as well as, sir."

"Um," Pallas said. Hostages were always shot in public, of course. But a hanging was different. He had a vivid mental picture of thirty thousand blood-hungry people marauding through the city, smashing windows, overturning cars, looting and burning and killing. "Any news of Porteous yet?"

"No, sir."

He's dead, of course, Pallas thought. And we'll be damned lucky if a lot more people aren't by this time tomorrow. "All right, Staff," he said. "Get it set up, will you. I'll be there in about half an hour."

"Sir."

"Oh, and Staff . . ."

"Sir?"

"Those three chaps who're going to be topped. See they get a decent meal tonight."

Matthew Levison ladled a generous helping of mutton stew on to his plate, dug his thumbs into a round, flat loaf, broke it open and used a piece of the warm bread to dip into the gravy. You didn't get rich following the Master, he thought. But you ate well. Nothing fancy, of course. And all the better for that. Just good, plain food you could get your teeth into. Decently cooked and plenty of it.

Like the others round the big table in the dining-room on the first floor of the house in Bazaar Street, Levison was wearing a collar and tie and a suit. Even the Johnson brothers, who seemed to live in woollen shirts and jeans, had put on suits for the occasion and sat hunched over their plates; big, bulky, rough-mannered men, their necks bulging over their collars, the knives and forks like toys in their hands.

There was a white cloth on the table and flowers in a vase. The soft lights shone on silver and china, glowed warmly in the bottles of wine. A pleasant room in the house of a wealthy man. Good food, good company. Warmth and light and wine. It ought to have added up to a festive meal.

But it was not like that.

The twelve men sat silently eating. No laughter between them. No conversation. Heads bent, their eyes on their plates, as if they were afraid to look at each other or at their young leader in the dark-grey, country-cut, slightly old-fashioned suit sitting at the head of the table.

Levison looked at him covertly under lowered eyelids, saw the face pale and withdrawn, shadowed by the beard and the thick brown hair; saw the eyes brooding, deep-set in their sockets. The long fingers crumbled the bread absently. But Davidson was not eating. The plate of food in front of him was untouched, the glass of wine untasted.

Levison frowned, his small, pointed face troubled. He thought of the many meals they had all eaten together in the last three years, starting with that magnificent, everything-must-go blow-out in his own house the day he had walked out of his job in the Taxation Department and taken to the road with Davidson. Wedding feasts, high teas with eggs and jam and honey in country cottages up north, six-course dinners in the houses of the well-to-do, alfresco breakfasts on the beach in Galilee, the juicy, fresh-caught fish hissing and spitting over the wood fire, picnic lunches in a boat anchored offshore, or up in the hills, or in a lay-by on one of the main trunk roads. Each one different. Each, in its own way, an occasion. Good food, good talk, a sense of destiny.

But none like this.

He forked meat into his mouth and wadded in bread, his cheeks bulging. Like a funeral, this was, and the Master sitting there, silent and white-faced as a dead man. No light in his eyes. No words on his lips.

Levison gulped and pushed his plate away, the food suddenly tasteless in his mouth, his appetite gone. He saw Davidson shake his head and say something. Those nearest to him looked shaken, afraid.

"What's he say?" Levison said quietly.

Beside him, James Zebedee said in a low voice, "Something about being betrayed."

"That again? I thought we'd heard the last of that nonsense." He shook his head. "He's not well, y'know. That's the top and bottom of it. Picked up a bug last Sunday I reckon. Hasn't looked himself since then."

On his other side Thomas Didymus said, "Who'd want to shop him, anyway?"

Levison nodded. "Who?"

The word went round the table in a whisper. "Who? Who?" Like a chill-fingered ghost touching the backs of their necks.

Sitting on Davidson's left, John Zebedee said awkwardly, "Is it me?"

"Or me?" Peter Johnson said.

"Or me?"

"Or me?"

On Davidson's right, in the place of honour, Judas Simson said calmly, "Is it me, Master?"

Davidson looked at him. The others were still asking, whispering among themselves, their faces anxious, the food forgotten on their plates. But Simson was aware of none of this. Only of those eyes looking at him, into him, through him. Eyes he struggled to meet and hold while the sweat broke cold on his forehead. Eyes that looked at him not in accusation, which he could have borne, but with a compassion which threatened to destroy him.

He ducked his head, pushed back his chair and stood up. "Excuse me. I have things to do," he muttered.

Davidson said, "Then be quick and do them, Judas Ishkerioth. Be quick and finish it."

The nickname was like a knife under his ribs. He looked up and said, "Gethsemane?"

"Gethsemane," Davidson said. "The valley of oil."

Simson smiled then, tears of relief pricking his eyes. Oil for anointing. Oil for a King. As once Samuel had anointed Saul. "Thank you, Master," he said quietly. "Thank you for that." And he turned from the table and went out.

6

The Jewish Army was a small, indifferently trained force principally assigned, under the terms of the Occupation, to guard, transport and pioneer duties. Sparsely equipped with outdated weapons and suffering from an acute shortage of good officer material, it was regarded with amusement by the Roman legions and with some embarrassment by the Jews themselves.

Except for the Temple Guards.

Hand-picked men, six-footers, magnificently equipped, the Temple Guards were the most photographed troops in Israel. Resplendent in their distinctive cockaded hats, with their white, wool-lined cloaks buckled round their shoulders over purple tunics and trews, they mounted a daily, round-the-clock guard at the Temple and the Palace of the High Priest. And, on rare occasions, at the Residency itself.

But they were not merely ceremonial troops. They were also battle-hardened veterans, disciplined, efficient. Steel-helmeted, in khaki drill and full webbing, they shared with the legions desert patrol duties and had gone into combat alongside some of the best Roman troops, defending their homeland against the marauding Bedouin tribes south-east of Eilat and up in the wild hill country of Gilead.

Major Gideon Sanballet, DSO, was typical of their officers. He was hard and weathered, with a big hooked nose and thick lips, his skin coarse and tanned by the desert sun. A fiercely correct, stony-eyed man who could come back from an eight-day offensive patrol in Sinai looking as though he had just stepped out of a bath and into a clean, newly pressed uniform.

At nineteen hundred hours precisely he marched himself into the entrance-hall of the Palace, was shown into the downstairs library, singled out Caiaphas from the company of rabbis gathered there, gave him a parade-ground salute and said crisply, in a muted shout, "Two platoons of Guardsmen at readiness, sir. Ready to move at two minutes' notice."

Caiaphas inclined his head and smiled. "Thank you, major. You'll take a glass of wine with us?"

"Thank you, sir." Sanballet took off his cap and accepted the glass. "Your health, sir."

Caiaphas said, "You've warned the men there's to be no shooting?"

"Maximum speed, minimum force, Your Grace." Off parade, his cap tucked under his left arm, Sanballet's voice dropped to a not unpleasant growl which gave his clipped manner of speech a certain brisk charm.

"Good. I don't anticipate there being any trouble. Davidson is surrounded by pacifists and drop-outs. You know the type?"

Sanballet nodded grimly. "Armed, d'you suppose?"

"I think it most unlikely. I understand his slogan is 'Love your Neighbour'."

Sanballet grinned. "He should go down to Akaba, Your Grace. There're some dark-skinned gentlemen there might change his mind for him. None too gently, either."

Caiaphas nodded, a wintry smile melting the ice in his eyes. "I think we can perhaps save him the journey, Major." He saw that Sanballet's glass was empty. "More wine? Or would you prefer whisky?"

"Thank you, Your Grace." He took a glass from the waiter's tray. "One thing, sir. This informer laddie."

"Simson? Yes?"

"I'd rather like to have him with us. Matter of identification, actually. These long-haired yobos all look alike to me."

"Of course, Major. An excellent idea. I'll leave you to make the necessary arrangements."

"Thank you, Your Grace."

"Anything else?"

Sanballet shook his head. "All we need now is the location."

Twelve miles south of Ein Gedi Seeker switched off the head-lights of the pick-up, drove another half-mile on the parking lights and turned off the shore road into the wadi that led to the caves. He drove slowly over the rough track to the dog-leg where the naked rock rose steeply on either side. There he stopped, flashed his headlights short-long-short, saw the answering flicker of a torch from a ledge eighty feet above him, and drove on to the camp.

Swinging the pick-up round in the open space in front of the caves he was relieved to see the five-tonner there, with the Romulus parked alongside it. Beyond the Romulus were a couple of fifteen-hundredweights and the Land-Rover.

As he cut the engine and got out of the cab the commandos came running to greet him. He walked across with them to the main cave, answering their questions curtly.

Inside a couple of pressure lamps lit up the scene. He gathered the men around him, accepted a tin mug of coffee and a cigarette and began the briefing.

"Big eats," the corporal said, unlocking the cell door and carry-ing in the tray.

The three men lying on the bunks sat up and looked at the food. Steak and eggs, fresh bread, fruit and ice-cream, two litre bottles of wine.

The corporal set the tray down on one of the bunks, pulled knives, forks and spoons out of his pocket and handed them round. "Eat, drink and be merry, gentlemen," he said, "for tomorrow . . ." He shook his head and smiled, not unkindly. "Ah well, like the man said, 'Tomorrow never comes'."

Barabbas prised the plastic cap off a wine bottle. "I'll drink to that, mate."

"Radio House. Can I help you?" The girl on the reception desk heard the pips stop as Simson pressed a coin in the slot.

"Is that Radio House?"

The girl sighed, raising her eyebrows at the night security guard leaning on the counter in front of her. "Radio House. Yes?"

"I want to speak to the News Department. Television."

"Your name, sir, please?"

"Never mind all that. Just put me through."

"I'm sorry, sir. I must have your name."

"Look," Simson said. "This is very urgent."

The guard said, "Who is it?"

The girl put her hand over the mouthpiece. "Some nutcase who won't give his name."

"Oh, ah?" The guard grinned. "One of those, eh? Heavy breathing and please, darling, what colour knickers are you wearing?"

The girl shook her head impatiently. "Says he wants to speak to TV News. Urgent, he says."

"That's what I'm here for," the guard said. He took the phone. "News desk."

"Well, it's about time," Simson said. "Look, can you get a camera-crew and an experienced reporter down to Gethsemane? Say about eight-thirty tonight."

"Gethsemane?"

"Yes."

"We might. Why?"

"And another standing by outside the Palace?"

"What for?"

"The end of the world," Simson said. "As we know it, anyway. And the coronation of the Messiah."

"Of who?"

"The Messiah." Simson said it simply, splendidly; a name to stand alone without need of explanation.

"Now wait just a minute," the guard said. "Who are you?"

"My name's Simson. Judas Simson. "I'm one of——"

"All right, Mr. Simson. Let's just take this calmly, shall we?"

"Take it how you like," Simson said. "Just so long as you're there." And rang off.

The guard put the phone down and shook his head. "He rang off."

"What did he want?" the girl said.

"God knows. One of these religious cranks. Something about the end of the world and the Messiah. You know. The usual stuff. Stark staring bonkers, poor devil."

189

Simson left the telephone kiosk, crossed the street and went up the steps into the Palace.

They made him wait in the entrance-hall and he stood under the arched ceiling, a slight, bespectacled figure lost, like a forgotten pawn, on the vast chess board of the tiled floor.

After a minute or two Caiaphas and Sanballet came out of the library.

"Ah, Mr Simson," Caiaphas said smoothly. "Have you got the information we need?"

Simson nodded. "It is Gethsemane, Your Grace. As I expected. He'll be there in about an hour."

"That is quite definite, is it?"

"Yes, Your Grace. He told me himself." And his heart lifted, remembering the clue about the oil.

"Good," Caiaphas said. "Oh, I'm sorry. This is Major Sanballet. He will be in charge of the—er—operation."

Simson nodded. "Shalom."

"He wants you to go along," Caiaphas said. "To identify the prisoner."

"Yes. Of course."

Sanballet looked down at him without respect. "Know him well, do you?"

"Yes."

"Don't want any mistakes, y'know."

Caiaphas said, "Mr. Simson has been with Davidson constantly over the last—er—three years, I think you said?"

"Yes, Your Grace." Ignoring the slur, biding his time, his time that was surely coming.

"Yes," Caiaphas said, rubbing it in. "Three years."

"One of his friends, are you?" Sanballet said.

"Yes."

Sanballet grunted, grim-faced. "Doesn't need enemies then, does he?"

Simson flushed.

Caiaphas said, "If you'll excuse us, Major? There are certain formalities to be observed."

"Your Grace." Sanballet put on his cap, saluted and marched out.

190

Caiaphas took Simson into a small office opening off the hall and indicated some papers set ready on the table. "If you will check those and sign them, please."

"What are they?"

"Just routine. The deposition affirming Davidson's claim to be the Messiah. And another affirming his claim to be our king. I think you'll find them in order." He pointed to the foot of the page. "Just there, please. Your usual signature." He watched Simson sign his name. "Thank you. It saves time later, you see, if we already have the evidence in writing. Now"—he put another paper in front of Simson—"this is just for our own records."

Simson looked at it. "What's this? Some sort of receipt?"

"Exactly. For fifteen pounds. I have the money here."

"Money?" Simson said, his hands shaking as anger and shame burned in him like a fever. "I don't want your money."

"Now, please," Caiaphas said. "It's not what you think."

"Blood money," Simson said. "That's what it is. Blood money."

"It most certainly is not," Caiaphas said coldly. "It is simply a perfectly normal legal fee. Like the stamp duty on a conveyancing document."

"I'm not selling anybody for fifteen miserable pounds," Simson said.

"Of course you aren't. That's understood." Caiaphas smiled. "Now, please. Sign the receipt."

Simson put his hands to his head. Somewhere deep in his mind a small, frantic voice insisted that something was wrong. But like the pilot of an aircraft who sees the end of the runway rushing towards him and feels the lift of air under the wings, he was committed and could not go back now.

"Fifteen pounds," Caiaphas said. "It's not important. A detail. Look—" he picked up an envelope and slipped it into Simson's pocket—"forget about the receipt. If it disturbs you that much we can dispense with it." He crumpled the paper and dropped it into the basket under the table. "The important thing is that you have helped to save your country from bloodshed and disaster. And for that, Judas Simson, we are more grateful to you than we can say."

Simson nodded. The crisis was passing, his head clearing, the frantic, inner voice silenced. The money was unimportant. The signed evidence irrelevant. It would never be used. An hour from now—less perhaps—Israel would have no need of courts of justice, evidence, fees paid for services rendered. Israel would have, instead, her King. Mercy and peace and the rule of God.

7

They went out through the Damascus Gate at four-minute intervals; an LWB hard-top Land-Rover and two five-ton troop carriers with the six-pointed star of the Temple Guards painted on their tailboards. Forking left they drove up the Rehov Hanevi'im, as if making for the barracks on the Shivtei Israel. But at the top of the Hanevi'im they turned right and began to work round the north-east corner of the city, down the Az-Zahara into the Jericho road, to rendezvous just beyond the junction with Shmuel ben Adiya.

Sitting in the front of the Land-Rover between Sanballet and the driver, Simson stared out at the strolling holiday crowds, the hooting traffic, the shop windows blazing with lights. He thought that this was how it must have been in Egypt that far, famous night when a nation of slaves shook off their chains and marched to freedom; people laughing and talking in the streets, eating and drinking and dreaming their dreams, unaware that the world they knew was coming to an end.

The traffic thinned along the Az-Zahara and they left the lights behind, skirting the valley below Mount Scopus, the city wall suddenly there on their right, vast and solid in the darkness. The headlights picked out the lay-by rendezvous and they pulled in off the road, cut the lights and engine and waited for the five-tonners to come up with them.

Ten minutes later, travelling together in convoy, they turned in through the gates of Gethsemane and drove up the twisting track between olive trees that were said to have been young when David was king. The gnarled trunks leaned back, thrusting out branches at odd angles, seeming to move stiffly in the white glare of the headlights like old men crippled with arthritis.

To the men sitting with Davidson on the little grassy knoll near the top of the garden, the lights of the trucks were like torches weaving up through the trees towards them. They stood up, clustering round him, and saw the Land-Rover swing off the track below them and stop, the two troop carriers nudging in behind it.

Sanballet opened the cab door and got out. The men dropped down from the five-tonners and fell in beside them, rifles in their hands, out of sight of the little group on the knoll.

"Right. Pay attention," Sanballet said. "Able platoon to give cover. Get up the slope under those trees on the right. Baker platoon to fan out and advance at a walking-pace. Mr. Simson and I will be in the centre of the line. As soon as he identifies Davidson, close in and take him."

Baker platoon sergeant said, "What if he makes a run for it, sir?"

"He won't run," Simson said quickly.

Sanballet nodded. "I don't think he will. But if he does, get after him. We want him alive, understand? And undamaged. Any questions?"

The sergeant said, "What about the others, sir?"

Sanballet shook his head. "Forget 'em. Not important. Now *they* probably will cut and run. Let 'em. It's Davidson we want. Nobody else. Right?"

"Sir."

"And remember, all of you, there's to be no shooting unless I give the order." He nodded. "Off you go, then, Able. Quietly now."

The men of Able platoon melted away into the trees.

Sanballet looked at Simson. "OK?"

"Yes."

"Right. Let's go."

There was no moon, but the stars were bright and close. In the strange quarter-light it seemed to Simson, treading the grassy slope, that Davidson alone in that shadowed clearing stood out clearly. It was as though he had gathered into himself all the light of the million stars above him. The men around him seemed to shrink away, dark blobs against the darker hillside. But he stood straight and shining, hands by his sides, head held high.

"Thank you, Mr. Simson," Sanballet said quietly.

Simson stepped out in front of the line of men, walked lightly over the springy turf and came to Davidson, smiling.

"Master," he said, and kissed his cheek; a kiss of hope and expectation; a kiss of homage to a king.

Davidson took a pace backwards and said something. But Simson did not hear him. He stood, arms outstretched, hands open, waiting for the transformation—the blinding light, the mighty voice that had spoken the word of Creation at the beginning of time, pronounced the Law from Sinai's clouded peak and would utter now the words of peace and life that would bring in the kingdom without end. The light, he waited for, and the voice. And the angel hosts in shining squadrons sweeping through the sky over the black hump of the Mount of Olives to stoop like hawks above the city, cleansing it, renewing it, making it ready in the starry night for the coming of the King.

But none of this happened. Ten seconds he waited. Twenty. Forty. A full minute. Two minutes. Nothing.

Gradually he became aware of a confusion of voices, the crack of a revolver, a cry of pain. The men of Able platoon came running out of the trees, leaping across the slant of the hill, rifles at their hips. And there were other feet running, down the slope and into the shadows. And the men of Baker platoon were all round Davidson. And the starshine had died in him and he was just another foolish young man who had thought to change the world, and failed.

8

(Excerpts from the script of the main news televised at 9 p.m. on Thursday 12th April from the Jerusalem studios of the Imperial Television Corporation.)

Video	*Audio*
CUT to Daniels M/CU	Subversive elements were again in evidence in the city today when three armed terrorists forced their way into the Antonia Fortress and attempted to free two prisoners, Jesus Barabbas and Peter Sorek, being held on charges of insurrection and murder. The attempt failed. One of the men was killed; the other two taken prisoner. Two men in a getaway vehicle were also killed.
MIX to shot of burnt-out troop carrier	More serious was an ambush earlier this morning on the Lod/Ramallah road. Thirty-eight men and two senior NCOs of the Tenth Legion lost their lives when their convoy was attacked in a pass west of Janiya. The men were acting as rearguard escort to a convoy bringing Colonel

196

Video	Audio

Video *Audio*

Victor Porteous, a senior SECPOL officer, to Jerusalem for talks with His Excellency, the Governor-General.

A statement issued two hours ago from the Residency confirms that the Colonel escaped unharmed from the ambush. His present whereabouts, for reasons of security, cannot at this stage be revealed.

CUT to Daniels
M/CU

Meanwhile, undeterred by these acts of violence and terror, pilgrims and visitors continue to crowd into the capital. Latest reports indicate that all hotels are now . . .

PART FOUR: Friday

1

Around one o'clock on the morning of Friday 13th April, the temperature dropped sharply.

In the black, moonless sky the stars sparkled with an almost frosty brilliance; a heavenly host indeed, but cold, remote, uncaring, and not as in Simson's vision. Serenity was there, but no pity; majesty, but without grace. A million men might die in agony without causing one of those distant angels to deviate by so much as an inch from his predestined orbit.

In Hinnon and Kidron the mist eddied, lapping at the old grey walls of the city like a milky tide. On iron gates and gold-leafed pinnacles the dew glistened in the starlight. People turned over uneasily in their beds and groped for eiderdowns.

But in the library of the High Priest's Palace the air was hot and stale, acrid with the musky scent of sweat and anger.

They had re-arranged the long, high-ceilinged room, grouping the chairs at one end in a series of concentric arcs round the high-backed wooden chair in which Caiaphas sat. From the far end of the room where the prisoner knelt on the polished parquet floor, the assembly of black-cassocked, black skull-capped priests curved outwards like enormous wings; the wings of an eagle poised to strike. In the centre, lifted above the others in that throne-like chair, Caiaphas was both beak and eyes, intent, cruel, infinitely patient.

"Tell us, Jesus Davidson." His voice reached out across the empty floor with measured clarity so that it seemed to Davidson to come from inside his own head. "Tell us you are not the Messiah, the Blessed One. Repent of your folly and confess that you are not He."

He had lost count of how often this had been said since they had brought him in three hours before. Three hours, or three years. For this was how it had all begun, three years ago in the desert beyond the Jordan when he had knelt, lonely and afraid, and heard the voice in his mind urging him to betray himself, deny his destiny, repudiate the power within him. There had been no Caiaphas to hound him then, no Judas to usurp his authority. Only himself and God and the voice in his head.

They had tied his wrists behind his back and he clasped his hands, interlacing his fingers, squeezing hard so that the knuckles cracked. The ache across his shoulders cramped his muscles agonisingly. He lifted his head, straightening his back, staring at the blurred faces set like stones against him, his tired eyes searching in vain for a hint of compassion in those bearded, hard-mouthed ranks.

A blinding pain stabbed into his kidneys as the guard behind him rammed the butt of his rifle into his back. "Bow your head when His Grace speaks to you," the guard growled.

His chin went down on his chest, coloured lights flashing behind his closed eyelids as the pain griped his stomach and bile rose bitter in his throat.

"I urge you to answer, Davidson," Caiaphas said. "I urge you to declare yourself no more than a man."

He bit his lower lip, tasting the saltiness of blood; a truncated, stoop-shouldered figure in the badly cut suit, his thick brown hair slicked with sweat. He had known for more than a year that it would come to this; accepted the knowledge, learned to live with it, shared it with his closest friends. What he had not known was the nature of it—the pain, the humiliation, the mounting, panicky dread of what was yet to come. He had identified himself with these people, discovered the appalling limitations of the human mind, forced himself to explore the twisted horror of pride and jealousy and hatred. Death and disease he had looked at, face to face and in shattering close-up. All this he had learned to accept as his human lot. And many times, sickened by the folly and senseless suffering, he had envisaged death as a release, a moment of liberation. What he had never anticipated was that he, like all men, would be afraid of it.

"Be quick and finish it," he had said to Judas Simson. But there was no hurrying Caiaphas.

The witnesses had come first. Pathetic little men with frightened eyes, mouthing their set speeches of blasphemy and law-breaking, the money for their willingness to lie clinking in their pockets as they stumbled and stammered and failed to agree the evidence.

"How do you answer, Jesus Davidson?" Caiaphas had said after each one had finished his miserable tale. But the question was only a formality. He had seen the contempt in Davidson's eyes and privately shared it. These men were not worth answering, their trumped-up evidence patently false.

But then had come the real test. The invitation, direct at first, later indirect, to declare himself in power. To call down the armies of heaven, blow the roof off this palace of lies and hypocrisy, raze the Temple, demolish the Praetorium, establish, in one mind-shattering stroke, the throne of God on the hills of Jerusalem.

"If you are the Son of God," the voice had said three years ago.

"If you are the Messiah," the voice was saying now.

But now, as then, this was not the way. It was what they all expected. But it was not the way.

The way was not conquest but suffering. Not the imposition of life upon death, like new paper pasted over a wall scabrous with dry rot, but the creation of life out of death.

And to do that, he must die, as all men must die.

He made to straighten his shoulders but stopped himself in time. He heard the rifle butt ground on the wooden floor behind him and was briefly thankful not to have felt its brutal thud.

"I urge you again, Jesus Davidson. Confess before this company of God's holy priests that you are not . . ."

Standing at the back on the extreme left, like a ruffled feather on the great black wing of priests, Simson stared down the long room at Davidson.

"Come on, man. Come *on!*" The words screamed in his mind, struggling to get through to that drooping, defeated figure kneeling in front of the guard.

The sweat glistened on his face, misting his glasses, as he concentrated all his will. As if, by marshalling his thoughts, he could even now see the miracle happen: Davidson on his feet, the cord snapped from his wrists, the radiance of power like a cloak around him.

But it was no use. He knew that. He had known it for the last hour or more.

When nothing had happened in Gethsemane he had told himself to be patient. The declaration of God's Kingdom was not a thing to be done in secret witnessed only by a handful of soldiers and a few ancient olive trees. Once they got him to the Palace, then he would speak.

Sandwiched between Sanballet and the driver on the front seat of the Land-Rover, with Davidson in the back guarded by four men, Simson had hugged the secret to himself, humming under his breath the triumphant psalms of his people.

"Lift up your heads, oh you gates

and be lifted up, you everlasting doors," he had sung as the blunt nose of the Land-Rover lifted towards the Lion Gate.

"And the King of glory shall come in."

But when he had come in, nothing.

Instead of glory, degradation. Instead of the great shout of praise, the mumbling inanities of the accusers. Instead of the word of life, the endlessly repeated questions.

Several times he had edged forward along the wall, hoping to catch Caiaphas's eye and be given the chance to confront Davidson himself. But Caiaphas had resolutely refused to look his way, had shown no sign of producing the written deposition he had signed. And in the end one of the rabbis had curtly reminded him that he was there on sufferance, and he had retreated to the back, frustrated.

He looked down the room with sick despair, no longer able to believe, as two hours ago he had, that the declaration would be made, if not in front of Caiaphas, then later, before Pilate. No longer able to believe in anything, except that yet again the longed-for Messiah had been revealed as a charlatan.

And yet, in spite of the failure of belief, he found himself still trying. The voice in his mind screamed louder. "Come *on! Come on!*" The sweat of hope where there was no hope dripped off his face and soaked the collar of his shirt. "Come *on!* Jesus, Master, *speak!*"

But when, a little after three in the morning, Davidson struggled to his feet, ignoring the shouts and blows of the guard, and finally answered the High Priest, it was not as Simson had expected it would be.

"Are you the Messiah?" The cultured voice, monotonous as a dripping tap, switched back to the direct question. "Are you, indeed, the Son of God?"

And Davidson was suddenly, unbelievably on his feet, head erect, back like a wall, oblivious to the thudding rifle butt. "I AM," he said, using the forbidden, secret name of God, his eyes bright, his voice clear and strong. "And you will all see me seated at the right hand of God, coming down through the clouds of the heavens."

Caiaphas rose, the beak of the eagle lifted for the kill. There was a rustling along the curved black wings, like the stirring of feathers, as the priests plucked in horror at the blasphemy ribbons stitched lightly to their cassocks, ripping them away in a gesture of shame.

"Blasphemy." Caiaphas's voice rang out. "We need no more witnesses, gentlemen. You all heard him. You all heard his wicked, lying words. What do you say?"

Simson stood like a stone as the priests rose up all round him, waving their ribbons like whips and shouting, "Guilty! Guilty! Kill him! Kill him! Kill, kill, kill!"

"Now," Simson said softly, his voice lost in the uproar. "Now, Father."

But again, nothing. No thunderclap. No lightning flash. No voice, no word, no sign.

The priests rushed down the room, the wings of the eagle hiding its prey, and hurled themselves on Davidson, kicking, punching, spitting. He went down on his back and rolled over, drawing up his knees, hunching his shoulders to cover his face.

They stooped over him, beating at him with their hands, tearing his clothes, showering him with spittle. Until the guard stepped forward, rifle across his body, and pushed them back and stood astride the huddled, bespattered man who moments before had claimed to be God.

2

Rosh stood by the window of the cell, staring out through the bars.

They had taken away the SECPOL uniforms and issued him and Jacobson with worn demin trousers and jackets. On Jacobson the clothes looked what they were: prison reach-me-downs, good enough to hang a man in. But Rosh wore them with a certain dignity; the patched and faded uniform of a soldier who, even in defeat, contrives a smart turn-out.

Behind him on the bunks Barabbas and Jacobson were sleeping. He listened without envy to their regular breathing, his grey eyes calm in the light of the low-wattage bulb screwed into the ceiling fitment.

The window looked out over a small, flagged quadrangle linked to the main courtyard of the fortress by a narrow passage. Above the opposite wall with its darkened windows the wheeling stars moved imperceptibly as the world turned through the night towards a new sunrise.

My last sunrise, Rosh thought, and was surprised to discover he was not afraid, as three years before he would have been. He had been wealthy then; a young man of position and promise with the golden years ahead of him. Too great a stake in the world to be able to accept the fact of death.

But not now.

He reviewed the events of the last few days, arranging them in a true perspective. He saw now that SLINGSHOT had been doomed from the moment of its inception, long before Hodor had sent out the abort signal. Freedom was not a prize to be won by violence at the expense of other men. Freedom was a gift to be accepted and shared.

But every gift, he thought, must have a giver. And where was the king who held the gift of freedom in his hands and was willing to share it with his people?

Until such a king appeared the only freedom was death, God's merciful gift to weary, disillusioned men.

A light came on in the little quadrangle outside the window. Rosh turned his head and saw the soldiers come through the passage, shouting and laughing with a prisoner between them. They gave him a push and he reeled across the flagstones, a scarecrow figure in an ill-fitting suit, the light shining cruelly on his bruised face and spittle-slimy beard.

Wakened by the noise Barabbas got up and stood beside Rosh, yawning and scratching his chest. "What the hell's going on out there? What time is it?"

"Quarter to four."

"Noisy bastards." Barabbas peered through the window. "Who's that?"

"Davidson. Don't you recognise him?"

Barabbas looked at the face, chalk-white, with black holes for eyes, like a death-mask under the light. "So they finally caught up with him, eh?"

"Caiaphas did. Those are Temple Guards."

"Then God help him," Barabbas said. "Everybody hates a Jew, but it takes another Jew to hurt one."

They watched in silence as one of the soldiers took an empty beer crate from a stack by the back door of the canteen and set it upside down in the centre of the flagged yard. He grabbed Davidson by the arm and forced him to step up on to the crate. The buttons had been ripped off his jacket and it hung loosely about his shoulders. He looked like a third-rate comedian playing a drunk.

The soldier struck a pose, arms outstretched, and shouted, "Gentlemen, the King."

The others stood in a group, laughing as he swung round, dropped on one knee and bowed his head. "Yes, Your Majesty. No, Your Majesty. Shall I kiss it for you now, Your Majesty?"

He leapt to his feet. "Come on then, lads. Get fell in. Smartly now."

The soldiers formed up in three ranks, stamping their feet and turning their heads; picking up the dressing with exaggerated gestures. The man beside Davidson sprang to attention, marched across to them, shouted, "Squad. Squad, atten-shun. Le-eft turn. By the right, quick—march." He fell in beside them, calling the time. As they drew level with the beer crate he shouted, "Eyes—left," and threw up a flamboyant salute.

They wheeled round the little yard, arms swinging, feet stamping hard on the cobbles. On the beer crate Davidson stood swaying, head down, hands hanging limply at his sides.

"Right, lads," the soldier shouted. "Sound off, damn you. Hail, hail, King Jesus. Come on, let's hear it then!"

"Hail, hail, King Jesus." The chant kept time with their marching feet, bouncing back off the fortress walls under the pitiless glare of the overhead lamp in the dark, cold hour before dawn. "Hail, hail, King Jesus. Hail, hail, King . . ."

"Dear God in heaven," Barabbas said softly.

"But not on earth," Rosh said. "That's where he made his mistake."

Barabbas nodded. "Us too, mate. Us too."

"King of the Jews?" Nicodemus said sharply. "That's not in the evidence."

Caiaphas tapped the document on the table in front of him. "I have a signed statement to that effect."

Nicodemus shook his head. "He claimed to be the Messiah, not a king."

Caiaphas sighed. He looked round the table at the fifteen members of the Inner Council. "I'm open to correction, of course, gentlemen. But I think it's a little late to be quibbling about words."

There was a muted chorus of assent.

"I'm sorry," Nicodemus said. "But a man's life is at stake here. It's not a matter of quibbling. It's——"

"The safety of our nation," Caiaphas said. "That's what's at stake, gentlemen. I'm sure we all respect Rabbi Nicodemus's concern that Davidson should be given the benefit of any possible doubt. But can there be any doubt? You have all heard his blasphemous avowal that he is the Messiah and——"

"Blasphemy," Nicodemus said. "Not treason."

One of the rabbis said angrily, "What's the matter with you, Nicodemus? Are you one of his supporters, then? A Galilean in disguise, perhaps?"

"I am a priest of God," Nicodemus said. "And as such I——"

"But my dear Jacob," Caiaphas's voice was like silk, new-cut, with a raw edge to it. "So are we all. All priests of God."

"I'm sorry, Your Grace," Nicodemus said. "I cannot vote for this man's death on a treason charge."

Caiaphas nodded. "I understand. And you, gentlemen? Are you ready to vote?" He looked round the table. "Yes? Then I put it to you that Jesus Davidson, having been convicted of blasphemy and treason, should be taken before the Governor-General with the recommendation of this Council that he be executed forthwith in the interests of public safety and the peace of the realm. All those in favour please show."

Fourteen hands were raised.

"Jacob?" Caiaphas said patiently.

Nicodemus shook his head.

"Do you wish to vote against the motion?"

Nicodemus hesitated, feeling their eyes on him.

"Well?" Caiaphas said.

"I prefer not to use my vote on this occasion."

Caiaphas inclined his head. "That is your privilege."

Nicodemus flushed. "It is my right, Your Grace."

"Indeed it is. To be cherished. And, if necessary, suffered for," Caiaphas said. "So, gentlemen, the motion is carried nem. con., one member abstaining." He looked at his watch. "Now, if you will excuse me, I must go and impress upon His Excellency the urgency of this matter."

3

Half-awake and evil-tempered Pilate said, "Won't come in? What d'you mean, they won't come in?" The early morning sun shining through the tall windows of the main hall of the Praetorium emphasised the puffiness under his eyes, the waxy pallor of his newly shaven face.

Max Sciotto said, "I'm sorry, sir. It's their religion. Apparently they're all ceremonially prepared for the Passover Sabbath and are prohibited by their law from entering non-Jewish buildings."

"For God's sake," Pilate said.

Largo smiled. "Exactly so."

Pilate scowled at him, resenting his fresh appearance, the elegance of his suit. He pulled down the tunic of his unpressed uniform. "I do not appreciate jokes, Senator, at this hour of the morning."

Largo inclined his head. "My apologies."

Pilate turned to Sciotto. "So what do you suggest, Max?"

"We could use the ground-floor balcony room, sir. They could stand outside in the courtyard and——"

"Oh, no," Pilate said with surprising firmness. "I'm not going to try a man for his life over a balcony rail. Not for fifty high priests."

"The prisoner could be brought into the room, sir."

Pilate hesitated. "What do you think, Largo?"

"Why not? It is Passover Friday. The big day. No point in making things difficult for yourself by offending their religious feelings."

Pilate nodded. "That's true. Oh, very well. It's ridiculous, of course. But if it keeps them happy . . ."

They went down to the balcony room at the front of the building. Pilate sat himself behind the table in a leather chair with the imperial crest embossed on its high back. Largo took a seat on the other side of the room which was spacious and cool, its pale blue walls softening the brightness of the morning light. He looked at Pilate with new interest as Sciotto put the document from Caiaphas on the table. It seemed to him that for the first time during his visit Pontius Pilate looked like a Governor-General, in spite of the creased tunic, the unhealthily white face. Something to do with the regal setting, perhaps; a room small enough not to dwarf him, yet possessing a certain, low-key splendour. Or it might have been a trick of the light, golden and blue-muted, flattering. He began to understand how the man had contrived to hold his position in spite of his reputation. There was a dignity about him now, a hint of presence. A vestige of original promise still gleamed, overlaid by years of failure but still there; submerged but not quite extinguished.

Sciotto opened the big glass doors and stepped out on to the balcony.

"It's a very serious charge," Largo said.

"If it's true," Pilate said. "I personally don't believe a word of it. Anything with Caiaphas's name on it has to be suspect."

Sciotto re-entered. "They're bringing him in now, sir."

Two soldiers of the Praetorian Guard opened the door and brought Davidson into the room, marching him up to the table.

"He's been searched?" Pilate said.

"Sir."

"All right. Wait outside."

When the soldiers had gone he said to Largo. "Can't be too careful. I wouldn't put it past Caiaphas to send some crazy gunman in here on a suicide mission." He looked at Davidson and raised his eyebrows. "This is the man, is it?"

Sciotto said, "Jesus Davidson. Yes, sir."

"Um." Pilate stared at the torn jacket stained with dried spittle, the baggy trousers, the crumpled shirt. "Doesn't look much like a king to me." He leaned forward. "Now listen to me, Davidson. His Grace, Lord Caiaphas has brought you to me on a very serious charge indeed. What have you to say?"

Davidson looked at him, steady-eyed above swollen, bruised cheeks. He said nothing.

"Come along, man," Pilate said. "You are entitled to speak in your own defence. Rome does not condemn a man without giving him that privilege."

Davidson pressed his lips together.

Pilate sighed. "You do realise, I suppose, that I have only to put my signature to this piece of paper and you're a dead man?" He saw the dark eyes blaze for a second and felt a little niggle of unease. He sat back in his chair. "So. You've nothing to say?"

Davidson stood silent, curiously composed.

Pilate said impatiently, "Oh, what's the use? The man's a complete fool."

He got up and went out on to the balcony. Caiaphas stepped out of a group of priests and walked towards him past the Jewish Army guards who had handed Davidson over to the Praetorians at the entrance.

Pilate stared down at him. "You'd better take him back and deal with him yourself. I can't get any sense out of him at all."

Caiaphas shook his head. "I'm sorry, Your Excellency, but that is not possible. We have already tried him and found him guilty."

"On what charges?"

"Blasphemy and treason, Your Excellency. It's all there, properly documented, in the signed statement."

"Then why come to me?"

Caiaphas lifted hands and shoulders in the age-old gesture of the Jew. "But, Your Excellency, treason is a capital charge, is it not? And we are no longer empowered under Roman law to execute a man." Behind him in the street a car drove past. "Time is passing, Your Excellency. The city is wakening. It is of paramount importance that this matter be dealt with as expeditiously as possible."

Pilate said, "I can't condemn a man without hearing his defence."

"I'm sorry, Your Excellency." The continuous use of his title, spoken with the faintest intonation of contempt, flicked at Pilate's nerves like a glove across the face. "We are all in your hands." Caiaphas drew himself up in his cassock, a black, ominous figure in the morning sunlight. "The safety of the nation rests with you."

"Hm," Pilate said and went back inside.

He sat down and said, "Are you the King of the Jews?"

Davidson's eyes gleamed in a small, tired smile. "Are those the words Caiaphas has put into your mouth?"

Pilate flushed. "I'm not a Jew to take orders from him. Let me remind you again of the seriousness of this charge. Being insolent is not going to help." The smile became a quick flash of anger. Pilate saw it, was disturbed by it and sat up straight in the chair, determined to dominate this oddly impressive scarecrow of a man. "I will ask you once more. And this time I want a proper answer. Are you the King of the Jews?"

Davidson said, "You wouldn't understand if I told you. My kingdom is in another place. Out of this world."

"Ah," Pilate said. "Now we progress. There is a kingdom, then?"

"Yes."

"So you are a king?"

The dark eyes, rimmed with tiredness, looked at him calmly. "Your words. Not mine."

Pilate met his gaze with an effort. There was something strange about this man, about this whole so-called trial. Something he couldn't quite put a finger on, but disturbing. Even dangerous. Perhaps Caiaphas was right, for once. Perhaps Jesus Davidson was a threat to the nation. But for the life of him he couldn't see how.

He said, "And what are your words, Davidson?"

With a kind of devastating simplicity Davidson said, "My words are truth."

"Truth?" Pilate said. "What is truth?"

But Davidson closed his mouth and said nothing.

"Oh, for God's sake." Pilate pushed back his chair and went out on to the balcony a second time. He saw that the number of people in the courtyard had more than doubled. A farm truck, piled high with vegetables, drove past on its way to the early morning market.

As Caiaphas came hurrying forward Pilate said, "He's not guilty."

"Your Excellency?" Caiaphas was shocked not only by the un-expected words but also by Pilate's bearing, the note of authority in his voice.

"The man is harmless, Your Grace. Not too bright, but harmless. I can see no good reason why I should sign his death warrant. I propose, therefore, to release him."

Caiaphas shook his head, thinking hard. "I'm sorry, Your Excellency, but that will not do. He cannot be allowed to go free. I beg you to reconsider."

"Nothing to reconsider," Pilate said shortly. "The man is innocent." Tall on the balcony he looked down at the fore-shortened figure of the High Priest, crow-black in his cassock on the coloured stone pavement. His ill temper had evaporated. In a curious way he was beginning to enjoy himself; as if, from that dark-eyed scarecrow called Jesus Davidson, he had caught an infection of confidence and power.

Caiaphas watched him warily. This was a Pilate he found disturbingly unfamiliar. He said slowly, "I'm afraid I cannot agree, Your Excellency. And I shall feel bound to say so in my report. With respect, of course. And regretfully."

"Report? What report?"

Caiaphas, looking up, saw Pilate's eyes cloud and permitted himself a brief smile. "My report of the trial held before the Sanhedrin last night, Your Excellency. I am instructed, as you know, to send in a full report of any proceedings of the Ecclesiastical Courts which uncover evidence of sedition. It goes, I believe, first to the Foreign Office in Rome and subsequently, if the contents are thought to be of sufficient importance, to the Emperor himself." He shrugged. "It will not be to my liking, Your Excellency, to disagree so fundamentally with your own view of this case. But one's duty to the Emperor must, I think you'll agree, take precedence over one's personal feelings."

Pilate looked at him and was suddenly very afraid, his confidence vanishing as it had done so often before, the old nightmare of suspicion closing around him. "Wait," he said, and turned back into the room.

Seeker dropped Hodor off at the corner and drove the pick-up round into the car park behind the Praetorium, running it in alongside the five-tonner which had brought fifty men up from Masada an hour earlier.

Hodor limped down the street and into the courtyard fronting the Praetorium. A number of cleaners and night-workers, going home to breakfast, had stopped to join the crowd of priests, soldiers and civilians. Hodor worked his way round the back of the waiting men, recognising several of the commandos who had come up in the troop carrier and were seeded in the crowd, inconspicuous in jeans and windcheaters. He found Simson over in the far corner and stood beside him. "What stage are we at?"

Simson turned to look at him. Hodor was startled by the change in his face. It was as if, overnight, he had aged twenty years. His eyes were sunk deep into his head behind his glasses, his cheeks were lined, the skin grey under the black stubble. Above his good forehead his hair looked lifeless, straw-dry, brittle, like the hair of a sick man. When he spoke his voice was thready. "I was mistaken." Tears crept out of the corners of his eyes and ran down under his glasses.

Hodor said, "Pull yourself together, man. There's still time. It's not over yet."

"It's over," Simson said. "His time came and he knew it. Looked at it, recognised it. And turned his back on it." He stood there in the loveliness of the morning with the colonnade of the Praetorium pink in the sunlight in front of him and the pinnacles of the Temple aflame behind him; a small, insignificant man trapped between Rome and Jewry, politics and religion; stood with the tears running down his face and his mind desolate and empty, that had been filled with the glory of the plan. "I was mistaken," he said again. "He was my friend and I thought he was God. But I was wrong."

Pilate drew hard on his cigarette and let the smoke jet out between his teeth. "He's outmanoeuvred me and he knows it."

"Caiaphas?" Largo said.

"Caiaphas." Pilate spat the name out like a curse. "Standing out there like . . ."

"Calm down," Largo said. "There's always a way out."

Pilate looked at him angrily. So cool, so poised, so damned sure of himself. Why worry about Caiaphas's report? Largo's would sink him in the first two paragraphs. "Not out of this," he said. "Whatever I do I'll be left holding a bomb. If I hang Davidson and he's subsequently proved to have been innocent there'll be some very awkward questions asked in Rome. If I don't, Caiaphas is quite capable of starting a holy war." He walked down the room, threw his cigarette into the empty fireplace and walked back. "I'm damned if I'll hang an innocent man. And I'm damned if I don't."

Largo said, "No. There really is a way out."

"What? How?"

"Let them decide. Don't try to make the choice yourself. Let those people out there make it for you."

"Here they come, boys," Hodor said. "Stand by."

Pilate and Davidson came out together on to the balcony; the soldier and the scarecrow. Around Caiaphas the priests set up an angry hissing sound.

Pilate lifted his hand. "Listen to me, all of you. I can find no reason to condemn this man to death. You say he is guilty and you may be right. But I can find nothing in the evidence to prove it."

Taking their cue from the priests the Temple Guards began to chant. "Guilty! Guilty! Hang-hang-hang! Guilty! Guilty! Hang..."

"All right," Pilate shouted. "Guilty then, if you like. But I'm not going to hang him. I'm going to release him."

There was a sudden silence. Caiaphas stepped forward, the wide sleeves of his cassock flapping, and looked up from below the balcony rail. "What trick is this, Roman?"

"Listen to me," Pilate said, ignoring him, looking out at the crowd. "It is the tradition at Passover time for me to set a prisoner free. Isn't that so?" He waited a moment and then said, "I set free Jesus Davidson."

"Now, lads," Hodor said urgently. "Let's hear it for the boss."

"Not Davidson." The voice rang out, echoing off the marble pillars. "Barabbas."

"Barabbas," the men from Masada shouted in chorus. "Barabbas! Barabbas! Give us Barabbas!"

Caiaphas thought quickly and nodded to his priests. "Barabbas! Barabbas! Give us Barabbas!" They joined in the chorus and the soldiers of the Temple Guard followed them. "Barabbas! Barabbas. *Give us Barabbas!*"

Pilate raised both arms and the chanting died. "And what shall I do with Davidson? What shall I do with your King?"

One of the priests called out, "We have no king but Tiberius!"

"Davidson says he is your king," Pilate shouted.

"Hang him," the priests shouted back. "Hang him!"

And the Temple Guard swung into their chant. "Guilty! Guilty! Hang-hang-hang!"

And since it would mean the freedom of their leader, the men from Masada, the commandos of SLINGSHOT, sworn enemies of the priesthood, added their voices. "Guilty! Guilty! Hang-hang-hang!"

The harsh words, ugly as their meaning, shattered the quiet beauty of the April morning. Pilate felt the sickness in his stomach and saw Caiaphas look up at him. "You have made your choice. The decision is yours, not mine. Is that understood?"

"Our choice," they shouted back. "Our choice!"

Pilate nodded. "Davidson hangs. Barabbas goes free."

A great burst of cheering welled up out of the crowd, rolling like a wave across the courtyard to break on the balcony, surging back and rising in volume until it seemed to fill the whole city with its sound.

Pilate took Davidson back inside and closed the doors. "I'm sorry," he said. "I . . . It's out of my hands now."

Simson pushed his way across the courtyard and gripped Caiaphas's shoulder, turning him round. He thrust an envelope into his hand.

Caiaphas looked at the tear-stained, desolate face. "What's this?" He felt the notes slide between his finger and thumb. "I can't accept this, you know."

"I did," Simson said. "And so must you. We share the guilt between us."

"Guilt?" Caiaphas said. "What guilt?" Around them the priests were laughing and talking excitedly. "He was no Messiah."

"Nor king, either," Simson said and turned and walked away.

4

The corporal swung open the door of the cell. "All right, lads. Let's have you, then."

Behind him in the corridor four soldiers of the Tenth stood ready; big, easy men, their faces not without kindness, rifles in their hands.

The corporal looked at the three prisoners. "Nice and quiet now, lads. No fuss, eh? It comes to us all, sooner or later, one way or another."

Rosh went out first, neat, cool, wearing his prison rags like an eighty-guinea suit. Then Jacobson, less certain, blinking a little, but upright, independent. Then Barabbas, slab-shouldered, cropped, rock-steady; there to see them right as he had always been.

They walked down the corridor between the soldiers and out into the main courtyard. The three-tonner was waiting to take them to Skull Hill.

As they stepped into the yard Gilder, waiting by the door, took Barabbas's arm. "Not you."

"What?"

"Not you. Not this time."

The other two were climbing over the lowered tailboard into the truck. Barabbas looked at them and back at Gilder. He shook his arm free. "What d'you mean? Not this time? We're all going together, aren't we?"

"They are. You're not."

"Like hell." Barabbas lunged forward; was stopped by the two soldiers and held.

The soldiers already in the truck pulled up the tailboard. One of them said something to Rosh. He and Jacobson turned, standing up under the canvas tilt, holding the metal roof-stay, their arms raised as if in salute.

"L'hitraot, sabra," Rosh called. "Like the man said, 'Tomorrow never comes'."

"Shalom," Jacobson shouted as the truck began to move out through the archway.

Barabbas shook his head and felt the tears warm on his face. "What the hell is this? What's going on?" He looked across at the empty archway where moments before the truck had been. "I ought to be with them. They're my men. My friends. I ought to be with them."

Gilder pulled a slip of paper out of his pocket. "Not this time, Barabbas. This time you're in luck." He gave the paper to him. "Governor-General's pardon."

Barabbas looked at the paper in bewilderment. "What?"

"You're it, boy," Gilder said and smiled. "The Passover prisoner who gets to walk out free."

"Me?"

Gilder nodded.

"Why me?" Barabbas said.

"By popular request," Gilder said. "Somebody out there loves you, boy."

When the other two were already there the soldiers brought Davidson. One on each side they half dragged, half lifted him out of the fifteen-hundredweight and supported him up the last gentle slope to the crown of the hill.

His feet were suddenly, maddeningly uncertain on the rough grass and he slumped a little, head up, eyes searching and searching and finding the three gallows silhouetted against the blue April sky like finger posts to eternity; new and unvarnished, white in the sunlight. Bone white on Skull Hill.

The ranks of the soldiers forming a hollow square opened briefly, holding back the watching crowd, making a corridor up which he walked conscious of a blur of faces, pointing fingers, the murmur of voices. Up the corridor, which closed behind him, into the lonely square of sun-scorched grass with the other two already waiting, and the gallows and the three wooden stools like the foot-stools before a throne.

"Hurry it up, sar'nt," Pallas said, very regimental in clean khaki drill, polished belt, polished shoes, polished leather holster, polished cap badge.

Davidson stood between the other two while the soldiers tied his wrists behind his back, took off his tie, unbuttoned the collar of his shirt. He told himself this was the worst part, the waiting part. Once across the grass and on to the stool there would be nothing to fear. He hoped, as the cord bit into his wrists and the knot was pulled tight, that he would not stumble during that last brief walk, that his feet would tread the grass as surely as once they had trodden the surface of the lake. He told himself that they were not taking his life; he was giving it. The life that had struggled for thirty-three years in the cramped prison of a human body. He was letting it go now, feeling it leaving him, escaping. Feeling the fear flooding in to take its place, alien, unimaginably powerful. He straightened his shoulders, astonished that men should find it possible to live with such fear inside them, hoping that he, like them, would find the will to die as a man should die, calmly, with dignity.

"Shalom, sir," Rosh said quietly.

He turned his head and nodded, recognising the face, unable to put a name to it. There had been so many faces, so many voices speaking of peace where there was no peace.

"Shalom." Was that truly his voice? The voice that had healed and inspired? That hoarse croak in his throat?

"I'm sorry, sir," Rosh said. "I'm glad it's not Barabbas. But sorry it has to be you." The words were not important. But the way they were spoken, the warmth, the kindliness—these things were weapons to fight the fear.

On his other side, his left side, the vulnerable, nearest-the-heart side, Jacobson said, "I hope you're satisfied now, damn you."

The bitterness in this voice cut into him and he looked to see who hated him with such passion on the threshold of death.

"Bloody coward," Jacobson said, fear twisting his middle-class, accountant's mind that was not equipped to face a gallows. "If you'd had the guts of a louse last Tuesday we wouldn't be standing here now."

Davidson looked at him without rancour, fascinated to discover that hate as well as love could be a weapon against fear.

"Right, lads," the sergeant said, keeping his voice down, making it casual. "Let's go."

Simson paid off the taxi and went down past the house through the vineyard, the grass dew-wet on his shoes, and into the barn. He made sure there was nobody inside, checking the two horse-boxes at the end and going up the ladder into the hay-loft. Satisfied that he was quite alone he took the coil of rope off the hook on the wall by the door and succeeded after two attempts in throwing one end over the heavy beam by the ladder. He tied a loop in the other end and drew it up carefully, measuring its height against the ladder. He tied it off then, knotting it securely round one of the upright posts.

He took off his jacket, folded it neatly and put it on the roll of blankets in his bed-space next to Thomas Didymus's. He pulled his tie loose and dropped it on his jacket, unbuttoned his collar and walked back to the door.

Throughout the preparations his face had been seriously intent but as he stood in the doorway and looked down that wild ravine towards the Dead Sea the intentness softened. His eyes opened wide behind the glasses and for a moment he looked young again.

He stood there for perhaps five minutes and then turned back inside the barn, closed the door and walked through the hay-scented gloom to the ladder. He climbed up until his chest was level with the loop on the rope, reached out and pulled it in towards him. He put his head in the loop and, steadying himself with his left hand, tightened the rope around his neck.

He hesitated then, balanced awkwardly on the ladder, his head pulled a little to one side. He felt there was something he should say; something important, memorable. He tried hard to think of something, his exhausted brain scrabbling in the dust of his memory. But nothing came.

In the end he said, quite simply and in a clear, contrite voice, "I'm sorry. I was mistaken," and stepped off the ladder, swinging out under the beam to freedom.

Davidson stood on the stool between the other two, grateful that he had managed the walk, that the fear, if not quite gone, had at least ebbed to a tolerable level.

"This is it, coward," Jacobson said. "Unless you've got one of your miracles tucked away for an emergency."

"Leave him alone, Andrew," Rosh said. "He's not like us. He's put new life into people. All we've done is kill them." His voice softened. "You once said I was not far from the Kingdom, sir. I've wandered a bit since then. Remember me now when we step into the dark."

Davidson tried to turn his head but the big knot under his ear prevented him. In a voice he was glad to hear sounding more like his own he said, "Today we'll be together in the Kingdom." And wondered for the first and last time if there was any truth in the words.

"Ready, lads?" the sergeant said to the men standing by to kick away the stools.

Davidson looked up slowly; a last, long look.

The faces of the crowd beyond the ranks of soldiers. They would all be there, somewhere. His mother. Mary of Magdala for whom love and faith were one. Peter and James and John, Matthew, Thomas, Andrew. All of them. Except Judas Ishkerioth.

His eyes lifted. The grey-walled city, the golden pinnacles of the Temple, the green shoulder of the Mount of Olives. The blue, eternal sky waiting.

The sergeant's voice saying, "Now!" and the stool kicked out from under his feet and the colours flowing and merging and searing his eyes with their brilliance. And darkness.

Pallas walked along the line. "Well done, lads," he said quietly. "Nice and quick."

The sergeant looked up at Davidson's body swinging gently, turning a little, the badly cut jacket gaping open, the trousers hitched high above the thick woollen socks, the dangling feet. "D'you think he was, sir?" he said.

"Was who?"

"The—whatsaname—Messiah?"

'As a matter of fact," Pallas said, "yes, I do. It doesn't make sense and it won't add up. But I think he was the Messiah."

Largo spread marmalade on a piece of toast. "They made the right decision this morning." He bit into the toast with relish.

"I'm glad you think so," Pilate said morosely. He pushed his plate away, the food scarcely touched, and lit a cigarette.

Largo watched him, smiling a little. "Still worrying about it?"

Pilate nodded.

"Barabbas?"

"Yes, Barabbas," Pilate said. "With a man like that loose in the city anything can happen."

Largo shook his head. "He won't bother you again."

Won't bother you, you mean, Pilate thought. But I've got to stay here and keep these people under some sort of control.

Largo sipped his coffee. "Davidson now, he's different. Or, to be precise, was different. With him around you could never be sure."

Pilate shook his head. "I don't agree. He seemed harmless enough to me. Odd, but harmless."

Largo smiled. "Not impressive in himself, perhaps. But as a representative figure, the embodiment of a dream—very dangerous indeed. People identified with him, you see. And that's always disturbing. Still, that's all settled now. He's dead and that's the end of it. Barabbases are two a penny. But men like Davidson don't come often. Be grateful you've seen the last of him."

In Rocci's office at the Red Stocking David Seeker slopped whisky into the glasses. "Come on. Drink up. L'hayim."

"To life." Hodor and Rocci raised their glasses.

But Barabbas sat still, looking at the play of light in his whisky, thinking of his five Pebble commanders who three days ago had been alive and were now dead. He stared down into the amber liquid as a medium gazes into a crystal, looking for their faces. But he saw only the scarecrow figure of Jesus Davidson standing on the upturned beer crate, his face a death-mask in the cruel light. The man he had believed the crowds would follow but whom they had rejected. The man who had taken his place on Skull Hill.

"Drink up, Jesus," Seeker said. "You're free."

Barabbas looked at him bitterly. Free? he thought. Free to do what? Not to live. Not even, it seemed, to die.

He turned his glass upside down and crunched it down on the table in a gesture of anger and despair. "Like hell I am," he said.

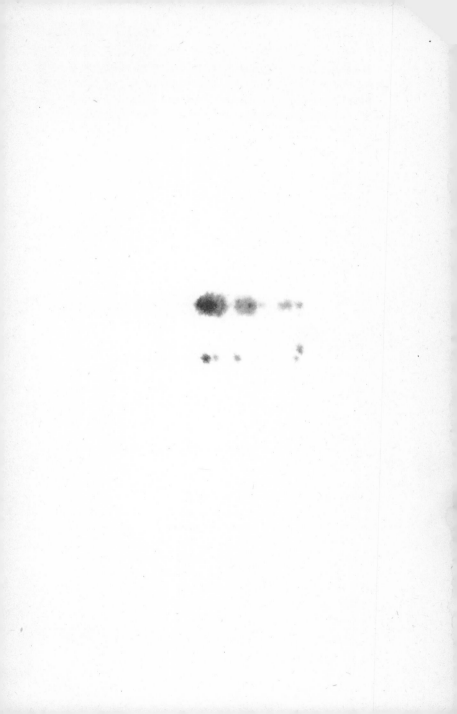

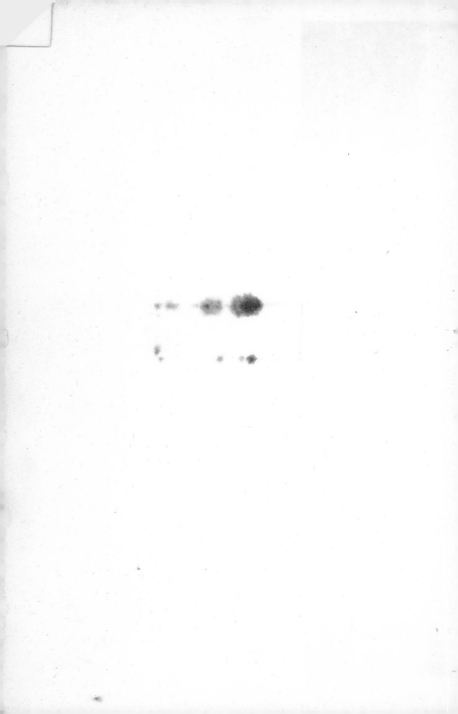